Sue Minix is a member of Sisters in Crime, and when she isn't writing or working, you can find her reading, watching old movies, or hiking the New Mexico desert with her furry best friend.

A Cover
for Murder

SUE MINIX

Published by AVON
A division of HarperCollins*Publishers*
1 London Bridge Street
London SE1 9GF

www.harpercollins.co.uk

HarperCollins*Publishers*
Macken House
39/40 Mayor Street Upper
Dublin 1
D01 C9W8
Ireland

A Paperback Original 2024
1
First published in Great Britain by HarperCollins*Publishers* 2024

A catalogue copy of this book is available from the British Library.

ISBN: 978-0-00865979-0

Set in Sabon LT Std by HarperCollins*Publishers* India

Printed and bound in the UK using 100% Renewable Electricity by
CPI Group (UK) Ltd

To Nancy

CHAPTER ONE

The month of January brought out all the many facets of my psyche. The joy of the holiday season was gone and the bills about to come in. Winter was at its peak, which in the current South Carolina climate meant thirty degrees one day and sixty the next. Still, the gray days outnumbered the sunny ones, and my mood fluctuated accordingly. Bipolar reactions to bipolar weather.

As I sat at my desk in the bookstore, beads of sweat trickled down my jawline, and I swiped them away. Whether they came from the unseasonably warm temperatures or the near-zero balance in my bookstore's bank account accusing me from the computer screen, I couldn't tell. I narrowed my eyes, willing a few extra zeros to appear next to those very single digits. I was no stranger to a diet of ramen noodles and PB&J—I was a college graduate, after all—but Ravenous Readers couldn't survive on chicken-seasoned pasta.

Christmas had brought plenty of cheer, but sales had plummeted like a cow in a dissipating tornado since the first day of the year. The Jen-solved-another-murder boom, as my manager Lacey Stanley—a mid-thirties mother of two with long brown hair she wore in a ponytail most days—liked to put it, hadn't lasted long enough this time.

The stack of unpaid bills grew higher every day, and my desperation flourished along with it. The next payment from the contest the original owner, Aletha Cunningham, had won to open the place was due to arrive next month. We had only two more coming after that, though. Then our survival depended solely on us. With a bit of luck, our new online sales plan would generate the boost we needed to make it through. The prospect of someday having to surrender made my stomach churn and bubble like it was filled with swamp water.

When Aletha died and left me the store, I had no idea what I was getting into, and pure unadulterated terror had consumed me. I was a mystery writer, not a business guru. I'd never even worked a real job before. Still hadn't, unless you counted the hour I spent waiting tables in the Dandy Diner last month when they were shorthanded. I chose not to, however, since I got fired before that hour was even over. The patrons weren't amused by my juggling act. Especially when it involved their food.

I ran a hand through my collar-length black hair and glanced at my German shepherd, Savannah, who snoozed in her bed beside my chair. "What do you think, little girl? You think we'll make it?" I asked her, hoping for some reassurance.

She opened one eye, thumped her bushy tail twice, and then went back to sleep. I couldn't help but laugh at her nonchalant attitude. She wasn't worrying about it, so I wouldn't either. For now, anyway. Nothing I could do about it, so why waste the energy? I had a limited supply and much more important things to do with it.

My current energy supply was earmarked for writing book three in my Davenport Twins Mysteries series. The second book, *Twin Terror*, wouldn't come out until April, so no way to know how well it would sell. Still, the first one, *Double Trouble*, was a huge success, so my publisher might make an offer for book three based on that alone. Fingers crossed, my writing would bring in some much-need income. Eventually.

I loaded chapter two onto my laptop and stared at the last paragraph I'd written, hoping my muse would return and my writing career could help save the bookstore. And me.

> *Daniel took a deep breath and shoved second thoughts out of his mind. His twin sister Dana was overreacting. Alpha Phi Alpha was the right fraternity for him, and everything would be fine. He clicked the submit button to send his registration application.*

Where should I go from here? Dana was the left-brained twin—logic, rules, and action gave her life meaning—and Daniel, the creative social butterfly, thrived on chaos. One complemented the other, each handling the situations most aligned with their individual skills. However, the boundaries weren't always so clearly defined. Enter the sibling squabble. My favorite scenes to write. Probably because I'd had no siblings of my own to argue with.

Before I could decide what to do next, Lacey tapped on the doorframe in her khakis and red Ravenous Readers polo shirt. "Hey, you got a minute?"

I closed my laptop and clasped my hands together on the desk. "Sure. What's up?"

She brushed the escaped hair from her ponytail away from her eyes and waved me out of my seat. "Come see what I have in mind for expanding the kids' section when we get our payment. I think you'll love it."

Expanding? That was news to me. My stomach did a backstroke, threatening to eject some of that swamp water. Love it or not, we had bills to pay. "I don't know, Lacey. That section takes up the whole back of the store already. There aren't that many kids in Riddleton."

"Yes, but our children's section is supposed to be our claim to fame, remember? And it accounts for the bulk of our sales. We should get the most out of it we can."

I rose from my chair and followed her past the stockroom onto the main floor. "True, but we have so many other things we need to do with that money." We maneuvered around the children's tables. The life-sized giraffes, bookending the rainbow Ravenous Kids painted on the back wall, observed our every move. "Like pay you and Charlie, for instance."

Charlie Nichols, our self-proclaimed barista-in-chief, lived in my apartment building and volunteered to help out for a pittance when I inherited the bookstore after Aletha's murder. We didn't get along well when we first met, but now I couldn't imagine managing without him.

In his other life, Charlie spent most of his time on his computer, doing I had no idea what. Probably playing games or hacking into secret government agencies, known only by their acronyms or not at all. I suspected he'd spent the majority of his high school time pounding on the inside of his locker door, begging to be let out.

"Charlie doesn't need the money. His parents pay his bills just to keep him out of their basement. He hasn't asked for anything, has he?"

I glanced at the coffee bar where Charlie leaned on the pastry case, tapping away on his laptop, his white, ten-gallon hat tipped back, revealing his unkempt black hair. Looked like we had Cowboy Charlie today. Hat, shirt, jeans, vest, boots, gun belt, and spurs all included for the low, low price of a percentage of the coffee bar sales. At least the holster tied to his leg was empty. For now. No telling what tomorrow might bring.

"No, but that doesn't mean he isn't entitled to it. And what about you?"

"We don't need the money, either. And working here gets me out of the house and keeps me sane. I was helping Aletha most of the time, anyway. Why shouldn't I help you, too?" She gave me a sideways grin. "Besides, I love hobnobbing with celebrities."

That deserved an eye roll. "One bestselling book and a couple of solved murders hardly makes me a celebrity." Although, it didn't seem to take much these days.

"It does in this one-horse town."

"It's only a one-horse town because Cowboy Charlie over there couldn't find a place to keep his."

Riddleton, South Carolina, was a typical small town, though. Lacey had that right. Once a stagecoach rest stop parked midway between the cities Blackburn and Sutton, the town had grown some after the dam created Lake Dester in the 1920s, but not as much as expected. Which was fine with me, although as a teenager, I hated having everyone in my business. I'd learned to appreciate the folksy, hometown feel since I returned a couple of years ago. It was comforting knowing that people cared about me, no matter what, even if it meant occasionally being fodder for the local rumor mill.

I grabbed my *Writer in Residence* mug from behind the urn and poured myself some coffee. "So, what did you have in mind?"

Lacey's face glowed as she pointed toward the wall. "You see how we have two-shelf bookcases lining the walls?"

"The perfect size for little bodies, right?" I stirred cream and sugar into my coffee while Charlie observed.

"Right," Lacey said. "But not all of their bodies are that little. We've got middle grade and teens to think about too."

"Okay. And?"

"What if we pulled those out and put in full-sized cases instead? We could put the picture books on the bottom shelves for the little ones, followed by the middle grade and teen titles at the top. Then we can sprinkle the small bookcases around the sales floor for special promotions and whatnot. We'll have more room for books in the kids' section and more books to offer in the rest of the store."

As much as I loved the idea, my swampy belly chilled my enthusiasm. "This all sounds great, but where will the money come from?" Money didn't grow on trees, as my mother loved to remind me when I was growing up.

"The contest payment we get next month."

I shook my head. "There's a stack of bills on my desk begging to be paid before their not-so-distant cousins arrive with the big red words PAST DUE stamped across them. Also, we need that money to get us through the slow times the rest of the year."

Her lowered eyebrows sent a clear message my way. "You're being short-sighted, Jen. We only have three more checks coming in. We must invest them in the future. Otherwise, when the payments stop, so do we. Is that what you want?"

"Of course not." A deep breath kept my gut in check. "I hear what you're saying, but we'll need a lot more inventory on hand to fill the shelves. Money we can't afford to have tied up in books we might not sell."

Charlie jumped in. "Isn't that where the online sales can pick up the slack? We'll need the inventory to get the orders out in two days like we promise on the website."

"Come on, guys. My last name is Dawson, not Bezos. We have to be careful how we spend our money." I considered mentioning how the Amazon founder spent his extra money on rockets, not books, but then Charlie would come in dressed like an astronaut tomorrow. Not that I had anything against astronauts. I couldn't afford to replace the glass display case when he shattered it with his helmet, trying to retrieve a ham-and-cheese croissant. "Let me think about it. I don't want to let Aletha down. She trusted me. Trusted us. I'd rather play it safe."

Lacey laid a gentle hand on my arm. "I loved her, too, Jen. But one of these days, you'll have to accept that the store is yours. It's been a year and a half. Now's a good time, don't you think?"

My cocked eyebrow reminded Lacey how adamantly she'd fought for things to remain as Aletha wanted them only a few weeks ago when I proposed cutting costs.

She blushed and waved me off. "I know, I know. That's not what I said before. But I've had time to think about it, and you were right. Not about charging for Story Time, but we don't know what choices Aletha would've made facing our current challenges."

I appreciated her making it not "you", but "we", as in we all went down with the *Titanic* together. I swallowed the last of my coffee and refilled my cup. "That's true, we don't. I do know, however, that the children's section was her favorite part of the store, so I really will think about it. I promise."

"Thank you." Lacey scrutinized her distorted reflection in the uppers of her black leather oxfords. When she looked up again, she said, "I have something to tell you guys."

"You want to put gold-plated fixtures in the restroom?" I asked.

"Ha-ha. But don't give me any ideas. I might surprise you one day."

"Have fun, as long as I don't have to pay for it." I let my grin fade. "Seriously, though, what's up?"

Charlie closed his laptop and leaned in, giving her his full attention.

Her eyes glistened, and her smile flashed every one of her pearly whites. "I'm pregnant!"

"Yeehaw!" Charlie yelled and galloped his imaginary horse around the coffee bar, waving his hat.

A surge of joy ran from my head to my toes and back again. I wrapped her in a full-body hug. "Congratulations! What does your husband think?"

"Ben is thrilled to death. He always wanted three kids. We've been worried it might never happen."

"I'm so happy for you."

She eased out of my grip to catch her breath. "I'm glad. I was worried you might be upset."

"Upset? Why?"

"Well, while I'm going to work for as long as I can, it's going to mean a big chunk of time off at some point. You'll have to make do without me."

Oh. I hadn't thought of that. Still, she was my friend, and I refused to make her joyous news all about me. "Don't worry about it. We'll manage."

Lacey poked me in the ribs. "Not too well, I hope. I'd like to have a job to come back to."

Still circling, Charlie guffawed. I shot him an open-mouthed glare as he passed. "It's not that funny! I could do a great job. You don't know."

We all laughed at that one. No way I could ever replace Lacey. "No problem. You have a place here for as long as you want it. I promise."

"Thanks." Lacey teared up, then fanned her face. "Sorry, it's the hormones."

I hugged her again. "You have nothing to worry about."

9

She pulled away and studied me thoughtfully. "Seriously, though, I think you'll do just fine without me. You're more capable than you give yourself credit for."

If only that were true. My history lent too much doubt to her words, but I appreciated the sentiment just the same.

Charlie galloped up to us, panting. "So, is it a boy or a girl?"

"We don't know yet. And we haven't decided whether we want to. Since we already have one of each, we might wait and be surprised. Personally, I'm hoping for a boy since I had all those blood pressure problems when I was pregnant with Brianna. No issues at all when I had Benny, though."

I took a large swallow of my tepid drink. Funny how I could enjoy my coffee after it'd cooled, but iced coffee didn't appeal to me at all. "What do the kids think about it?"

"We haven't told them yet. I'm a little nervous. I think my daughter will take it well. She's already been through it with her brother. Him, I'm concerned about. He's been the baby of the family for six years. And he likes it that way."

"I bet he'll be fine," Charlie said. "He'll probably love having a little brother or sister to boss around."

Lacey sighed. "I hope you're right." She glanced over her shoulder. "Well, I'd better find something to do before the Saturday rush hits."

Saturday rush? I followed her glance around the empty store. "What's that old expression? From your lips to God's ears?"

She shrugged. "No kidding."

I wandered back toward the giraffes, gauging how the area would look with full-sized bookcases. Smaller, most likely, as the side walls would each seem a foot closer to the center than they currently were. Still, there'd be more than enough of an area for the kids to play with the toys stashed in the imitation pirate's chests spread strategically around the space. And plenty of room for Queen Lacey's throne and the semicircle of chairs arranged for Story Time. It all came down to whether we dared spend the money. Whether *I* dared spend the money.

I wiped my sweaty palms on my jeans and returned to the coffee bar, brow furrowed.

Charlie's gaze followed my travels. Then he reached into the pastry case and retrieved a chocolate chip muffin. "Here you go, boss. This should help you make up your mind. Chocolate solves everything, right?"

I wish. "Right," I said and took a bite. A chocolate morsel melted on my tongue, and a groan escaped as I closed my eyes.

"Have you heard anything about that skeleton you found in the tunnel under St. Mary's last month?"

My eyelids flew open again. The memory of being trapped and lost underground tainted the enjoyment of my snack. I set it on the counter. "Not much. They still don't know who it is, and Riddleton PD passed the case off to Sutton County. They have a cold-case squad over there that specializes in these kinds of things."

"Too bad." He shrugged. "I was hoping you'd break out your pipe and magnifying glass for another investigation. And I could play Watson."

I leaned on the counter and broke off a chocolaty piece of my abandoned muffin. "I've thought about it a lot, to be honest. I'd love to know who it was and how he got down there."

"He?"

"Yeah, the medical examiner in Sutton said he could tell by the hips or pelvis or something like that. But the cool thing is they know he was murdered execution-style with a slug to the back of the head." I pointed to the back of my skull halfway between my neck and the top. "Right here. They also retrieved the bullet, and last I heard they're running it through the system, but they don't expect to get a hit without also having the murder weapon."

Charlie grinned. "Sounds like you're already looking into it."

"Well, maybe a little. It's a mystery, and you know how much I love mysteries."

"Everyone knows how obsessed you are with mysteries, but that's why we love you."

Savannah poked me in the back of the leg with her favorite stuffed bone. I threw it toward the front of the store for her to chase at the same instant a fortyish guy, whose head almost brushed the top of the doorjamb, walked in holding a little girl's hand. Oops. The dog skidded to a stop at the "Do Not Cross" tape we put on the carpet about ten feet from the door and sat, rear end wiggling.

Lacey greeted the man and his daughter, and Savannah trotted back, bone hanging halfway out of her mouth. I took it and led her around the side wall, past the cherry bookcases with carved wooden plaques above indicating the genres. Not that she would hurt anyone. I wanted our guests to shop without distraction, and a full-grown German shepherd wanting to play would be a real distraction.

I sat on the brown and gold couch near the front window and scratched her chest while light classical music from the ceiling speakers drifted over me. Lacey would be gone soon. When did pregnant people go on maternity leave? Would she wait until she couldn't see her shoes or until she went into labor restocking the Self-Help section?

Then for how long after the baby was born? Weeks or months? It must be several months total, at least. What would I do without her? I'd learned some of the management end of running the bookstore, but I was nowhere near ready to take over. Guess I'd have to step up and learn the rest by the time she left to have her baby.

I kissed Savannah on the head. "What am I going to do, little girl?"

She licked my cheek.

That made it all better. Savannah kisses always did. Second only to chocolate, of course.

Movement across the street flickered in the corner of my eye. I turned my head and caught two men going into Antonio's Ristorante. The restaurant had been closed since the owner died last summer. What was going on? Guess I'd better wander over there and find out.

CHAPTER TWO

I wandered across Main Street, blinking against the sixty-degree sunshine pouring down from a clear blue sky. An almost spring-like January day. It was unusual for this time of year to be so warm, but I relished the relief from the winter cold. Way too soon, though. Old Man Winter wasn't near through with us yet, despite what my eyes were telling me today. But I could enjoy it while it lasted.

The closed blinds obscured my view through the restaurant's windows, but I knew those guys were in there, just not what they were doing. My boyfriend, Eric, would tell me to mind my own business, but I couldn't help myself. Like the beaver that gnawed off the branch it was standing on, dropping it into the stream below. However, tall, scarecrow-thin Eric O'Malley had an astonishing lack of curiosity for a police detective. In my mind, people messing around in a building closed for months, directly across the street from my bookstore, *was* my business.

14

I hesitated for a moment, questioning the wisdom of what I was about to do. In truth, I had no idea who those guys were. The lack of forced entry proved they had a key to the building, so, more likely than not, they were relatives who'd inherited the restaurant. Still, a bit of caution on my part wouldn't hurt anything.

The front door eased open when I gently pulled on the handle. After a quick survey of the dining room, I stepped inside and waited for my eyes to adjust to being indoors again. Ladder-back chairs rested upside down on all the tables, and the Tiffany-style lamps hanging from the ceiling were coated with dust. Antonio's had been Riddleton's "fancy" restaurant until last summer when the owner died. I'd only been in it a few times when it was open, some visits more enjoyable than others.

A shadowy blob near the double doors leading to the kitchen said gruffly, "Can I help you?" The blob materialized into a swarthy, fortyish man with thinning black hair and a thick black mustache concealing his upper lip. The guy looked a bit like Tony Scavuto, the previous owner, only a lot taller. Tony was a little bitty guy, height-wise. He made up for it in muscle-driven girth, though.

Was the man a relative come to claim his inheritance? I plastered on a smile and stuck out my hand. "I'm Jen Dawson. Owner of the bookstore across the street."

He wiped his hand on the back of his jeans and shook with a firm yet not overpowering grip. "Fredo Di Rocca. Nice to meetcha. I'll be reopening the restaurant in a few weeks. You want a drink or a coffee? No food yet, but the fountains work."

A chill ran down my spine as if a ghost had spoken. The man sounded like Tony. He must be from Chicago, too. "No, thank you. Are . . . were you related to the previous owner?"

He smoothed his mustache, almost covering both lips with it. "Son-in-law. His daughter Mara is my wife. Me and his son are gonna run this place together when we get it back in shape. Gotta get it cleaned up first."

Better get a psychic or a medium in here too. "That's great! Riddleton's been missing a high-end restaurant. We have to go all the way to Sutton or Blackburn for anything other than diner food. Well, there's the bar and grill too, but being surrounded by drunks watching sports isn't really my idea of a romantic dinner."

Fredo took a handkerchief out of his pocket and mopped the back of his neck. "We'll be happy to fix that problem for you. And we'll be keeping the menu the same. For now, anyway."

The front door opened, and a short, wiry guy with slicked-back hair so black it could've been coated in shoe polish came in carrying two Piggly Wiggly bags. He unloaded cleaning supplies onto a table in the dining room.

"Hey, Gilberto!" Fredo called.

The man looked up, examined me with coal-black eyes, and flashed his even, white teeth. "I'm sorry. I didn't see you there." He advanced toward me with his hand extended. "Gil Scavuto. I'm so happy to meet you!"

16

Scavuto? A direct relation to Tony. He definitely had his eyes. And lack of height. "Jen Dawson. I run the bookstore across the street."

A look of recognition skimmed over his face, and he pushed his black-rimmed glasses up to the bridge of his nose. "Oh, yeah. My father mentioned you. He said you were trying to help him." Gil knitted his eyebrows. "Guess they got to him before you could."

Something like that. Tony died last summer after he'd been named a suspect in the police chief's murder. He'd asked for my assistance in clearing his name, but I was unable to help him before he became another victim. I'd tried my best, though. "I'm sorry for your loss."

He lowered his head for a second, then met my gaze through his thin, black wire-frames. "Thank you." He regarded his brother-in-law. "Did Alfredo here offer you something to drink?"

"He did, thank you."

"Yeah, Fredo can cook like nobody's business, but he isn't much in the customer service department. That's my job." Gil grinned and pointed his thumb at his chest. "I'm loving this town. I've met so many terrific people."

I turned to Fredo. "Is your wife around? I'd love to meet her too." I caught Gil's scowl out of the corner of my eye. Had I said something wrong?

Fredo gestured toward the back of the dining room. "No, she's over in her shop getting it ready to open."

A new shop? Exciting. Riddleton needed something different. "Really? Where is it? And what's it going to be?"

17

This time Fredo wore the scowl. "It's gonna be a disaster, that's what."

Gil frowned, his black eyes unreadable. "She's opening a bookstore over by the vet's office. I was hoping she'd work here with us, but she didn't want to."

A bookstore? My knees betrayed me, and I took a step to catch my balance. There weren't enough customers for the one we had, let alone another one. I saw serious trouble in my future. Maybe I was the one who needed the psychic. I balled my fists at my sides and sealed my lips against the oncoming explosion.

The look on my face must've given Gil pause because he smiled. "Don't worry. It's a *used* bookstore. It won't be any competition for you. You only sell new books, right?"

My face heated so quickly that it seemed I stood before an angry flamethrower. Of course it would be competition. More than competition. The cheaper books would put us out of business. "Yes, but—"

Gil's smile broadened. "There, you see? Everything's fine. There's more than enough business to go around."

"In Chicago, maybe. But you're not in Chicago anymore."

Gil's puzzled expression proved he truly didn't understand my problem. And I was too furious to explain it to him. Transplants from the city couldn't understand how different life was in a small town like Riddleton until they'd lived here a while. The same held true in reverse, as I'd learned when I moved to Blackburn for college. But Blackburn was no Chicago.

The Scavuto clan was in for a huge culture shock. The water moccasin trying to survive in the desert kind.

I looked to Fredo for help. "Can't you talk to your wife? There are plenty of other products she could sell. Things people here would be thrilled to not have to leave town to get. How about shoes or sporting goods? Anything but a bookstore!"

Fredo shrugged. "I wanted her to work here with us, too. Make the restaurant a real family business. Mara wants to sell books. It'll make her happy. If she's happy, she's not making me miserable. So, she'll sell books."

Gil narrowed his eyes and pressed his lips together.

Clearly, Gil was no happier about his sister's choices than I was. Or maybe Fredo was the problem. Hard to tell at this point. Either way, Mara was the one I needed to be talking to, not these two clowns. I pried my fingernails out of my palms. "Well, it was nice meeting you. Good luck getting the restaurant back open. I'm looking forward to eating here again."

I bolted out the door before either could respond. I had no interest in anything they had to say. It wasn't their fault, though. Mara had decided to destroy everything I'd worked to achieve for the last year and a half. I could only hope she didn't understand the full impact of that decision. Didn't realize there was no room for a second bookstore in town. Mara had to listen to reason. And I had to find a way to be reasonable.

Fortunately, I had a three-block walk to help me calm down. I hung a right at the corner of Main and Walnut. Leaves from the trees the street was named for crunched under my feet as I marched down the sidewalk, struggling to get my temper under control. Mara would never listen if I spewed my venom on her. Deep breaths helped, and I focused on relaxing my muscles. Little by little, the boiling anger cooled to a simmer.

By the time I reached Bannister's parking lot on the corner of Second Street, I could think in complete sentences. Progress. Now I had to calm down enough to make those sentences make sense. I had to acknowledge, though, the anger was only the outward manifestation of the fear roiling in my stomach. Fear that piggybacked on my dread that the bookstore might fail. That I might fail.

I turned right onto Second and weaved around the folks heading to the bar and grill for lunch. I briefly considered stopping in for a drink but decided against it. I had a low tolerance for alcohol, and approaching Mara while intoxicated wouldn't help her understand my predicament. Assuming my words made any sense to begin with.

Once across Pine Street, I slowed as I passed the gas station. Mara's shop was two doors down on my right, and I still had no idea what to say to change her mind. If Fredo was correct, and this was her dream, nothing I said would make any difference. But I had to try.

I stopped in front of the shop with no sign and windows that hadn't seen a drop of glass cleaner in at least a year next to the Riddleton Veterinary Clinic's backyard. I'd calmed some, but not enough. It would only take a tiny spark to set me off again. I hesitated at the front door and fell back on the mantra my shrink, Dr. Margolis, had taught me for occasions like this:

Deep breath in, slow breath out.

Once more, and I was as ready as I would ever be. The doorknob turned easily in my hand, and I pushed the door open and stepped inside. Once my eyes adjusted, it only took a second for me to realize I'd entered an empty room. She didn't even have bookcases yet. I might have a chance to change her mind.

"Can I help you?"

I turned to face a petite, black-haired woman around my age, wearing jeans and a plain white T-shirt with the sleeves rolled up, and holding a broom. It was showtime. I pasted a smile on my face and moved toward her. "Hi, are you Mara?"

Her lips twitched into a hesitant grin, giving her a striking resemblance to her father. She fingered the pendant depicting scales resting against her chest. "Yes. What can I do for you?"

Give up your lifelong dream? "I'm Jen Dawson—"

Mara's smile broadened. "The writer. I've heard people talking about you."

"Yes, ma'am. But I'm not just a writer. I also own Ravenous Readers, and I was hoping we could talk about your plans for a used bookstore."

She pinched her eyebrows together and tipped her head toward her shoulder. "How did you hear about that?"

"I stopped by Antonio's, and your husband and brother told me about it."

Her grin evaporated. "Men never know when to keep their mouths shut."

Was it supposed to be a secret? Why? "I was bound to find out sooner or later. I'm only glad it was before you got all stocked up and ready to open."

She leaned on her broom. "Why? What difference does that make?"

I rubbed my hands down the front of my jeans. "Well, I was hoping I might be able to change your mind. Riddleton is a small town. Definitely too small for two bookstores."

Mara's knuckles blanched on the broom handle. "I disagree. I think there's plenty of business here for both of us. I'm going to sell used books, not new ones. They can buy them new from you and trade them back to me when they're done. I don't see a problem."

The flamethrower reappeared. I took a deep breath. "I don't think it's going to be that simple. We don't only sell newly published books. Our inventory is quite varied, including some that people might find here instead."

She shrugged. "There's nothing wrong with a little healthy competition, is there?" She gave me a cheeky wink. "It's good for everyone."

My closely clipped fingernails created half-moons in my palms again. "Maybe, but there are so many other products people here need more. I hate having to drive for half an hour just to get a pair of shoes or a new couch. Or how about a dress store or jeans? Riddleton already has a bookstore and a library. Why do you think there's enough demand to support more book sales?"

"You make a good point." She paused for a second, just long enough for hope to peek out of the mire. "But

I'll take my chances. I think if given a choice, people will come here first. Maybe that's what you're worried about."

Damn right, that's what I'm worried about! "Maybe, maybe not, but why not get into something that will benefit the town and leave room for both of us?"

She gave me an I've-got-a-secret smile. "Who says I want to leave room for both of us?"

My mouth fell open. "This is personal? Why?"

"You killed my father, and I'm going to make you pay for it. Now, get out of my store!"

My feet froze in place, confusion flooding my brain. "I had nothing to do with your father's death."

"If that's what helps you sleep at night, good for you." She pointed the broom handle toward the door. "Get out! And don't come back unless it's to hand over your inventory for free, 'cause I sure as hell won't give you a dime for it."

I forced myself out the door, squashing the impulse to wrap my hands around her throat and squeeze. I rarely had violent impulses, but some people brought out the worst in me. Mara was one of those people.

Once outside, I took a few more deep breaths and lifted my face into the sunshine to calm myself, then pulled out my phone. It was ten after one, and I was supposed to meet Eric at the diner for lunch ten minutes ago. Half my brain told me I should hurry because Eric didn't like it when I was late. The other half said to take my time so I didn't erupt all over him the instant I arrived. I went with the take-my-time half. Things had been great between Eric and me the last few weeks.

We'd only been seriously dating for a few months, but we loved each other. While I still wasn't quite sure he was "the one", I shouldn't risk messing things up by throwing a temper tantrum in public.

I made a right on Oak Street, past the vet's office, and strolled to Main, focusing on my breathing. As I crossed Main toward the diner on the corner of Pine, my phone buzzed with an email. I halted in front of the Goodwill and opened it. It was from an attorney.

Dear Ms. Dawson,

This notice is to inform you that the Your Life Contest has filed for bankruptcy, and no further payments will be issued. You may file a claim by contacting us before March 31. Any claims received after that date will not be considered by the court.

You will receive a written copy of this notification within three weeks.

Sincerely,
Paul Holcomb
Holcomb, Holcomb, and Klein, Attorneys at Law

Could this day get any worse?

CHAPTER THREE

My legs buckled. I leaned back against the Goodwill window, blocking the view of an old Remington manual typewriter displayed behind the glass. My hands shook so much I almost dropped my phone while stuffing it back in my pocket. Tears pushed their way into my eyes. Pinching the bridge of my nose helped keep them back for the moment, but it was only a matter of time. However, I couldn't walk into the diner a bawling mess, so I stood in the middle of the sidewalk, shoppers dodging me like magnets with the same poles, as I tried to regain my equilibrium.

When I woke up this morning, the bookstore was in trouble, but it was the only one in town, and the contest would prop it up for a couple more years. We were the only one within twenty miles, so we only had to convince people it was better to *stay* in town than run to the malls in Blackburn or Sutton.

Now the contest was bankrupt, a new bookstore almost guaranteed to steal all but the most loyal customers was about to open, and the referee had hit number eight of a ten count. We could probably hang on for a little while, but Mara would be basically selling most of the same books we were for half the price or less. And trade-ins would reduce the cost even more. It wouldn't be long before we were knocked out. Despair crept through every muscle fiber in my body, but I refused to give in. There had to be a way out of this mess.

My phone buzzed with a text from Eric, wanting to know where I was. A fair question. I was almost thirty minutes late now, which would try the patience of Mother Teresa. Might as well get it over with. Perhaps a double bacon cheeseburger and an extra-large chocolate milkshake would make it all better. For a minute, anyway.

Forcing one foot in front of the other into the diner, I waved at the proprietor, Angus Halliburton, in his usual place behind the counter. He wiped his hands on the condiment-splashed apron covering his ample midsection, then pointed toward the back corner with his black combover flopping like a fish that had escaped its tank when he turned his head.

My boyfriend frowned alternately at his drink and watch. He hated when I arrived late, something I was prone to. Unfortunately, I had a good excuse this time.

I maneuvered around the tables of mostly Riddleton residents, along with a few strangers passing through. Even if I didn't know everyone in the room, the visitors stood out like watermelons in a pumpkin patch. They wore the frazzled demeanors of travelers or the aloof disdain of people from the city here on business. Today we had six tourists and, despite the khakis and polo shirt he wore, an obvious businessman. He had collar-length brown hair, a matching beard, and his nose buried in a copy of the *Wall Street Journal*. Not your average Riddleton reader.

I slid into the orange booth opposite Eric. "Sorry I'm late. It's been a busy morning."

He ran a hand through his close-cropped orange hair, which contrasted with the freckles spread across his cheeks. "What's going on? You're not usually *this* behind schedule."

It all came crashing down. Unable to stop myself, I burst into tears.

His expression softened, and he reached for my hand. "Jen, what is it? I'm sorry I got upset. I didn't mean it."

My breath hitched, and the tears trickled to a drip. I grabbed a napkin out of the table dispenser and blew my nose. "It's not you. I should have said terrible instead of busy."

He came around and sat beside me. When our waitress, Penelope, approached our table, she did an immediate U-turn as Eric waved her away. "Tell me what happened."

I sniffed, then blew my nose again. "Well, I saw some people in Antonio's this morning, so I went over to check it out. Tony's son and son-in-law are reopening the restaurant."

Eric squeezed my hand. "That's a good thing, isn't it? Now we won't have to drive all the way to Sutton for a decent meal."

"I'd like that too. The problem is that Tony's daughter, Mara, is opening a used bookstore over by the vet's office. I went to try to talk her out of it, but she's adamant. She wants to put us out of business because she thinks I killed her father."

His jaw dropped. "That's absurd!"

"I know. We had a big argument, and she threw me out."

He put his arm around my shoulder and pulled me close. "That's all right. We'll figure something out. Don't give up just yet."

A new wave of tears soaked the shoulder of his Riddleton Police Department T-shirt. I breathed in his freshly showered man-scent, drawing comfort from his strength. "But there's more." I pulled away so my runny nose wouldn't leak on him and reached for another napkin. "On my way over here, I got an email from a lawyer informing me the contest is going bankrupt. We won't be getting any more payments."

He inhaled sharply. "No wonder you're so upset. That puts a whole new spin on things. I'm so sorry, Jen."

I buried my face in my hands. "I've done a lousy job with the bookstore, and now I'm going to pay the price for it."

"That's not true. You've had other priorities, that's all. Your writing is important too."

"But Aletha trusted me, and I've let her down." More tears flowed, and I felt as if my whole body had been turned inside out, exposing my most vulnerable parts.

Eric hugged me again. "Honey, there's no way you could have predicted this, and Aletha couldn't have either. She'd be in the exact same position you are, and I doubt she'd have any more ready solutions than you do."

He had a point. "Probably not."

"Look, I have a little money saved. Not much, but it's yours if you want it."

"Thank you." I sat up and dried my eyes. My chest filled. "I couldn't take your money. You've worked too hard for it. But I love you for offering."

He gazed into my eyes, and butterflies took off in my midsection. "I love you too. Please let me help. At least keep it in the back of your mind, okay?"

I looked away, trying to pull myself together. "I will."

Penelope swished to our table again, in her short black skirt, took one look at my swollen red face, and said, "Are you all right, Jen?" She aimed her golden eyes at Eric. "What'd you do to her?"

Eric lifted his hands in surrender. "I had nothing to do with this."

I sniffled. "It's true. It's not his fault. I've just had some really bad news."

Her expression shifted into concern. "Oh, bless your heart." She retrieved her pad and pen out of her apron pocket. "A good hot meal will make you feel better. Give you a whole new perspective. How about we double size that milkshake today? Chocolate can fix anything."

If only that were true. Eric ordered for both of us and returned to his side of the table. He took my hands again. "Have you considered getting a loan from the bank?"

"I haven't considered anything yet."

"Well, what do you think?"

"I think it'll help for now, but the used bookstore will still be stealing all our sales, and then I'll have a loan to pay off on top of everything else."

"True, but at least it'll buy you some time to figure out what to do next."

"I'll think about it. The bank doesn't open until Monday anyway. That gives me all day tomorrow to figure out what to do. Right now, I just want to forget about it for a while."

Our food arrived, and we ate in silence. I could feel his worried glances between bites, but stubbornly refused to acknowledge them. My fragility wouldn't allow it, lest I fall apart like a cracked glass in a dishwasher. As hard as I tried, I couldn't forget. "You're a loser" went round and round in my head. The world's worst daily affirmation.

Writing *Double Trouble* was the only thing I hadn't failed at in my life. The only thing I'd ever started that I'd actually finished. I'd made a mess of everything else, and now the bookstore was about to join the ash heap. Another bestseller would help bail me out, but *Twin Terror* didn't release for another three months. Way too late, I suspected.

I broke from my reverie to find Eric studying me with a solemn expression on his face. "What? Why are you looking at me that way?"

He smiled. "I was just thinking. Mara can't possibly believe you killed Tony. No facts ever supported that theory."

"Since when do facts matter these days? People believe what they want, regardless of whether there's any proof."

"Maybe. But what if she wants something from you, and she's only using that nonsense to get your attention?"

I cocked one eyebrow. "You're kidding, right? What could she possibly want from me?"

He shrugged. "I have no idea. There's only one way to find out, though."

"You mean ask her?"

"Yup. You need to have a calm, reasonable conversation with her."

My crumpled napkin landed in the pool of ketchup on my plate. "No way. After the way she treated me the last time I tried to talk to her? If I go back there, she'll either beat me with that broom, or I'll end up killing her, which won't be good for either of us."

Eric laughed. "Yeah, right. Like you could kill someone."

I crossed my arms. "Anyone can kill if the motive is strong enough. Just ask any mystery writer. Or homicide detective."

"I'm a homicide detective."

"Then you should know better."

He sat back and draped an arm over the top of the booth. "This is silly. You're telling me that you would be motivated enough to kill someone to save a failing business that isn't even your number-one priority in life?"

I hated when he got all logical on me. "Maybe."

He laughed again. "Baloney. If someone stole your laptop, and you hadn't saved your completed manuscript anywhere else, I could totally see it. Otherwise, you're being ridiculous."

I snickered and blew my nose again. He was good for me. Like fresh fruit and broccoli.

"Go talk to her. See what she has to say. The worst that can happen is she throws you out again. At least you'll know you tried everything."

I hated when he was right too. "Fine, I'll go see her. Will you come with me?"

"You don't need me there. Mara might be more amenable if it's just the two of you."

"Is amenable another word for violent?"

The skin beside his eyes crinkled. "You're the writer. You tell me. I'm just a dummy police detective."

"Yeah, right. Detectives aren't necessarily stupid."

"Tell that to all the investigator characters in your books."

"Very funny." I reached for his hand. "Seriously. Please come with me. I'll feel safer if you're there. Less likely to say something stupid."

"I can't. I promised Ingrid I'd run a few laps with her this afternoon since she couldn't make it to our group run this morning. I can make it after that, if you want."

Ingrid Kensington was the town doctor slash medical examiner and a member of the Riddleton Runners. I playfully pushed his hand away. "Okay, I get it now. You'd rather spend time with her than me."

He put a finger up to his lips. "Shhhh. Marcus will hear you. You know he gets jealous."

I glanced at the tall, muscular man conversing with Angus behind the counter. "Marcus Jones doesn't have a jealous side. Besides, he likes you. And he trusts Ingrid. They're perfect for each other. And now that Angus has promoted him to assistant manager, they have a real chance at a future together."

I couldn't help but wonder if Antonio's reopening would take some of the diner's business. If Angus lost enough customers, he wouldn't need an assistant manager, and Marcus would have to be a cook again. Not that Ingrid would care. She loved him for himself, not what he did for a living. And she adored his two little girls as if they were her own. Marcus would take a demotion personally, though. He'd worked hard to make a better life for his family than he had growing up. He'd see it as a failure.

Eric flashed an impish smile. "Speaking of Angus, I heard he has a girlfriend."

I peered at him from under my eyebrows. "You're not only speaking of Angus; you're speaking like him. When did you hitch a ride on the gossip train?"

"I didn't. I just wanted to change the subject."

"Okay, I'll bite. Who's he seeing?"

"I don't know. That's what makes it so interesting."

"It's only interesting if it's true." I rested my elbows on the table. "I guess he'll tell us when he's ready. Maybe he's waiting until he decides it's serious."

Eric grabbed the check and stood, the waistband of his cargo shorts settling on his hip bones. "I'd better get going. I told Ingrid I'd meet her at three, and I still have to go home and change."

33

"All right. You two have fun."

"Call me later to fill me in on how it went?"

"Will do. Fingers crossed I'll have good news!"

He kissed me, his lips soft on mine, setting the butterflies into motion again, then he headed for the register while I pushed French fries around my plate. I didn't want to see Mara for a second time today, but Eric was right. She might have a different motive for wanting to put me out of business. One I could address. Unfortunately, the only way to learn what that might be was for me to go back to that store.

I got a to-go box from Penelope and threw a few fries in there for Savannah. Angus flagged me down with a glint in his brown eyes as I passed the counter on my way to the door. "Hey, Jen. Have you heard they're reopening Antonio's?"

"I met them this morning. I thought they were robbing the place so I went over there to check it out. Turns out it was Tony's family."

Angus nodded. "I was so disappointed when they turned down my offer to buy the place. They said they were reopening, but honestly, I wasn't sure I believed them. Guess I was wrong."

My eyebrows shot up my forehead toward my hairline. "I didn't know you wanted Antonio's."

"Yeah. That's one of the reasons I promoted Marcus. I was going to run that place, and he would take care of this one for me. I've always wanted a fancy restaurant. You know, la-di-da wines and such. I was really looking forward to it."

I squeezed his arm. "I'm sorry you didn't get it. It looks like we're both getting shortchanged on the deal."

"How so?"

Dread crept back up my throat. "Tony's daughter is opening a used bookstore while her brother and husband run the restaurant."

His mouth fell open, revealing perfect white teeth. "What? I hadn't heard about that."

"You mean I beat the gossipmongers for a change? First time for everything."

"I'm so sorry, Jen."

Me too. "Thanks. I'm on my way over there now to try one more time to talk her out of it. Wish me luck."

"Luck!"

I shook my head and scooted out the door to drop off the fries at the bookstore and fill Lacey in on the new-bookstore-opening-soon news while Savannah inhaled them. I couldn't handle another "What are we gonna do?" discussion, so I ducked out before she could respond. And I wasn't even close to ready for the "the contest isn't sending any more money" conversation, so I didn't mention it. Only one more errand today before I could go home and drown myself in the brand-new bottle of white Moscato I had stashed in my refrigerator.

Suicide by alcohol inhalation. That would be a first for Ingrid.

Not quite ready to face Mara again, I took the long way around and strolled up Walnut, around the cul-de-sac at the end, and back to Second Street. The detour added about twenty minutes to my journey, giving me time to conquer the fear and anger and consider what I would say to her. What *could* I say that wouldn't set her off again?

I paused for a moment in front of the door, steeling my nerves for the uncomfortable encounter to come. Was meeting with her again a good idea? Wouldn't it be like swatting at a beehive? Probably, but if I waited too long, she might be too far into the process to change her mind. And I had to convince her to change her mind. No matter what.

I swallowed my trepidation and reached for the doorknob. The door opened soundlessly, and I stepped inside the empty room. The broom was leaning on the wall, but no sign of Mara anywhere. "Mara?"

An open doorway caught my eye, and I moved in that direction. It was a storage room full of empty bookcases and boxes I presumed contained books. She was much further along than I'd realized. No wonder she wouldn't consider doing anything else. I owed her an apology, but I had to find her first.

"Mara?" I called out again.

I spotted a fire exit straight ahead and another closed door on my right. Bathroom? Maybe. It could be an office, too. I tapped on the door and listened. No answer. I tried the doorknob, which was unlocked. It turned out to be an office with file cabinets lining the walls and a desk against the back wall by the window. Someone was sitting in the chair in front of the desk. I tapped on the doorframe. "Mara? It's Jen. Can I talk to you for a minute?"

No response.

"Listen, I know you're upset with me, and you have every right to be. I came to apologize. Please hear me out."

Still no answer.

I stepped around the remains of a carryout lunch from the Dandy Diner scattered on the floor. *What happened here?* "Mara?"

One more step, and I saw her slumped over the desk, a yellow silk scarf wrapped around her neck. I sprang forward. "Mara! Mara, are you okay?"

I moved the scarf away from her bare neck, adorned with a red line around it. The idea that something wasn't quite right, other than she seemed to have been strangled, flashed through my mind, but I didn't have time to deal with it right now. I checked her pulse. Nothing. She was dead. With a hand shaking so hard I could barely control it, I pulled my phone out of my pocket and dialed 911. Before they answered, the front door crashed open, and people rushed in.

I turned around, and two uniformed Riddleton Police officers burst through the doorway into the office. Their guns were drawn and pointed toward us. Their eyes volleyed between Mara, face down on the desk, and me. Then their guns both pointed at me. "Freeze! Let me see your hands!"

After placing my phone on the desk, I lifted my hands to the level of my ears.

My day had just gotten much worse.

CHAPTER FOUR

The room seemed smaller than I remembered from my interrogation during Aletha's murder investigation. But my arms handcuffed to the table this time might have something to do with it. That and the hour or so I'd had to wait. No way to know for sure how much time had passed since they took my phone, and I didn't wear a watch.

However, enough time had passed for me to understand how much trouble I was in. Mara was dead. Murdered. And I was found standing over her body. Sweat broke out on my palms. Too bad it wasn't enough for me to slip out of the cuffs and escape. Not that I would. Where would I go?

I hear Venezuela's nice this time of year.

No way. I'd done nothing wrong. Havermayer would have to see that eventually. Fear crept into my throat, and my hands vibrated against the steel surrounding them. Eventually could be a long time. Like life-in-prison, or death-by-lethal-injection long.

I studied my reflection in the mirrored window, and a tired and haggard version of myself stared back. I'd aged ten years since this morning. It'd been that kind of day. Finding another dead body was nowhere on my to-do list when I woke up, yet here I sat, marinated and seasoned, waiting to be grilled by a detective who hated me already. And scared out of my mind.

Detective Francine Havermayer had been my nemesis since the day we met a year and a half ago, and she wore her animosity like a badge of honor. Her starched and pressed suits contrasted with my jeans and sweatshirts, as did her "I'm right, and you're wrong" approach to life in general and me in particular. Her greatest disappointment had been her inability to pin a murder on me. She'd be desperate to do so now. Unfortunately, this time she might succeed.

The wobbly hard plastic chair cut off the blood flow to my bottom, and I squirmed to ease the tingling in my legs. Nothing I could do about the sweat rolling off my forehead into my eyes. My shoulders could only reach so far. My belly churned, and I desperately needed to use the bathroom. Nobody to ask, though. And even if there was, I wouldn't give them the satisfaction. My mother always said my pigheadedness would be my downfall one day. I refused to let *her* be right, either.

Havermayer finally came in and dropped a manila folder on the table. She stood silent, hands in the pockets of her crisp black suit pants, glaring down at me through fierce green eyes nestled under dark eyebrows. Didn't she ever take a day off? Her outfits always appeared brand new. She must have a considerable clothing budget. Or an award-winning dry cleaner.

"Hi, Jen. How're you doing? You need anything? Something to drink, maybe?"

I met her gaze head-on. She was playing nice to throw me off guard. Fat chance I'd fall into that trap. "No, thank you."

She glanced at my handcuffed wrists and pulled a key out of her pocket. "How about we take those off?" Her tone dripped more syrup than even my sweet tooth could stomach. Unfortunately for her, I wasn't stupid enough to fall for it. I knew full well how Havermayer really felt about me.

The detective released my hands, and I rubbed the deep red dents on my wrists. "Thank you." Might as well keep things civil for a bit longer.

Havermayer pulled a chair from the other side of the table close before sitting and pulled out a sheet of paper with *MIRANDA RIGHTS AND WAIVER* in big bold letters across the top. I was a bit player in her own personal TV cop show, and she loved every minute of it. I wished I could say the same. I made another fruitless attempt to clear the perspiration dripping down the side of my face.

She held the paper at arm's length in front of her and squinted while she read. "You have the right to remain silent."

Time for reading glasses, Detective? "I was already read my rights."

"And I'm doing it again. You have the right to remain silent. Do you understand?"

40

I considered exercising that right, just to irritate her, but played along instead. "Yes."

She turned the form to face me and pointed to a line. "Initials here."

Once I scribbled my *JD*, she promptly moved on to the next line.

"Anything you say may be used in a court of law. Do you understand?"

"Yup."

Another set of initials.

She continued that way until the bottom line. "Knowing these rights, are you willing to waive them and speak to me? If so, sign here."

As soon as my pen left the paper, she flipped it around and signed with the date and time before slipping it into her folder.

"Where's your partner? Shouldn't Eric be here, too?"

She laughed. "In the real world, unlike in your books, that's against protocol. Plus, I like my cases to not end in a mistrial. He's not coming anywhere near this investigation. If you're expecting him to rescue you, forget it. It's not going to happen." She opened her file and slid a photograph of Mara Di Rocca's body in the chair by her desk toward me. "You want to tell me about this?"

I forced back bile and glanced away. The image was still fresh in my mind. I didn't need to look at Havermayer's attempt at intimidation. I pushed the photo back to her side of the table. "There's nothing to tell. I stopped by to speak with her and found her like that. Then the police busted in and arrested me. I had nothing to do with her death."

"You were heard arguing with her minutes before we found you."

"Someone may have been heard arguing with her, but it wasn't me. I had just arrived. It had to be somebody else."

Havermayer shook her head. "A tech from the vet's office was in the yard and heard loud voices arguing and then a scream. She called 911. Officers arrived within two minutes and found you standing over the body with the scarf in your hands. Who else could it have been? Did you see anyone else there?"

"No." I massaged the back of my neck. "Maybe whoever killed her went out the back door when they heard me come in the front."

"Without us seeing them? Not likely. The vet tech was waiting for us outside. She didn't see anyone either."

"She couldn't have paid too much attention while she waited, or she'd have seen me go in the front *after* she called. I'm not surprised she didn't notice the killer leaving." I hid my clenched fists in my lap. "Unlikely or not, the murderer had to have slipped out the back door because I didn't see anyone come out the front, and I didn't kill her. And I only had my phone in my hand, not the scarf. I'd just called 911 myself when your officers burst in. Why would I do that if I'd murdered someone?"

She sat back in her chair and clasped her hands behind her head. Her pristine black jacket fell open, exposing the gold detective's shield clipped to her belt.

"You expect me to take your word for that? Maybe you were just trying to throw us off. Make us think you're innocent because you called it in."

"I've never lied to you before."

"Something else you expect me to take on faith."

Deep breath in, slow breath out.

"I guess so since you've tried multiple times over the years to prove I was lying and failed every time."

Havermayer pressed her lips together, and fire shot out of her green eyes. I glared back. She blinked first. *Score one for me.*

"Let's start at the beginning. Why did you want to talk to Mara Di Rocca?"

"I came by to apologize. We'd had an argument earlier. Well, more like a heated discussion. I wanted to talk her out of opening a used bookstore that would put Ravenous Readers out of business."

"And what did she say?"

Uh-oh. No way to tell the whole truth without putting a big red guilty sign on my back. So be it. I did nothing wrong. Stupid, maybe, but not wrong. "She said 'no'. She said she intended to put me out of business because I killed her father. Her words, not mine."

"Her father?"

Shouldn't she know this by now? What'd she been doing for the last hour? "She's Tony Scavuto's daughter. Her husband and brother are reopening Antonio's."

Somebody rapped on the glass. I looked up to see who, but of course I only saw myself and the detective's back.

Havermayer stood and pushed Mara's picture back in my direction. "Sit tight. I'll be back in a minute."

My belly clenched, and I turned the photograph face down, the scene still vivid in my mind. How could anyone think I'd do something like that? It was Havermayer, though. She'd believe anything. Especially if it was something negative about me. I'd never figured out her problem with me, but whatever it might be, she brought it with her the first time we met. Nothing I could do about that.

My legs tingled again, and I stood, stretching my arms above my head. My stomach roiled with uncertainty. What was she going to do with me? If she locked me up, I'd never be able to prove my innocence. With Eric off the case, nobody would fight for me. I might even end up on trial for something I didn't do. And be convicted for it. How could I prove a negative?

If I were found guilty, what would happen to the bookstore? Lacey would keep it going for as long as she could, but we were almost out of money, and the contest wouldn't bail us out this time. And she was pregnant. How much longer would she be able to work, anyway? A few months, maybe. Then what? No way Charlie could handle the day-to-day and online sales too. We'd have to close the doors for good. The only answer was to find the real killer.

Detective Havermayer came back in and sat down with an angry scowl on her face. "Sit down!"

I showed her the palms of my hands. "Jeez, okay! I wasn't going anywhere. Chill!"

The look she sent me was more chili with extra jalapeños than chill. "Is there any reason we might find your fingerprints at the crime scene?"

"Of course. I was there. I'm sure I touched something, although I don't remember it."

"We found fingerprints on Mara Di Rocca's neck. Any reason they might be yours?"

"Yup. When I saw her slumped over, I checked for a pulse."

"And the DNA on the scarf that strangled her? Is that going to be yours too?"

"Some of it might be. I had to move the scarf out of the way to get to her neck. The rest will belong to the killer."

She glared at me. "You've got an answer for everything, don't you?"

"Because I'm telling the truth. I didn't murder Mara Di Rocca."

Havermayer pulled her chair forward until we were nearly knee to knee and leaned toward me with her elbows on her thighs. "Look, I want to believe you. I do. But you have to give me something. The vet tech said she recognized your voice arguing with Mara before the scream. Why would she say that if you weren't there?"

I took a deep breath. We'd reached the dangerous part of the conversation. "If she said that, she was mistaken because I arrived only a minute before your officers did. Perhaps she heard us arguing this morning and got confused about the time." I matched Havermayer's lean. "But frankly, I think you're lying to me, and she never said that at all."

She sat up and glanced at her notepad. "Eric told me you left the diner over twenty minutes before you say you arrived at the store. That gives you plenty of time to argue with Mara and then strangle her. I think we caught you red-handed, and you'll say anything to get out of it."

"Eric left the diner before I did. How would he know what time I left?"

"And if I told you Angus confirmed it?"

I twisted my lips. "I'd say you got an amazing amount of investigating done in a short period of time. Much more than you usually do."

She narrowed her eyes. "What were you doing during those twenty minutes you say you weren't arguing with Mara?"

"First, I stopped at Ravenous Readers to drop a treat off for Savannah. Then I walked around. I went all the way down Walnut and came back before turning onto Second. I needed to compose myself and figure out what I was going to say. That's where I had to be when Mara was murdered. Nowhere near the crime scene."

"Did anyone see you there?"

"Not that I noticed, but I wasn't looking for anyone else."

Havermayer crossed her arms. "So, you have no alibi for the time of death."

"No. If I'd known I needed an alibi, I'd have made sure I had one. I'm not stupid. I'm a mystery writer, for Pete's sake. I wouldn't make that kind of mistake."

"You would if you committed the crime in the heat of the moment." She leaned in again. "I know you didn't mean to kill her. You asked her not to open a bookstore. She said 'no' and gave you that ridiculous story about you being responsible for her father's death. You lost your temper and grabbed her scarf, trying to talk some sense into her. Maybe you pulled a little harder than you realized, and she died. It was an accident. It could happen to anyone."

She pushed a yellow legal pad and pen toward me. "Just write down what happened. I'm sure you didn't head over there with a plan to murder her. Put it in your own words so we can understand what went on that led to her death."

Eric had been trying to convince me that Havermayer was an excellent detective ever since he went into training with her. For the first time, I saw what he did. Unfortunately for her, her tricks were wasted on me.

Pushing hard against the fear creeping up my spine, I took the pad and pen with trembling hands and printed the word "LAWYER" in large block letters. I showed the pad to the person behind the window, then the camera in the corner by the ceiling, and gave it back to Havermayer. No way would I go down for a murder I didn't commit.

The person behind the window rapped again. Havermayer grabbed the pad from the table. "That was a wasted opportunity, Jen," she said as she stormed out.

I wiped the sweat off my forehead and struggled to control my bouncing leg. Adrenaline had my heart racing, too. My breath came in short gasps, unable to provide enough oxygen to my brain. I rested my head on my forearms, determined to remain conscious and in control.

Deep breath in, slow breath out.

Havermayer opened the door and stood in the doorway.

After one more deep breath, I looked up to find her eyebrows reaching for her nose and her jaw bulging from teeth gritted together so hard you'd think she was trying to crack a walnut.

She waved her hand toward the hallway and said, "You're free to go."

I released my breath and bolted out of there.

CHAPTER FIVE

Eric wore a track in the linoleum by the duty sergeant's desk, pacing, arms folded across the lettering on his T-shirt. When I came around the corner, he reached me in two strides, pulled me into his chest, and kissed the top of my head while I struggled to control my feelings. Fear, dread, and panic along with relief and the sense of safety provided by Eric's arms, all jumbled into a nauseating emotion stew. I didn't know whether to cry or throw up. I struggled not to do either.

I held on to him, soaking in his scent, jaw clenched against giving in to the tears of frustration, anger, and exhaustion. I'd already cried more today than I had in years, and I'd had enough. I took a deep breath and lifted my chin. No more wallowing. It was time for action.

I let go and pulled him by the arm toward the door. "Let's go. We have work to do."

Once outside, he stopped and turned me to face him, hands lightly gripping my shoulders. "What are you talking about? You're going home to get some rest. You've had a rough day."

He had a gift for understatement. "No kidding." I checked my phone. There was a string of unread texts from concerned friends I didn't have the mental bandwidth to deal with, and it was 5:47. "I need to get Savannah. Lacey's leaving soon."

He glanced over at the bookstore, shaking his head. "I'll get Savannah for you and pick us up something to eat. Go home, take a hot bath, and relax. We'll get all this figured out. I promise." He tipped my chin up with his forefinger. "You trust me?"

The last time a guy asked me that was in high school, and he wanted something I wasn't ready to give. But this was Eric and, strangely, I did trust him. Trusting people had never been easy for me, but I knew deep in my heart he'd never do anything to hurt me. I gazed into his earnest green eyes, then nodded and smiled. "Okay, you win. Get my girl something special. She's had a hard day too."

Eric laughed. "Oh yeah, I'm sure. Bacon treats from Lacey, cookies from Charlie, and neck scratches from everyone else. Definitely a hard day." He kissed my forehead. "I need a job like that."

I dropped my hands onto my hips. "But none of those things were from me, and that makes a big difference. You should understand that by now."

He snapped off a mock salute. "Yes, ma'am."

After a quick kiss, I turned toward my apartment, my chest filling with warmth. He really did love me. A fact I found more incredible every day. I'd come to believe, on some level, that a successful relationship with a man would never happen for me. That nobody would ever care about me because of who I was, not who they wanted me to be.

Eric knew all my faults—my stubbornness, my fierce need for independence, my insecurities—and loved me anyway. He saw something in me I couldn't see in myself, and I loved him for it. He made me smile inside. I'd never had that in any relationship before. Except maybe with my father, but he died in a plane crash when I was six.

I forced my legs up the steps of my building, clamping both hands on the rail for support. The day's events whirled around in my head, adding tangible weight to my limbs. I couldn't remember the last time I'd felt this exhausted without having just survived a life-and-death struggle. Perhaps I'd been in a life-and-death struggle of a different kind. One I was still fighting. And stood an excellent chance of losing.

My apartment seemed extra empty when Savannah didn't greet me at the door. I'd grown to adore that little girl more than I ever dreamed possible. When the woman in Georgia gave me a puppy to "keep me out of trouble," I couldn't imagine the tremendous place she'd soon have in my heart. Growing up, I'd had no pets—my stepfather wouldn't allow it—and I never understood people's fascination with them. Now I couldn't conceive of a life without that big, goofy dog.

My keys landed on the coffee table amid the unread mail, receipts, and miscellaneous junk. I flopped on the couch, leaned my head back, and closed my eyes, just for a minute. One by one my muscles relaxed, and I drifted into a light doze.

After a few minutes, I prodded myself awake. Eric would be here soon. I had to get up. My legs balked, but I propelled them into the kitchen, where I retrieved a glass and a bottle of wine from the refrigerator. Then I headed for the bathroom and turned on the water in the tub.

The thick robe my mother gave me hung next to the thin, silky one from Eric. Today, Mom's gift won. Stripping off my clothes gave me the sense of peeling away all the day's troubles, though I knew that was just wishful thinking. The warmth of the robe cocooned and soothed me like a joey safely tucked in its mother's pouch. I poured a generous glass of wine to further calm my nerves.

Soaking in a hot bubble bath wouldn't solve all my problems, but it would relax me and bring a little peace to my mind. Something I desperately needed right now. A hot bath, a hot meal, and a receptive ear would help me plan my defense against all the problems I'd had dumped on me today. Assuming there was a defense to be had.

I removed my robe and slipped into the steaming water. The lavender-scented bubbles covered me up to my chin, tickling my nose when they popped. A large swallow of wine burned all the way down, and I relaxed into it. My eyelids grew heavy. I let them close and focused on my breathing. Nothing like bathtub meditation to clear my mind and wash away the horrors of the day. For a little while, anyway.

Half an hour later, the front door opened, Savannah pawed at the bathroom door, and stuck her nose in the space between the door and the floor, sniffing and whining.

"All right, little girl. I'm coming. Hold your horses."

She yipped and tried to dig underneath in response.

I reluctantly abandoned my bath, toweled off and slipped back into my snuggly robe, and opened the door to a furry onslaught. Full-grown Savannah came up to my chin when she stood on her hind legs nowadays. I tried to hug her, but she pulled away and zoomed around the apartment. Somebody didn't get enough exercise today. Maybe tomorrow would be better. For both of us.

Eric unwrapped our dinner in the kitchen, and I peeked around him to see what he'd brought. Fried chicken in one Styrofoam tray, meatloaf in the other. Mashed potatoes and green beans in both. Apple pie for dessert. And a plain hamburger with no bun for Savannah. Not bad. He'd remembered everything.

I slipped my arms around him from behind and stretched on my tippy-toes to kiss his cheek. "Looks great. Thank you. Why don't you pick out a movie while I go throw some clothes on?"

He grinned and waggled his golden eyebrows. "I think what you're wearing is just fine."

My cheeks heated. Why did I still get embarrassed when he said things like that? "I'm sure you do. I'll be back in a minute."

"If you insist."

I pulled on fresh sweats, along with my Pat Benatar T-shirt—my last clean one. Time to do laundry. Another chore on the list for tomorrow. When I returned to the living room, he'd laid out our dinner on the coffee table, poured me another glass of wine, and scrolled through Netflix.

"What would you like to see?" he asked, then forked mashed potatoes into his mouth.

I settled on the couch beside him. "I don't care. You pick. Something that doesn't require a lot of brain power. I don't have any left, at the moment. I think my brain got fried along with that chicken. I don't imagine it would taste nearly as good, though."

Eric scrolled through a few more selections. "How about *Julie and Julia*? You've seen that a few times, so no thinking required." He bumped me with his elbow. "And you might learn something."

I turned and tipped my head back to look at him. "Very funny. You complaining about my cooking?"

He chuckled. "Can't complain about something that never happens."

"Well, excuse me for not wanting to be arrested for poisoning a police officer on top of all my other legal problems." Fatigue-driven tears welled in my eyes. I swiped them away.

Eric put his arm around my shoulders and pulled me toward him. "Oh, honey, I'm sorry. I was just teasing."

I snuggled against his chest, wishing I could disappear into it. I craved the safety and security I knew lay within. "I know. It's been a difficult day. Not a terrific time for poking at sore spots."

54

He kissed my forehead and released me. "You're right. It was a bad joke. Let's just eat and watch the movie, okay?"

"Sounds good."

About a third of the way through the film, a knock on the door interrupted our dessert. Savannah bolted toward the entrance with a flurry of deep, growling woofs.

I called out, "Come in," knowing nobody who hadn't met my German shepherd would even consider entering.

The growls immediately turned to excited yips when my best friend, Brittany Dunlop, flyaway blond hair poufing out in the humidity, and her boyfriend—also my ex from high school—Police Chief Stan Olinski, stepped through the doorway. Brittany stuck her hand out in a "stop" gesture, and Savannah sat with her whole body wriggling. She could barely stand it, but she stayed. *That's my girl.*

"Hey, guys," Brittany said, pulling a bottle of white wine out of a paper bag. "Here, I figured you could use another one of these." She slid her oversized, tiger-striped glasses back up her nose.

Brittany and I had been friends since kindergarten, and she usually knew what I needed before I did. She'd been there for me through all the significant events in my life, beginning with my father's death when we were in the first grade.

I took the bottle from her and set it on the coffee table. "You figured right, as always. Thanks."

She grabbed another glass from the kitchen, then dropped onto the couch beside me, smoothing her ankle-length floral-print dress beneath her thighs. Savannah laid her head in Aunt Brittany's lap, thumping her tail on the floor while Brittany stroked her between the eyes. "How are you holding up?"

What made her think I was holding up? "Me or the dog?"

Brittany trained her caesious blue eyes on me. "You, doofus."

"As well as can be expected, I guess."

Olinski slid a finger under his dark-rimmed glasses to rub his eye, then handed Eric a beer from the six-pack he'd brought and settled into the cracked-leather recliner by the sliding glass doors to the balcony. We'd dated throughout high school, and everyone, including Olinski, expected us to marry after graduation. Everyone but me, of course. I wanted to be a writer, so when I was offered a scholarship for college in Blackburn, I grasped it with both hands and ran like someone was chasing me.

Olinski took ten years to forgive me for leaving, but we'd finally made our peace a couple of years ago. Now, I considered us friends. I still wasn't sure how *he* felt about it, though. But we got along, for Brittany's sake.

Brittany laid her rose-painted fingernails on my arm. "Well, I'm just glad Havermayer didn't arrest you. She's been trying to get you in a jail cell for years."

Eric and Olinski exchanged glances, but neither said anything. Afraid of how I'd react, probably. I didn't blame them.

"It's not over yet. She's got a fairly solid circumstantial case against me this time. Maybe more than circumstantial since my fingerprints were on the body, and she's almost guaranteed to find my DNA on the scarf. All the other times were just conjecture and wishful thinking. I still can't figure out why she let me go. I got the feeling she didn't want to." I glanced at Olinski, who averted his murky brown eyes, suddenly finding his unmanicured cuticles fascinating.

Brittany smiled at her boyfriend. "I'm pretty sure my man over there had something to do with it, but he won't confess to it."

I watched him from the corner of my eye. "Well, that's fine. If he won't admit it, I don't have to thank him."

Olinski raised his bottle and said, "Here's to not having to say thank you."

I laughed. Something I didn't think I'd be capable of at the moment. Amazing the healing good friends could provide. My heart swelled with gratitude.

Brittany changed the subject. "How's the new book coming along?"

"Okay, so far. I didn't have much time to work on it today. Doubt I'll get much done anytime soon, either. It seems I have another murder to solve."

Olinski sat up and pointed at me with one bushy black eyebrow cocked above the level of his glasses. He looked like he had caterpillars parked between his forehead and his eyes. At least there were two of them now, as opposed to the one stretching straight across his face he used to have. An accomplishment of Brittany's I assumed.

I ignored him. I wanted to tell Brittany about the email from the lawyer informing me about the bankrupt contest, but Olinski could see it as another motive for me to kill Mara Di Rocca. That would have to stay a secret between best friends once I could safely share it. Eric would be forced to tell Olinski if he asked or lose his job, but I didn't think he'd volunteer the information, knowing how it might be construed. I hoped not, anyway. Another one of those trust situations that made me so uncomfortable.

Olinski fixed his gaze on mine. "Another murder to solve? What do you mean by that?"

A frustrated sigh escaped my lungs. He was about to give me the lecture on staying out of police business, and I was in no mood to hear it. "I mean, Havermayer has me in her sights, and she's not going to search very hard for the real murderer when she's positive I did it. We've been through this routine before. Eric's off the case, so unless you're going to order her to look elsewhere, which you really can't do because of our prior relationship, I'm on my own."

He tipped the beer bottle to his lips and swallowed. "Don't worry, she'll do her job."

"Really? You didn't see the expression on her face when she had to let me go. She'll arrest me the first chance she gets. I'm sure of it."

Olinski leaned forward, elbows on his knees, holding his beer with both hands. "You know, Jen, first off, what makes you think I didn't see her expression, or that I wasn't the cause of that expression? Second, I'm invested in making sure that *all* of my officers do their work thoroughly and with integrity. Third, I'm getting real tired of having to warn you off interfering in our investigations." He turned to Eric. "This time, I'm warning both of you. Stay out of it, or one of you will be in jail, and the other will be unemployed. It's just that simple."

Eric rested a warm, moist hand on my knee, and I bit back an angry retort. "Fine. I have enough other things to worry about right now. You need to make sure Havermayer does a diligent search for the real killer. You know I could never hurt anyone unless they were about to hurt me first."

Olinski nodded. "I know that. The truth will come out. I promise."

Brittany lifted her glass and said, "Here's to the truth coming out."

"Hear, hear," we all said as our glasses and bottles met in the middle.

CHAPTER SIX

I woke up early Sunday morning and couldn't go back to sleep. Dreams of dead bodies, come back to accuse me, marred my rest, and when I awoke from them, reality wasn't much better. My bookstore was on the brink of disaster, and I was under suspicion of murder. Again. Only this time, they had real evidence I couldn't dispute. I pushed away the anxiety.

The coffeemaker did its job while I escorted Savannah around the block for her morning walk. Another unseasonably warm morning tricked me into believing spring had arrived, but the calendar told a different story, and that fantasy wouldn't be a reality for quite a while yet. No need to put away my winter things. It'd be cold again soon enough.

Savannah completed her rounds—checking her pee-mail and leaving suitable replies—and we trotted up the stairs for our rewards. Breakfast for her and coffee for me. I filled my "Creativity Begins With Coffee" mug while she licked her bowl clean. Nothing could convince her she wasn't malnourished. Thankfully, her sides had filled out, so I no longer had concerns about the ASPCA showing up at my door.

The next step in our morning routine involved me at my desk, pretending to write, and Savannah sleeping off her breakfast belly on the couch. I opened my laptop and brought up chapter two again. Daniel Davenport had just submitted his fraternity registration application. I stared at the screen. Now what?

As usual, the words lay hidden deep in my subconscious. I waited for them to wend their way to the surface like photons of light escaping the sun's gravity. A picture of Mara Di Rocca as I'd last seen her popped in instead. I pushed it away. No time for that. Olinski promised he'd oversee the investigation. Make sure the wrong person wasn't indicted for the crime. I had to trust him too. Our history made that a little more difficult than trusting Eric, though.

Perhaps Dana should voice her opinion again. No, they'd already had a massive blowout. The reader would get the point. I had to think of something to keep them busy until Daniel's fraternity brother died in the tunnel. Like the skeleton I'd found. I really needed to look into that. The cold-case squad in Sutton didn't seem to be doing anything to discover who he was or how he got there. Although I wasn't exactly kept informed about their progress.

I shook the distraction away.

Focus, Jen.

Okay, I'd introduce the new friend Dana would meet in her freshman English class. She had a secret too. One that would keep the twins occupied for a while. As soon as I figured out what it was. What could Dana's new friend Elaine's secret be? And what would make Dana interested enough to investigate? I should have figured all this out before I started writing, but what's the fun in that? Fewer headaches, though. And less opportunity for my old friend writer's block to reinsert itself into my life.

My interview with Havermayer yesterday niggled at the back of my mind. She was positive I'd killed Mara in a rage, and while I trusted Olinski mostly, I'd never trust Detective Havermayer. Did I dare put my future in her hands? Eric had faith in her. He always tried to convince me she was an excellent detective. I wanted to believe him. Especially now, but she'd demonstrated a propensity for tunnel vision far too often in the past. And this time, I was trapped in that tunnel with no way out.

I'd told Olinski I'd stay out of it. A promise I made for Eric's sake, so his job wouldn't be at risk. However, first thing tomorrow I'd go to the vet's office and talk to the tech who made the 911 call. There was no way she heard me arguing with Mara yesterday afternoon. It had to be somebody else. Perhaps the other voice was female so she assumed it was me? More likely Havermayer made the story up. I didn't know, but I had to find out one way or the other. Too bad Dr. Felton didn't work on Sundays. I could get it out of the way today.

In the meantime, a little research couldn't hurt anything. I had to know what I was up against. Who I was dealing with. I had no information about Gil, Mara, or Fredo. I'd had no idea Tony even had any children.

He never mentioned them, which was strange enough to begin with. He talked about distant relatives but never his own kids. The only parent I'd ever met who didn't have a phone full of photos. At least not that he showed anyone.

I brought up my search engine and typed in *Gilberto Scavuto*. Nothing relevant surfaced, but his Facebook page came up. I clicked on it, and a slew of pictures of a smiling Gil and Mara together in various places appeared. No photos of Gil with anyone else and no mention of any other family. Not even a post about his father's death. *Strange*.

The photographs revealed little other than the younger Scavutos liked to travel together. Picture after picture of them with arms around each other, grinning into the camera in front of the Eiffel Tower, or on the beach, or at sea on a cruise ship. Tony had more money than I'd realized. And his kids enjoyed spending it for him. That much seemed normal, though.

Mara's page included much the same, with the addition of her and Fredo's wedding picture. At least her husband got a mention. According to the date on the post, they'd only been married about a year last month. Perhaps they hadn't had time to do anything interesting together yet. Didn't they take a honeymoon trip, though? If so, Mara hadn't documented it. Maybe Fredo didn't photograph well. Or refused to have his picture taken for some reason. Or maybe they didn't have a honeymoon. Not everyone did.

Another Facebook search produced only one Alfredo Di Rocca, who had no photos of any kind, not even a profile picture. Perhaps he really didn't like having his picture taken. Back to the search engine. Only the one Facebook page and fettuccine Alfredo recipes. Nothing useful. I'd have to hand this one off to Brittany or Charlie.

Time to quit stalling and go back to work. I had to finish this book since my writing might soon be my only source of income again. A scary thought. Even if *Twin Terror* sold as well as *Double Trouble*, I still would see no substantial royalties from it until this fall. Book three would produce only a minuscule advance, assuming my publisher wanted it soon, until next year. No way I could support the bookstore under those circumstances. I'd barely be able to support myself. I might even have to get a real job. My mother would *love* that.

I rubbed my temples to push back the burgeoning headache. Wallowing in my troubles accomplished nothing. Especially when I could do nothing about them. I'd never been much good at handing off my problems to others, however. I had to find my own solutions somehow. Unfortunately, I had no idea where to start.

As soon as I returned my attention to chapter two, my phone rang. My mother with her Sunday morning call. I answered it.

"Hi, Mom. How are you?"

"Fine. How are you?"

I hesitated. Should I tell her about everything happening in my life right now? Probably, but she had enough issues of her own to worry about. And I wasn't up for a repeating string of "I told you so." I replied with forced cheer. "I'm great."

"Huh," she replied. "It's way too early for you to be that happy. What's going on?"

I crossed my fingers to absolve my fib. "Nothing. Everything's fine."

"Now I know you're lying. You're never fine. What're you hiding?"

"How's Gary?" My stepfather had recently completed his last round of chemotherapy for colon cancer.

"Much better. He's getting stronger every day."

"That's terrific! I'm so happy to hear it."

My mother inhaled deeply. "Jennifer Marie Dawson! If you don't tell me what's wrong, I'm coming over to shake it out of you."

Uh-oh, the dreaded middle name. "All right, I'll tell you, but you have to promise not to get upset. I'm handling it."

"All right. Tell me."

My turn for a deep breath. "You remember the guy who used to own Antonio's?"

"You mean the one who was murdered?"

I took a swallow of my cold coffee. "Yeah, him. Well, his kids are going to reopen the restaurant. His son and son-in-law, anyway. His daughter was going to open a used bookstore by the vet's office."

"Was?"

"She was found dead in her store yesterday. By me. Now the police think I killed her to eliminate the competition." My stomach twisted into a knot, determined to send the coffee back.

She laughed. "That's ridiculous. You wouldn't hurt a fly. Except in one of your books."

"Thanks for the vote of confidence. You can be a character witness at my trial."

"Get serious. They can't possibly think you're guilty. What about Eric? Isn't he standing up for you?"

My mother was Eric's biggest fan. Second to me, of course. "He would if they'd let him. They kicked him off the case. If he tries to help me in any way, Olinski will fire him."

"No! He can't believe this nonsense. Where is that Olinski? I'm going to give him a piece of my mind!"

I leaned back in my chair. "No, Mom, you're not. Just let it go. It'll sort itself out."

"Well, it better, or he's going to be one sorry young man. And to think, I treated him like he was family all those years."

Better than family. She actually *liked* him. "It's not Olinski's fault. All the evidence points to me right now, but he made Detective Havermayer let me go after our interview yesterday, even though she wanted to arrest me. So, he must believe me."

"Of course he does. He's a good boy. So is Eric."

I chuckled. "Neither one of them are boys. They're both in their thirties, remember?"

"Whatever."

I chose not to remind her I'd just turned thirty too. If I said it out loud, it would be real. "Well, I'd better get dressed. I need to go to the bookstore today."

"Why? It's Sunday. Don't you deserve a day off?"

"I take plenty of time off. More than I should, given the circumstances. And I need to talk to Lacey and Charlie about something."

"What's so important it can't wait until tomorrow?"

A sigh escaped. I didn't want to tell her, but she'd find out sooner or later, so better she heard it from me. "The Your Life Contest is going bankrupt, which means no more payments. We have to devise a plan to keep the store open somehow."

"Oh, honey, I'm sorry. I wish we could help, but Gary's medical bills are so high we're struggling to make it ourselves."

What? No snide comments about my shortcomings? Now I felt guilty for not helping them. Not that I had any money either. "Don't worry about it. We'll manage. I have a royalty payment coming in a few weeks. Maybe it'll be enough to help us both."

"We're fine. Just take care of that store of yours."

"I'll do my best. Talk to you later."

I disconnected the call and sat with elbows propped on the desk and my head in my hands. *Double Trouble* had been out for two years now. That payment probably wouldn't be enough to keep me fed for six months, let alone keep Ravenous Readers afloat. My phone screen flashed 9:38. Time to break the rest of the bad news to Lacey and Charlie.

The bookstore had no customers when I walked in at ten. No surprise. I'd never seen a line waiting outside at opening. Lacey fussed around the cash register, straightening the bookmarks in the case beside it. Savannah wound up her tail and sprang toward her favorite treat dispenser. Lacey already had the bag out.

"Here you go, little girl," Lacey said, scratching the German shepherd's chest while she chomped down the bacon snack. "I know you haven't eaten in weeks. I hope this holds you for a minute or two."

"Only until you can get the next one out of the bag." I smiled. Savannah adored her friends. As did I. "How's it going?"

She glanced around the empty store. "The usual." She fed Savannah one more treat, then put the bag away. "It's early yet. We won't get busy until after lunch."

Hmmm. "In that case, maybe we should consider not opening until then. If we won't do any business anyway, why be here so early?"

She thought about it for a moment. "That's not a bad idea. It wouldn't be unusual for a place in a small town like this to not open until one on Sunday."

"Let's do it, then. You can have Sunday brunch with your family."

A smile spread across her face. "I like it. I don't get to see enough of my kids, and it'll be nice to spend more time with them before the baby comes."

Oh, yeah, the baby. The problem I keep forgetting about. "Have you told them yet?"

Lacey shook her head. "Ben wants to wait until I'm showing, and they ask questions. We'll have to tell them then. They're old enough to think I have a tumor or something."

Her daughter had recently turned nine and was fascinated with the internet. "No kidding. All they have to do is chat with Dr. Google, and they'll learn all the worst-case scenarios."

"We definitely don't want that."

"I don't blame you."

Disco Charlie pushed through the door, carrying the box of goodies from Bob's Bakery across the street, wearing a lavender satin shirt, tight leather pants, and purple platform shoes. I helped him unload the cookies, muffins, and croissants into the pastry case connected to the coffee bar, snagging a chocolate chip muffin for myself to go with the coffee I poured from the urn. I needed the chocolate to get through what was about to come next.

"Okay, guys. Before we get busy, I need to tell you something."

"You're pregnant too?" Charlie asked, a bite of ham and cheese croissant stuffed into his cheek like he was a chipmunk.

"Not funny." I blew air through my lips. It never got easier. No matter how many times I had to repeat the story. "I received an email from a lawyer yesterday. We're not getting any more payments from the contest."

Lacey's jaw fell. "What? Why?"

"They're bankrupt. We can file a claim, but from what I know about it, creditors and employees will come first. We might get a few cents on the dollar. Not enough to make a difference. Probably not even enough to pay a lawyer to do it for us."

Lacey turned with a determined expression on her face. "That's okay. We'll manage."

"I don't see how."

Charlie swallowed another bite. "I'll get our sales sites up and running. And we can buy the books when they're ordered instead of stocking up. Our service times won't be what we wanted, but we'll have some money coming in."

"Thanks, Charlie. Every little bit will help. I'm going to talk to the bank tomorrow and see about a loan to keep us afloat for now. Making the payments will be tough, but it'll buy us some time to develop a better solution." And, with luck, I wouldn't be arrested for murdering Mara Di Rocca. That would put a definite crimp in the plan.

"That's one option," Lacey said. "Would you consider taking on an investor?"

I'd never thought about that. Then again, I'd never had to before. "Maybe. It depends on the terms, I guess. Do you know anyone who might be interested?"

"I might. My husband knows people in Blackburn with more money than they can spend in two lifetimes. Maybe he can convince one of them to part with some of it."

I chuckled. "That doesn't mean they'll give it to us, but it's worth a try."

The bells over the front door jingled, and Fredo and Gil entered.

Good grief! What do they want? I had enough trouble already. They could only bring more. I turned to face them.

CHAPTER SEVEN

As Fredo and Gil made their way down the aisle, Savannah took up a position midway between them and me. Lacey and Charlie fell in behind like in a scene out of *West Side Story*. No singing or finger snapping involved, however.

Gil stopped before reaching the dog, who had her hackles up, but Fredo pushed right by her without a glance. The venom behind his scowl radiated across the space between us. A chill enveloped me as if someone had opened all the windows in the world, and I shivered, wiping slick palms on my jeans. I'd never admit it out loud, but something in his eyes turned my guts to a pile of mush. His pupils had engulfed the benign brown irises, leaving me peering into an evil abyss, within which I didn't want to know what resided.

Fredo pointed at Charlie and Lacey, pulling his black leather jacket away with his other hand to reveal an automatic pistol stuffed into the waistband of his jeans. "You two, get lost!"

They stood their ground, ready to do battle on my behalf. But this was my fight. I couldn't risk either of them being injured because of a problem Fredo had with me. "Charlie, would you and Lacey put Savannah in the office, please, and close the door?"

"But . . ." Charlie folded his arms across his chest.

Without breaking eye contact with Fredo, I said with a slight quiver in my voice I hoped nobody else could hear, "Just do it, please. I don't want any of you to get hurt."

"We don't want you to get hurt either."

I seconded that concept, but guys like Fredo fed on fear. I didn't dare allow him to see mine. "I'll be fine. Just please do it."

Charlie nodded and whistled for the dog. "Come on, girl. Let's go back here."

She reluctantly responded, ears back, tail down. Even though she was scared, in her mind, her job was to protect me, and Charlie wanted her to run away. I could tell she didn't like that one bit. But she obeyed.

Lacey pulled her cell phone from her pocket and followed. If I knew her, she was about to call 911. I only had to keep Fredo civilized for a few minutes. Then we'd all be safe.

Fredo leaned his face close to mine, his breath coating me with a mixture of stale whiskey, coffee, and bacon. "You made a big mistake killing my wife, and you're gonna pay for it. The cops may have let you go, but I never will. You understand me?"

I stuck my hands in my pockets so he couldn't see them vibrate and fought to hold his gaze. "I didn't kill your wife," I said with the same tremor in my voice.

He poked me in the chest with his finger. "I don't believe you. Everywhere you go, I'll be there. And one day, I'll take care of you. You'll never see me coming. You hear me?"

I crossed the line between courage and stupidity and batted his hand away. "Don't threaten me, or I'll call the police." I hoped Lacey already had. They should be here any minute.

I held my breath when Fredo closed the gap even further. "Just so you know, we don't deal with the police. That's why we're here. To get to the bottom of this and settle the score."

Gil stepped up beside him, fear apparent in his red-rimmed eyes. He touched Fredo's arm. "Take it easy."

He pushed Gil back. "Bug off!"

Gil raised his hands and stepped away. "Okay. Just relax, will you?"

Sweat pooled on my brow, but I refused to wipe it away for two reasons. Number one: I didn't want Fredo to see how frightened I was. Number two: I was shaking so hard I might poke myself in the eye.

"Let's hear what she has to say," Gil said. "I want to know why she murdered my sister too. Mara never hurt anybody."

I forced down the golf ball that had appeared in my throat and looked Fredo directly in the eye. "I didn't kill her. I swear! She was dead when I got there. All I did was find her."

Gil issued a short, sharp laugh. "C'mon, lady, you can't expect us to believe that. We're trying to be reasonable. Just tell us the truth."

There was nothing I could say they would accept, so I said nothing. I couldn't prove to Fredo I didn't kill Mara any more than I could Havermayer.

After a moment, Gil turned to Fredo. "Let's just go. She's not gonna tell us anything."

Fredo took a threatening step toward me. I held my ground. Backing down to him would be suicide, and I wasn't depressed today. Yet.

"She'll tell us, all right."

He reached for me, but Gil grabbed his arm in an unexpected show of bravado. "That's enough, Fredo!"

Fredo jerked his arm away. "Get lost, weenie boy! She was my wife. My wife! Just because you two acted like you were married half the time doesn't mean you were."

Gil's jaw dropped. "You just couldn't stand it, could you? Mara and I were practically twins, closer than the two of you, and you were jealous. Nothing was the same after she married you." He jabbed his forefinger toward Fredo. "You know what I think? Maybe this lady didn't kill Mara. Maybe owing money to the wrong people in Chicago has finally caught up to you. Or should I say caught up to Mara?"

I stood there, watching, thankful to no longer be on the receiving end of Fredo's laser-like glare. Over his shoulder, I saw the businessman from the diner walk by, wearing a suit this time, looking in the window as he passed. I willed him to come inside and break the tension. They would do nothing rash with a witness around. Charlie and Lacey were in the office with Savannah. A customer would keep them from hurting us or each other.

As the man disappeared from view, two RPD officers, the same two who arrested me yesterday, came in.

"We got a call about a disturbance," the taller one asked as he scrutinized me.

I glanced at Fredo, who stepped back. Should I tell them he'd been threatening me? They'd arrest him, but he'd be out by this afternoon. Even angrier than he was now. Then I'd really be in trouble. I couldn't take the chance. "I think this was a little misunderstanding. Everything's fine. We've got it all straightened out now." I gave Fredo a pointed look. "Right?"

He glanced from me to the officers and back again. "Yeah, right. We were just leaving." He stomped toward the front of the store with Gil trailing behind. When he reached the door, he turned and aimed two fingers toward his eyes, then turned them back to me. *He's watching me.*

"Thanks for coming so quickly, guys." I gestured a shaking hand toward the coffee bar. "How about a cup of coffee and a muffin before you go?"

"Are you sure you're all right?" the officer asked again, tucking his thumbs into the top of his duty belt.

For the moment. "I hope so. No harm done so far. He just lost his wife and needs some time to process. Since I found her body, it's only logical he'd believe I had something to do with her death. If he comes back again, I'll let you arrest him." *If I live long enough.*

75

While they hesitated, Eric burst through the door, tie askew. "Jen! Are you okay? What happened? Did they hurt you?"

My shoulder muscles relaxed for the first time since Fredo and Gil charged in. "I'm fine." I took his hand in my sweaty one, allowing his strength to bolster mine.

Eric turned to the waiting officers. "I've got it from here, fellas."

They nodded and left.

He gathered me into his arms. "I was so worried when I heard the call." Easing me away from him, he inspected me from head to toe. "Are you sure you're okay?"

I smiled, feeling protected and loved. "I'm sure. It was only a misunderstanding."

He stepped back with a grin. "What'd you get yourself into this time?"

Holding up one finger, I said, "I'll tell you in a minute."

I went to the office and released Charlie, Lacey, and Savannah from captivity. "It's safe to come out now. They're gone."

"Are you all right?" Lacey asked. "Who were those guys? And what did they want?"

I gave them the rundown as we walked back onto the sales floor. Eric sipped coffee, and I poured a cup for myself. "Those are the two guys reopening Antonio's. They wanted to know why I killed Mara."

Savannah whined and pawed at my hand. I scratched her neck to calm her.

Charlie's eyebrows pinched. "What? Who's Mara? And when did she die?"

Lacey stared at me like I was a candidate for the loony bin. Apparently, the water wheel at the Riddleton Rumor Mill had broken down, and they hadn't heard about my adventurous Saturday afternoon.

"Mara is . . . was the lady I told you about yesterday. The one I went over to talk to about not opening the used bookstore. When I arrived, she was dead, and the cops found me standing over her body. Now everyone thinks I murdered her to keep her from opening the store. As if I'd kill to eliminate competition." I shook my head.

Lacey smirked. "Everyone like Havermayer, I assume." She eyeballed Eric. "What are you doing about it?"

He slipped an arm around my shoulders. "There's nothing I *can* do about it. They pulled me off the case."

She turned back. "Those two guys were her family?"

"Her husband and brother. And they believe I killed her, too. It's crazy. Like I don't have enough other things to worry about, I need to be the focus of a murder investigation."

An older couple came in and browsed the Biography section. Lacey went to offer her assistance while Charlie put tongs on all the trays in the pastry case. The store was open. We needed to finish setting up.

I took Eric by the arm and led him to the couch by the front window.

He encircled my shoulders and pulled me close. "What can I do?"

I snuggled in, feeling safe for the first time today. "I don't know. Fredo, Mara's husband, is convinced I murdered his wife. Gil, her brother, made it seem like Fredo had ties with organized crime. Said he 'borrowed money from the wrong people,' and maybe that's why she's dead. All I know is it wasn't me."

"They were both upset. It probably didn't mean anything. Besides, if he did borrow money from a loan shark, it wouldn't have anything to do with you."

"No, but Gil said he thought Mara might've been killed to make Fredo pay the money back. What if a hitman is wandering around Riddleton? Nobody's safe."

Eric squeezed me closer. "You're letting your imagination run away. First of all, a loan shark wouldn't go straight to murder. He'd break a few bones first to make his point. Second, even if he did hire a hitman, the guy would have no reason to stick around after his job was done, right? And why would he go after you or anyone else even if he did?"

"He wouldn't, but if Mara's death was a professional hit, there's almost no way to prove it. I might end up being convicted for his crime."

He shook his head. "I highly doubt Mara was killed by a professional because her husband didn't pay back a loan. I'd be more inclined to look hard at the husband himself."

"I know. The spouse is always the first suspect. How's that worked out for you so far?"

"Just because they're not always guilty, doesn't mean it's not a valid place to start."

I sat up. "Okay, so let's look at him."

He turned me toward him. "I'm not allowed to be involved in this case, Jen. You know that. Are you trying to get me fired?"

"No, of course not. But technically, you can't *work* the case. Nobody said you couldn't talk about it."

"You're splitting hairs."

I gazed into his emerald-green eyes. Butterflies took off in my stomach. "If you can honestly say you're positive Havermayer will do everything she can to find a suspect who isn't me, I'll let it go. I'll never bring it up again. Given what you know about her, can you tell me that? Honestly?"

Eric flushed, which contrasted with his orange hair, and provided a solid red background for his freckles. He opened his mouth, then closed it again.

"Well? What's your answer?"

He ducked his head. "You know I can't say that. Havermayer's going to conduct the investigation the way she sees fit. However, I can't condone you investigating on your own, either. That's only looking for trouble."

"I understand that. I'm not asking for your permission, only your help. Will you help me prove I didn't kill Mara?"

"I'll do what I can, but I'm not making any promises."

I kissed his cheek. "Fair enough. Thank you." I scooted around on the couch so we could talk face-to-face. "Now, what do we know about Fredo Di Rocca?"

"I only know what you've told me. He was Tony's son-in-law. He's from Chicago and wants to reopen Antonio's with his brother-in-law."

"That's all I know. Can't you get information from the Chicago Police Department? See if they have anything on him?"

"If I knew somebody over there, maybe, but I don't. I can suggest it to Havermayer. She can request information as part of her case. I can't make her follow up on it, though."

I crossed my arms. "Nobody can make Havermayer do anything she doesn't want to do. Except maybe Olinski. Why don't you suggest it to him instead and see what he says?"

"Because I like my job."

The elderly couple left, armed with two books each. I gave Lacey a thumbs up, wondering how many of those books were her doing. My store manager was a superstar at convincing people to buy more than they came in for. What would I do without her? Fortunately, I wouldn't have to find out for a few more months. Assuming we could stay open for that long. I rubbed grit out of my eyes. Too tired to worry about that right now. Maybe tomorrow.

Before the door closed all the way, a hand grabbed it, and Gil squeezed through, almost catching his jacket on the doorknob.

Terrific. What did he want this time? To have me decapitated? Drawn and quartered, maybe? Although, he did defend me in the end. I scrunched into the couch cushion as if I could blend in like a chameleon. No such luck.

He marched directly toward us and stopped, rubbing the back of his neck like he had no idea what he'd come to say.

Eric stood, hands on his hips. "What do you need?"

Gil put his palms up. "I don't want any trouble. I came to apologize for Fredo. He had no business acting that way."

I rose to stand beside Eric. "You weren't exactly little Sally Sunshine, either."

"I know. I'm sorry. I'm not thinking straight. My sister and I were very close."

Eric stepped toward him and waved toward the door. "All right. You said what you had to say."

Gil nodded and turned to leave.

I stopped him. "Wait." This might be my only chance to learn more about the family dynamic and who had a motive to kill Mara. "I appreciate you stopping by, and I accept your apology. Let me get you a cup of coffee."

Eric jerked his head in my direction. I put a hand on his shoulder, and winked at him. "It's okay."

Understanding dawned in his eyes. "Right." He turned to Gil. "How do you like your coffee?"

"Black, no sugar, please."

Eric took off for the coffee bar, and I invited Gil to sit in one of the matching wingback chairs across from the couch. "First, let me say how sorry I am about your sister. I swear, I had nothing to do with it. I was so shocked to find her I froze, and then before 911 could even answer my call, the police showed up."

Gil studied his well-manicured fingertips. "Thank you for saying that. I believe you, but it will take more than your word to convince Fredo."

"I'm determined to find the real killer. That will convince everyone. Including Fredo."

He nodded. "I hope you do. I want him to pay for what he did."

Ditto. "You said something earlier about Mara possibly being killed because Fredo owed money to the wrong people. What did you mean by that?"

He smiled and dismissively waved his hand. "I shouldn't have said that. I was angry and unhappy and trying to find someone to blame for my misery."

I leaned forward. "So, Fredo didn't borrow money from someone in Chicago and leave without paying it back?"

"No, he did, but not like that. Nobody who ever would've . . ." He pinched the bridge of his nose between his fingers.

"I'm sorry. I didn't mean to upset you."

"It's okay. I'm not ready to talk about it yet. I thought I was, but I guess I was wrong."

I needed to change the subject to keep him talking. "Are you and Fredo still going to reopen the restaurant?"

"Yes, it's what my father wanted when he left it to Mara and me. He wanted us to work together. To use all the skills he gave us while we were growing up."

"But Mara was opening a bookstore instead. How did that happen?"

Eric returned with our coffees and handed one each to Gil and me. We thanked him, and Eric settled on the couch beside me. "What did I miss?"

"Nothing," I said. "I was just asking Gil about the restaurant, and he was about to tell me how he ended up working on it with Fredo instead of Mara."

Gil cleared his throat. "It was simple, actually. Mara didn't want to work in the restaurant, and Fredo did. That's not how I preferred it, but nobody asked my opinion. The two of them decided without me. I had no choice but to agree." He set his cup on the end table beside the chair. "I'd better go."

Eric stood with him. "Just one more question, Gil, if you don't mind."

Gil turned. "Sure."

"Where were you yesterday afternoon between one and three?"

Gil lifted his chin. "At the restaurant, getting things ready for the opening. All afternoon until we got the call from the police. You can ask Fredo. He was there, too."

CHAPTER EIGHT

Eric and I held hands all the way to the diner for a late lunch, ignoring the glances from the people we passed. I could almost hear the thoughts they dared not say aloud.

"What's that killer doing walking around free?"

"Look at that. A cop and a murderer walking down the street like nothing ever happened. I can't believe they let her out already. And that he would dare to be seen with her!"

"There's no way she did this. They're treating her like it's one of her mystery novels."

The small-town mentality. No getting away from it. The incessant need to know everything about everyone else. To compare their lives with others', hoping to be able to feel superior. To judge without having all the facts. Or, sometimes, any facts at all. At least they weren't acting on it. No snide comments or flying produce. Only the stares. Long, unapologetic, uncomfortable stares.

I squeezed Eric's hand, and he responded by releasing mine and putting his arm around my shoulders. I leaned into him, grateful to have someone who believed in me. Someone who only needed my word to decide on what to believe. In reality, he knew no more about the case than the old man who sneered at me, but he had my back just the same. I could live with that.

When we walked into the diner, Angus was working with the new grill cook, and Marcus and Ingrid were huddled in a corner booth, enjoying his lunch break together. They waved us over to their table.

Ingrid stood and hugged me when we arrived. "Come, join us."

Eric shook his head. "We don't want to intrude."

"Don't be daft," Ingrid said. "You two are always welcome."

Ingrid had moved to South Carolina from London when the state offered to pay her medical school tuition in exchange for five years as a small-town doctor. She picked Riddleton for some reason. I always imagined her sitting in her dorm room in Charleston, throwing darts at a state map. No other rational explanation. Still, we were happy to have her. We'd had no doctor in town before her arrival. At least now we didn't have to drive twenty miles for a checkup.

She was a welcome addition to our population as well. A good person who'd do anything for anyone in need. And her accent threw me straight into a PBS episode of *Miss Scarlet and the Duke* or *Rumpole of the Bailey*. Two of my favorite places to be.

Eric and I slid into the orange seat across from them and grabbed menus from the condiment holder. On the wall beside us hung a black-and-white ad for *The Thin Man*, starring William Powell and Myrna Loy. One of my go-to movies when stress threatened to swallow me whole, and I needed to decompress. We should've watched it last night. Too bad I didn't think of it before Eric made his selection.

"What're you going to have?" Eric asked, studying the lunch side of the laminated card he'd retrieved from the condiment stand.

Ingrid laughed.

Smart aleck. I narrowed my eyes and pursed my lips at her. "Bacon cheeseburger, fries, and a chocolate milkshake." Otherwise known as "the usual."

"Again?" He studied me over the top of his menu. "You had that yesterday."

And your point? "Yup. And I'll probably have it again tomorrow."

Marcus shook his head. "Man, one of y'all needs to learn how to cook."

"What, and put you out of a job?"

He pointed his thumb at his chest and flashed his perfect white teeth. "I'm the assistant manager now, thank you very much."

Eric pretended to sip tea from a tiny cup with his pinkie extended. "Well, la-di-da. You know that only means you're expendable, right? A cook is necessary for a diner. An assistant manager? Eh, not so much."

Ingrid leaned on the Formica tabletop. "Like a detective?"

Eric's face turned a new shade of beet, but his laughter was genuine. "You got it."

The merriment subsided when the server, Penelope, came up to take our orders. She spoke to Marcus and Ingrid first. "Yours should be up any minute now." Then she regarded Eric. "What would you like today?"

She jotted down his chicken sandwich, extra mayo, with fries, and a Pepsi, then turned back toward the front counter.

I sat up in my seat. "Hey, what about me?"

Penelope rested the end of her pen on her lower lip. "Well, I heard about your day yesterday, so it's safe to assume it's a shake day. Nothing else ever changes, does it?"

"Well, no, but . . ."

She said, "There you are," and walked away.

My mouth flopped open and closed like a fish trolling for plankton. I hated being so predictable, but I loved bacon cheeseburgers, so they'd just have to get over it.

Ingrid touched my hand. "Speaking of yesterday, how're you holding up, luv?"

"I'm all right, I guess. Frustrated at feeling like I need to solve another murder to save myself, even though I had nothing to do with it."

"I understand, but it beats spending time at His Majesty's pleasure."

I sighed. "In English, please."

"Spending the rest of your life in prison." Ingrid grinned. "And that *is* English. Not my fault you don't speak the proper language."

I wrinkled my nose at her. "That'll only happen if His Majesty is Detective Havermayer."

"How can we help?" Marcus asked. "You've done so much for me; I'll do anything you need me to do."

"Thanks, Marcus. But I don't think it's a good idea for you to be involved. You're still on probation. You can't afford to get in trouble."

He slapped his hands on the table. "I'd be in prison now if it wasn't for you. Just tell me what you need. You want me to give you an alibi? I can say you were here all afternoon if you want me to."

"No, thank you. You need to behave yourself for another eight months. Then you'll be clear." I pointed my index finger at him. "And you'll still have to behave even then."

Marcus grinned. "Yes, ma'am."

Penelope brought all our plates together and laid them in front of us.

Eric took his from her hand. "That was fast."

"Our new cook, Jacob, has been practicing his meats today, so everything was ready. All we had to do was assemble it how you wanted it." She checked our drinks, then asked, "Y'all need anything else right now?"

"It looks delicious. Thank you."

Penelope left. I slathered my fries with ketchup and added an extra dollop to my burger. Fruits and vegetables were a necessary part of any proper diet, right? Before I took my first bite, I considered whether Marcus could do anything for me. I needed all the help I could get, but not at the expense of his freedom. His daughters, Larissa and Latoya, needed their father.

Perhaps a general discussion would be best for now. I hadn't quite reached desperation yet, though I suspected that might be right around the corner. "Ingrid, have you done Mara's autopsy yet?"

She sipped her tea, then said, "I finished it this morning. Nothing unusual, though. She was strangled with the scarf, as we expected. I took a few DNA samples, but we won't know who they belong to for a week at least. Too bad we can't just snap our fingers and get the results like on TV."

"No kidding," Eric replied around a mouthful of chicken sandwich. "Those shows make it seem like everything is instantaneous. It gives people the wrong idea. Makes it look like we're not doing our jobs."

I downed my bite of burger and wiped ketchup off my mouth with a napkin. "Well, until then, the fastest way to know the killer is to know the victim. What do we know about her?"

Eric swallowed. "Not much, really. I spoke to one of my buddies this morning, and as far as they can tell, she's led a relatively low-key life. Nothing in her past stands out as a motive for murder. Nothing they could find here in Riddleton, anyway."

"Okay. They haven't been here very long, though. What about her husband?"

"We didn't talk about him. I didn't want to push my luck."

"What do you mean?" Marcus asked, then pushed a French fry into his mouth.

"They're afraid I'll manipulate evidence or something. Like I'd ever do that. So, I've been kicked off the case since Jen's a person of interest."

"Which in Havermayer's world means Grade-A Prime Suspect," I added. "She's thrilled to finally have me in her sights."

Ingrid's eyes widened. "Should we be talking about it now?"

Eric shrugged. "I don't see why not. None of us knows anything that isn't common knowledge, so we're not interfering in the investigation, just having a conversation."

And if it led to something, that would be a bonus. "Sounds good to me. What do we know about Alfredo Di Rocca?"

Ingrid and Eric shook their heads. The guy was like a ghost. Here, but not here.

Marcus said, "He's been in a couple of times. In fact, he came in yesterday afternoon to pick up some food to go."

I perked up. "Really? What time?"

"I don't know. Two, two thirty, maybe?"

Right in the time-of-death window. I exchanged a glance with Eric. Gil's alibi just blew up. Fredo's, too, now that I thought about it. Definitely Fredo's, since I'd had to step around the remains of food on the floor of Mara's office to get to her desk. If lunch made it to her, so had Fredo. And he'd have had plenty of time to strangle her before I arrived. But why would he murder his wife?

"I think I'll put Charlie to work finding out more about him when I get back to the bookstore. He's great at digging up dirt on people."

"Excellent idea," Eric said. "Wish I could help. I hate being on the outside looking in."

I tapped his ribs with my elbow. "Welcome to my world!"

The front door opened, and the mysterious businessman, wearing jeans and a white long-sleeve button-down, entered with a newspaper tucked under his arm. When did he change his clothes? And where? He settled into the booth in the opposite corner from us.

I jutted my chin in his direction. "Anybody know that guy? This is the third time I've seen him in two days. Who is he? And more important, what's he doing here?"

Marcus forked up a fry. "First time I saw him was Friday night. He came in for dinner. No idea why he's here, though."

"Where's he staying, I wonder? Riddleton doesn't have a motel. Is he driving here every day just to hang out at the diner? That doesn't make any sense." I put down my burger. "Unless he's here for Fredo."

"What are you going on about?" Ingrid asked.

"Well, when Gil and Fredo came to the bookstore to accuse me of murdering Mara, Gil made a comment about Fredo borrowing money from the wrong people in Chicago and skipping out on the loan by moving here. He denied it when he came back to apologize, but what if he was covering up something he shouldn't have said in the first place? Something incriminating?"

Eric added more ketchup to the pool on his plate. "What would that have to do with that guy over there? He seems pretty harmless to me."

"Well, Gil also said that maybe the loan shark, or whoever, sent someone to 'convince' Fredo to pay. Perhaps killing Mara was supposed to be a warning."

"That's way more than a warning. Don't they start with a toe or finger first? Seriously, Jen. Don't get carried away. This is Riddleton, not New York or Chicago. We don't have any gangs or Mafiosos here. This town doesn't even have a drug problem, prescription or otherwise."

"I didn't say he was *from* here. He could have followed Fredo from Chicago."

"Sounds like you're dreaming up another bestseller to me."

I leaned back and crossed my arms. "Thanks a lot. You're supposed to be on my side."

"I am on your side. It's just, you know, you like to run off half-cocked and get yourself in trouble. I'm trying to save you from yourself."

"I'm no damsel in distress, Eric. I don't need you to ride in and save the day."

"Believe me, I know." He slammed two fries into his ketchup, breaking them both.

What's going on with him?

Marcus interrupted what was about to turn into a fight. "I'll tell you what . . . since the guy is eating all his meals here, how about if I try to find out more about him? I'll chat him up some tonight at dinner. He might tell me something helpful. How does that sound?"

I gave him a grateful smile. I hated fights with Eric but always seemed to instigate them, anyway. Even when I had no idea how. "Sure. That would be great. Thanks."

Ingrid squeezed Marcus's arm. "And I'll try to pry something out of Havermayer when I deliver the autopsy results. She might know something about the husband's background."

"I'll talk to my buddy again," Eric added. "Maybe he'll let something slip."

"Sounds like we have a plan. Let's hope it works. Orange isn't my best color."

Nancy from the Snip & Clip wandered up to our table. "Hey, guys, what's up?" She ran her fingers through the bottom of my hair. "Look at these ragged ends. You're way past due for a trim, Jen."

"I am. I haven't had time to make an appointment, but I will."

"Nancy, your scarf is positively lovely," Ingrid said, admiring the red silk draped around Nancy's neck.

"Thank you," Nancy said, fingering it. "I love this material, but it's so slippery. I can't keep it on unless I tie it."

"It's beautiful, though," Ingrid said. "I'd love one in blue. Where did you get it?"

"Actually, I've started selling them at the shop. I'm sure I have something in blue that'll suit you."

"Brilliant! I'll stop by tomorrow and have a look-see."

Nancy grinned. "You should hurry, though. They've been quite popular." She leaned forward with her hand beside her mouth as if she had a secret to tell. "Angus even bought one. In yellow. He said it was for his niece in New Hampshire, but I think he has a lady-friend."

I shifted in my seat. "Angus bought a yellow scarf?"

She frowned. "Yes, just last Thursday. No, wait, Friday. I remember because I was super busy and had to make Mrs. Firosa wait. Boy, was she grumpy about it."

Huh. Angus bought a yellow silk scarf. Like the one Mara was strangled with after she'd turned down his offer to buy Antonio's. No way Angus murdered Mara Di Rocca, though. Not for a silly reason like that. It had to be a coincidence, right? But I didn't believe in coincidences. Especially not in a murder investigation.

CHAPTER NINE

My alarm blared me awake Monday morning with the Beach Boys musing about how nice it would be if they were older. *Good for them.* I was too old already as far as I was concerned. I'd definitely aged ten years in the past two days. I slapped the off button, and Savannah, who slept attached to my side all night, flopped her head onto my chest.

I stroked the space between her eyes while she blinked at me. "Good morning, little girl. Did you sleep well?"

She thumped her bushy German shepherd tail against my leg. It was like being beaten with a flexible club.

"Yeah, me too."

Eric had stayed late last night. We discussed all the angles of my current situation, concluding there wasn't much I could do about the murder investigation without bringing the wrath of Havermayer down on my head. No solutions for Ravenous Readers' financial problems either, although he repeated his offer to give me his meager savings if I thought it would help. It would, for about fifteen minutes. Then we'd be right back where we started. But I loved him for the offer.

I struggled to sit up, but Savannah's head suddenly gained fifty pounds. She trained her liquid brown eyes on me. I scratched her behind the ears. "C'mon, kid. We have to get up."

Two more tail thumps and ten more pounds.

My little girl enjoyed our snuggle time only slightly less than wolfing down her meals. "I'd love to lie here all day and pet you, but I have things to do."

Thump, thump.

"You're no help." With a hand under each side of her jaw, I lifted her head off my chest and slid out from under the comforter, catching my foot in it and lurching toward the dresser. My hand caught the corner just in time to avoid a nasty gash on my cheek. Graceful as always. Back on both feet, I shook out my wrist. Even a sprain was worth having avoided the alternative, though. It would be nice if I didn't always have to make those kinds of choices. Too bad I flunked out of charm school.

Savannah jumped up, stretched, and zoomed a couple of laps around the apartment. I froze in place until she dropped her favorite stuffed monkey at my feet when she completed her last round. It was the only safe way to ensure I didn't get trampled on lap three.

"You gotta be kidding me."

She leaped onto the bed, clamped a pillow in her mouth, and flew off the other side back into the living room. I threw on my sweats and searched for my Nikes, finding them under the coffee table beside my cell phone. Savannah sat by the door, leash in her mouth, pillow at her feet, and sides heaving. Subtlety was never her specialty.

I finished dressing while the coffeemaker gurgled, filling the pot with my personal ambrosia. Although, the way things were going lately, the prospect of immortality seemed less and less appealing with each passing moment. Wouldn't stop me from drinking it, though.

Savannah bounced the pillow off the doorjamb, trying to take it with her on her walk, and I put it on the counter to convince her to leave the thing behind. I should have let her try, however. The challenge of her attempts to get out the door with it would've been hilarious. Too late now.

We trotted down the steps into the pale light of the early morning winter sun to the oak tree in front of our building. She reclaimed it with a long squat, and we proceeded around the block for the remainder of her elimination process. Her favorite number two place was on the corner of Riddleton Road, by St. Mary's Catholic Church. No worries about offending anyone, though. A plastic grocery bag occupied my jacket pocket, waiting to spring into action.

My coffee had perked by the time we vaulted back up the steps. I fed and watered the dog and poured myself a cup, savoring the fresh-brewed aroma on the way to my desk. I blew steam off the top and sipped as chapter two reappeared on my laptop screen. A quick scan of what I'd written so far, and my fingers took off across the keyboard. My muse had showed up this morning.

I might actually write something worth keeping for a change.

Two cups of coffee later, I'd pounded out a thousand words. Daniel was on his way to Greek Week and his fraternity initiation, and I'd reached chapter three. Overall, a good morning's work, and it wasn't yet nine o'clock. I took a lap around my apartment track and stretched my arms and neck. I'd learned the hard way not to spend too much time sitting at my desk without a break, a stiff neck for two days being the price for disobedience.

I'd settled back in for another round when my phone rang. Ruth Silverman filled the screen. I hadn't heard from my agent in months—since I'd finally submitted *Twin Terror* to my editor. Intrigued, I swiped the green button.

"Hi, Ruth. How've you been?"

Her Eastern-European accent of unknown origin blasted across the airwaves. "I'm doing very well, *bubbele*. Very well, indeed. How are you?"

I smiled at the Yiddish endearment she always used when addressing me. At a whopping four foot ten, she comforted me like the little blue-haired grandmother I'd never had. "I'm doing all right. Working on book three in case they decide they want it."

"That's why I'm calling. They sent me an email this morning. They want two more books. Same deal as last time."

My heart tried to leap out of my chest. "That's wonderful! I needed a reason to celebrate. It's been a tough weekend."

"Well, before you get too excited, there are some conditions."

A blanket of dread covered my heart's excitement. "Like what?"

"They want book three by June thirtieth and book four at the end of December. Can you do that?"

Six months each? Uh-oh. "That's not very much time. What happened to one book a year? Isn't that what they told us in the beginning?"

Ruth sighed. "The market is changing. Too many other series out there to choose from. Readers don't want to wait anymore."

It still seemed like a lot to ask. Could I do that with everything else I had going on? Maybe, if people stopped killing each other and blaming me for it. What about Lacey's maternity leave? Or worse. What if she decided not to come back? Could I write on a schedule and still run the bookstore? I had enough trouble writing on a schedule without any other distractions.

Being a successful author was my dream, though.

"I think I can do it."

"You have to be sure. They won't tolerate delays like you had last time unless you are sick or have a true emergency. They want these books out on schedule. If you need more time, you should say so. They'll decide whether they can give it to you or not. Then you can make an informed decision."

Part of being a successful author was dedication to the work. I had to prove myself to them again. This might be my last chance. If I failed, my dream would be lost. "Tell them I'll do it. And I will. I promise."

"It's not me you have to convince, Jennifer. You must convince yourself. The only one who doubts you is you."

Grandma strikes again. We'd spoken directly so little over the years, yet she knew me so well. "Convincing myself will take a bit more work, but I'll get it done, somehow. My editor might have to earn her keep this time, though. The end product probably won't be my usual stellar work." I laughed.

Ruth joined me with a chuckle of her own. "I'm sure she'll manage. Just make certain you get it in on time. Otherwise, you're finished. *Kaput.* We don't want that, yah?"

No kidding. "Yah. We don't want that."

"I'll let them know we accept."

"Thank you." I laid the phone on the desk and tried to focus on the screen before me. My left leg bounced, and my palms were sweaty. No good. I was too excited. "Savannah, we got two more books! Let's go tell Aunt Lacey and Uncle Charlie."

She lifted her head off the couch when I stood, jumped to the floor, and beat me to the door as if she understood what we were excited about. I grabbed my phone. I had to let Eric know, too. It would hurt his feelings if I told anyone else first. After snapping on her leash, we skipped down the steps, and I pressed the icon beside his picture. He answered on the second ring.

"I got two more books!" I blurted.

"What?"

"Two more books! My publisher wants two more books!"

I could hear the broad smile in his voice. "That's great, honey. I'm so proud of you."

"Thanks." I won a fight with Savannah to use my leash hand to push stray hair out of my eyes. "I'm thrilled."

"I can tell. We'll go out tomorrow night and celebrate. Where do you want to go?"

Oh, I hadn't thought about that. Where did I want to go? Someplace with champagne and chocolate cake, for sure. Not at the same time necessarily, but I considered both a requirement for a decent celebration. "I'm not sure. Let me think about it."

"Okay. Let me know soon in case I need to make a reservation."

"I will. Talk to you soon." I hung up, and the sensation I'd forgotten something waltzed through my mind. What was I supposed to do today? I fast-forwarded through the events of yesterday, hoping to trigger a memory. When I reached my conversation with Havermayer, it came to me. I needed to go to the vet's office and talk to the tech who made the 911 call.

I tugged on Savannah's leash. "Come on, little girl, change of plans." We were right outside the diner, and she pulled me toward the entrance. "Sorry, kid, not right now. We have to go to the vet."

She jerked her head toward me. Apparently, she knew that word. "No, not for you. But we'll pretend it is, so somebody will talk to me. Don't worry, you'll be fine."

I eased her across the street and headed down Pine to Second, then made the right toward the vet's office. My muscles tensed as we passed Mara's store, and I stared straight ahead, catching flashes of yellow crime scene tape out of the corner of my eye. Nope. Not going in there. Maybe never again.

The entrance to the Riddleton Veterinary Clinic was around the corner on Oak. When we entered, the waiting room was empty, but I could hear voices in one of the exam rooms.

The tech behind the front desk, Amanda, looked up and smiled. "Hi, Jen, what can we do for you today? Is Savannah okay?"

I reached down and patted the subject of our conversation on the head. She pulled me toward the door. I told her to sit, and she complied, leaning against my leg for protection.

Her weight pushed me off balance, and I righted myself. "She's fine. I misplaced her heartworm pills, and I need to get some more."

Amanda retrieved a tan box off the shelf. "You usually get a six-pack, right?"

"Right." I glanced out the front door. "Hey, did you hear about the ruckus down the street yesterday?"

She settled at the desk and tapped on her computer keyboard. "I not only heard about it, I *heard* it! It was so bad, I called 911."

I leaned on the front counter. "Really? What happened?"

Setting the box on the counter beside me, she said, "That's going to be $49.99."

Ouch! That was fifty bucks I hadn't planned on spending today, but at least she'd have enough pills to

102

last for a while. I dug in my wallet for a credit card. "So, what did you hear?"

Amanda took the card I offered and plugged it into a machine. "There was all kinds of shouting and then a lady screamed. That's when I called the cops."

"Huh. Could you tell who it was?"

"Not really. I heard the lady who works there died, so I assume she's the one who screamed. I couldn't tell who she was fighting with, though."

Nice try, Detective. "Was it a man or a woman?"

The transaction was approved and she handed me back my card with a receipt. "I don't know. I think it might've been a man, but I couldn't swear to it."

I stuffed the card in my pocket. "Interesting. I wonder who it was?"

"I wish I knew. Then I could've been more help to the police."

I released a relieved breath. She didn't see them haul me away in handcuffs. "Well, it was nice chatting with you. We'll see you for Savannah's next checkup."

Amanda stood and poked her head over the counter. "Bye, Savannah."

I smiled and followed my grateful German shepherd out the door for the walk to Ravenous Readers. Amanda had been very helpful and, as I suspected, Havermayer had lied to me about my voice being identified. I'd like to say I was surprised, but that would be a lie too.

The bookstore sales floor was empty when we arrived, so I released Savannah as the door closed behind us. She went searching for her friends. Lacey popped out of the storeroom in response to the opening door, and my spoiled rotten German shepherd gently grabbed her hand and led her toward the cash register, where the coveted snacks were kept.

"Where's Charlie?" I asked, glancing around the empty store.

"He went over to Bob's to pick up the pastries. I was just getting some more crowns for Story Time." Lacey eased her hand out of Savannah's mouth and wiped slobber on her pants, leaving a wet streak down the front.

I checked my phone to find it was after ten. "Oh, is it that late already? I had no idea."

Lacey tilted her head back and squinted at me from across the room. "You look flushed. Are you coming down with something?"

A grin stretched across my face. "Nope. I just got some news, and I'm excited."

She smiled. "Are you pregnant?"

Why does everyone want me to be pregnant all of a sudden? "Good grief, no! How could you even suggest such a thing?"

"Then what's going on? Did you inherit a million dollars or something?" She fed Savannah a bacon treat.

"No, thank goodness." I gestured toward the empty sales floor. "I'm still trying to recover from my last inheritance."

"Yeah, but a million dollars would help with that."

"True, but no such luck."

"Well, are you going to tell me, or what?" She carried the crowns back toward the kids' section. "If it's supposed to be a secret, you're not hiding it very well."

104

I glanced out the window for a sign of Charlie as I followed her. "No, I want to wait until Charlie gets back so I can tell you both at the same time. It'll affect both of you."

"Now I'm really intrigued." She laid the crowns on the chairs that didn't have them yet and collected the crayon boxes from the stand beside the throne.

Savannah poked me with her stuffed bone. I grabbed the end, and she growled and pulled back. A good game of tug might help burn off both of our extra energy. I growled back, and she shook her head, trying to yank the toy out of my hand. I held on tight with both hands. "Nope. Not this time, kid."

She lost her grip, and I scuttled backward onto my butt for the second time today. When I regained my feet, I tossed the bone toward the front of the store, and she took off after it, toenails scrabbling against the carpet. She reached the toy, snatched it up, and zoomed around the perimeter of the store. The Riddleton 500 part two.

Lacey stood at the coffee bar, enjoying the show. She turned to me. "You know, if we could bottle all that energy, we'd be rich."

"Don't I know it. Although, I suspect I'd consume a big portion of the product."

Charlie bustled through the door, wearing khaki pants and his red Ravenous Readers polo shirt and carrying the box of goodies from Bob's.

My jaw dropped as he set the carton down on the pastry counter. "What's wrong with you?" I asked him.

"Huh? I'm fine. What are you talking about?"

"You're wearing your uniform. Are you sick?"

He chuckled. "No, I just thought I'd change things up a little. People are getting tired of seeing the same old outfits. I need some time to think up something new."

I rolled my eyes. "Can't wait. I'm sure it'll be interesting. And wildly inappropriate."

Lacey came over to help him load the pastry trays. "All right. We're both here. What's your exciting news that's going to affect us?"

Charlie shot me a puzzled glance.

"My publisher offered me two more books."

I held up a hand to cut off their congratulatory remarks. "But, there's a catch. They want them both written by the end of the year. And I can't be late."

Lacey's mouth formed a circle. "Oh. That sounds tough. Can you do it?"

"I can, but it'll take up a lot of my time. I'll have to really focus on it, so I won't be around here as much. Not that I'm much help, anyway. But I haven't signed the contract yet. If you have any objections, now's the time to let me know. I don't want you to feel like I'm taking advantage of you."

"Don't be ridiculous," Charlie said, handing me a chocolate chip muffin on a napkin. "We got your back, Jack."

I bit into the chocolaty cake and wiped crumbs off my chin. "Lacey?"

She wore a concerned expression. "I'm thrilled for you, and I'll take care of everything for as long as possible. But remember, I won't be here for at least a few months. Will you be able to handle it while I'm gone?"

Crap. I'd forgotten about the maternity leave. Again. No way I could do both. I could barely handle the store without having my writing to worry about. And vice versa.

Charlie spoke up. "I can take care of it with a little help during the busy times. Instead of training Jen before you leave, Lacey, train me."

"Are you sure?" Lacey asked.

Charlie puffed out his chest. "You bet. It's about time I stepped up around here."

A lump formed in my throat. I didn't deserve such good friends. I turned to Lacey. "What do you think? Will it work? Assuming we're even still open by then."

She dropped a hand on Charlie's shoulder. "Sure, it'll work. I'll teach him everything he needs to know. Sign your contract."

I hugged them both, finally having something to look forward to. Once I found the money to keep the store going and cleared myself of Mara's murder.

CHAPTER TEN

Veronica Winslow set off the front-door bells as she strode in with a twin preschooler in each hand. Veronica, recently elected mayor in a closely contested special election, released the boys, Peter and Parker, and tucked her mid-length auburn hair behind one ear. She waved at us. "Hi, y'all. We ready to read?"

Savannah galloped toward them, screeched to a halt, then sniffed the boys all over, searching for breakfast remains. They squealed and hugged her, which she didn't like, but tolerated for friendship's sake. That, and she knew there'd be cookie crumbs in her future if she treated them right. My dog was no dummy. She knew how to get the good stuff.

Lacey walked over, collected the twins, and led them back to the kids' section where Story Time would soon begin. Today's selection was *Waiting Together*, and she'd already placed a stack of copies beside her throne for parents to buy. Once Lacey had seated the boys, Charlie brought a plate of cookies for each, and Savannah took her position at their feet for crumb collection duty.

"How's it going?" Veronica asked me as she poured coffee for herself. "Heard you had an exciting weekend."

"That's one way to put it."

"Don't worry; they'll get it figured out."

I smirked. "With Havermayer in charge? As far as she's concerned, she's already figured it out. I can't imagine her devoting too much time and energy to investigating anyone else. I'm lucky she didn't charge me on the spot. She would have if Olinski hadn't stepped in."

Veronica shook her head. "One thing I know about Francine Havermayer is she's a stickler for the rules. She'll do her job."

I grabbed a cup and studied Aletha's smiling face as it filled. Lacey wanted me to have new cups printed with me sitting in the chair reading instead of Aletha, but I'd balked. It just didn't seem right. The bookstore was *her* dream. She should be a part of it for as long as it lasted. "Maybe she will, but I still feel like I need to help clear my name. That won't be a priority for her in any case."

"What are you thinking?"

A couple of other groups of children were led in by parents, who then headed for the coffee bar. We moved to a table by the Mystery section. "I'm not sure what I'm going to do. What do you know about Fredo Di Rocca and Gil Scavuto? Fredo was the victim's husband, and Gil her brother. They're the most likely suspects. Besides me, of course."

She furrowed her brow in thought. "Not much. They moved here from Chicago to reopen the restaurant. And I've been told Gil's been making the rounds introducing himself to everyone. He hasn't made it to me yet, though. He's pretty well-liked from what I gather. Why? What have you heard?"

"Well, Gil accused Fredo of being affiliated with organized crime. Said he borrowed money from someone and didn't repay it before he left town, so they sent an enforcer to inspire him to make good on it."

"And killing Mara was supposed to be that inspiration?"

I shrugged. "Maybe. It's worth looking into."

"Have you mentioned this to Detective Havermayer?"

"Not yet. I haven't seen her since my interview, and I generally don't go looking for her unless I have to. She probably wouldn't listen anyway."

"You should tell her. She might not know any of this."

I pursed my lips. "Eric knows. Perhaps he'll tell her."

Veronica sipped her coffee. "It's my understanding he's been removed from the case. Apparently, for some strange reason, they consider having your girlfriend as the prime suspect in a murder you're investigating a conflict of interest. Imagine that." She smiled over the top of her cup. "You need to talk to her."

I gave an exaggerated sigh. "Fine. I'll do it this afternoon." Right after I had all my teeth pulled out with pliers, which would be considerably more fun.

The front door opened, and two teenage girls chattered their way to the Romance section.

Shouldn't they be in school? Must be a free period. I hoped, anyway. I certainly didn't want Ravenous Readers becoming a haven for truants.

I ran a quick inventory check in my mind to ensure there was nothing over there they were too young to see. I couldn't think of anything. We ran a clean place. No pornography or gory violence in that section.

I turned back to Veronica. "Have you seen that strange guy hanging out at the diner lately?"

"You mean other than Angus?"

We shared a laugh. "Angus isn't strange. He's unique. Like Charlie."

"True. So, strange in what way?"

"Strange in that I've never seen him before a few days ago. He just turned up out of the blue. The nearest motel is on the outskirts of either Blackburn or Sutton, and he drives here every day to walk around town and eat in the diner. I haven't seen him in a car, but it's safe to assume he's not hiking twenty miles each way to get here and back."

She nodded. "You know, I think I have seen him. No law against checking out the town, though. And maybe he's staying with friends or at a vacation rental."

"True, but that doesn't mean he's not the hitman."

"Come on, Jen. That's a stretch. And even if he is, why would he still be here?"

"I don't know. To remind Fredo what happens when he doesn't pay?"

"Could be, but Havermayer will handle it. You need to trust her to do her job."

When the door opened again, Detective Havermayer strolled in and glanced around, her face wearing its usual acerbic expression.

My face matched hers. "Terrific. I guess we said her name one time too many."

Veronica waved me away. "Well, you wanted to talk to her, so go talk to her."

I stood and moved in her direction, saying over my shoulder, "Yeah, but I absolutely didn't mean it."

Havermayer picked imaginary lint off the lapel of her black suit jacket. She had as much chance of having a dirty jacket as I did of wearing a ball gown to a baseball game. Or anywhere else, for that matter. She tugged on the collar of her crisp white blouse and smoothed back her sandy-blond hair. "Hi, Jen. Got a minute? I have a few more questions."

Yippee! I can't wait. "Sure, why not? It's either answer them here or have you drag me back to the station, right? But my request for a lawyer hasn't changed."

She dropped her hands onto her hips, pulling her jacket back to expose her badge and gun in the standard police intimidation move. "I'm sure you want off the suspect list, so you'll cooperate, right?"

"I want off that suspect list as much as you want to keep me on it. I know you're hoping I'll incriminate myself. Well, I won't, so have a seat, and let's get this over with. If you still think it'll get you something."

"I'll take my chances." She occupied a chair at a table near the Craft section, pulled the obligatory cop notebook out of her pocket, and flipped through the pages. "You mentioned you'd argued with Mara

Di Rocca earlier on the day she died. What was that about?"

I settled across the table from her, struggling to mask my irritation. Poker wasn't my favorite card game. "As I told you already, I wanted her to open any other business than a bookstore. Why do we have to go over it all again?"

She trained her lackluster green eyes on my blue ones. "Because you described it as . . ." She flicked through a few more pages. "A heated discussion. Correct?"

"That sounds about right."

"Well, her husband says it was a lot more than that. He says his wife told him you threatened her, and she was afraid for her safety."

"Good thing that's hearsay because it isn't true. Either he's lying to you, or she lied to him. Or, you're lying to me. You're allowed to do that, right?" I shifted in my seat. "I never threatened her. Even after she told me her intention was to put me out of business, which makes no sense at all."

She crossed her arms, exposing the gold badge clipped to her waistband again. "Why would he lie to me?"

"To deflect suspicion from himself, obviously. Everyone knows the husband is the first one you look at. Perhaps he's just trying to get ahead of it."

"I've found no motive for him to kill her. He came down here to open a restaurant that his wife and her brother own jointly. Without her, he's her brother's employee."

Has she even looked for a motive? "Unless he gets her half when she dies. Then he becomes an owner, instead of what he was before she died: the husband of one of the owners. And an employee. Sounds like motive to me. And he brought her lunch, making him most likely the last one to see her before she died." The detective should've already considered that possibility. Eric repeatedly told me she was sharper than I gave her credit for. It didn't seem like it at the moment. What was she up to?

Her lips twitched to suppress a smile. "She wanted nothing to do with that restaurant. He was as good as an owner already."

"As good as, but not quite. And what about his associates in Chicago?"

"What about them?"

I relayed what Gil had said about Fredo's money problems.

"I spoke to Mr. Scavuto. He said nothing about any of that."

No surprise. "He returned here to apologize for Fredo's behavior yesterday and retracted the statement. I didn't believe him. I think he just let a family secret slip. Well, what if that secret got his sister killed?"

Havermayer sat back in her chair. "What do you mean by that?"

"Gil suggested Mara was murdered because Fredo ducked out on a loan from someone in Chicago. And there's been a strange guy hanging around Riddleton the past few days. You should check him out. Maybe he has something to do with it."

"I will, but Fredo's not the only one having money problems, is he? The contest that's been supporting you

114

went bankrupt. Another bookstore in town would've been the end of this one, wouldn't it?"

"Possibly, but—"

Havermayer pointed her pen at me. "So, you got rid of the competition. You murdered Mara so she couldn't open that used bookstore. Then you might have a chance to keep this one going a little longer."

I stood, shaking from barely controlled anger. "I didn't kill Mara Di Rocca. Now, I think you should leave. I have nothing more to say."

She sighed as if I were a recalcitrant child. "Sit down, Jen. I still have more questions."

"Am I under arrest?" I asked, hoping Olinski would require more than hearsay and supposition to let her charge me.

Havermayer narrowed her eyes. "No, but keep in mind your ex-boyfriend isn't going to be able to protect you forever. Eventually, I'll find something even he can't ignore." She stood and adjusted her jacket, flashing the butt of her police-issue, nine-millimeter automatic one more time.

Another attempt to intimidate me. She really needed to find a new move. I wasn't falling for that one. "Well, until then, I'm done talking."

"Just give me one more question, and I'll leave you alone."

"That depends on what it is."

She met my gaze. "You mentioned Fredo brought his wife lunch yesterday. How do you know that?"

"Marcus told me Fredo picked up food at the diner that afternoon. The remains of it were all over the floor

115

when I went back and found Mara dead. So, he had to have been there."

"Thank you." She stood and dropped her notebook into a pocket.

I watched until the door closed behind the detective and ambled back to Veronica's table, rubbing my neck and twisting my head to release the tension. Story Time had concluded, and she had a twin on either side, excitedly discussing the story.

Oh, to be three years old again. When the worst thing that happened was bedtime came before you were ready. Or you knocked over your milk, and Mom got mad.

Veronica lifted her smile toward me and pointed to my seat. I lowered myself into it, and she hugged her energized twins, then handed them their almost empty cookie plates. "Why don't you boys bring these to Savannah for her to clean, so Miss Jen doesn't have to empty them?"

"Okay, Mommy," they chorused and ran off with the plates, dumping most of the remaining crumbs on the chocolate-brown carpet.

She rolled her eyes and shook her head. "Sorry about that."

"No problem. Savannah's middle name is Hoover. She'll take care of it."

She smiled and nodded. "So, what did Havermayer want?"

I planted an elbow on the table and propped my head in my hand. "She said that Fredo said his wife said I threatened her the day she died. Wow, that's a lot of saids. You get the idea. It sounds like one of Angus's stories."

"And she believed him?"

"She'd believe anything if it brought her closer to being able to arrest me. Thank goodness for Olinski. He won't let her do anything to me without real proof."

"It's nice to know people in high places." She grinned.

"Yeah, it helps sometimes. I'm friends with the mayor too, if you ever need anything."

Her expression sobered. "Speaking of which, if it comes down to it, and I sincerely hope it doesn't, Ted will represent you. Don't worry about that."

Veronica's husband, Ted Winslow, was a high-powered defense attorney with an office in Sutton. If I had to have a lawyer, he was the one I'd want. "Does he know that?"

"He will as soon as I tell him." She winked at me.

I laughed. "Thank you. Hopefully, it won't come to that."

She raised her coffee cup in a toast. "Here's to Havermayer finding the real killer."

I tapped my cup against hers and took a large swallow. I needed all the help I could get. Things were looking bleak at the moment.

Veronica pried her twins away from Savannah and led them to the door, stepping out of the way when a red-faced, sweaty Eric burst in. She sent me a lifted-eyebrow glance, shrugged, and left. Eric scanned the room until he located me. Four strides later, he was seated on the other side of my table.

I gave him a second to catch his breath, then asked, "What's going on?"

His scowl relaxed. "Nothing. I'm mad, that's all. Angus just told me Fredo's been going around telling people you killed his wife and threatened him to keep quiet about it or you'd kill him too."

My eyebrows pinched. "That's absurd. If anything, it was the other way around."

He took my hand. "I know that. I'm frustrated because I can't do anything about it. He has a right to say whatever he wants, even if he knows it isn't true. And I'm not allowed to interfere in the investigation, which means I can't even talk to him about it or risk losing my job. It's a lousy position to be in."

I reached across and took his other hand. "Thank you for wanting to defend me, but I'm perfectly capable of caring for myself. And nobody with any sense will believe him anyway."

He smiled. "You're taking this better than I am. It makes me so mad! I just wish I could do something about it."

Giving his hands a squeeze, I said, "I get it. It makes me mad too, but I suspect he's only trying to deflect attention from himself. So, because of that, I'm more intrigued than angry. He's putting an awful lot of effort into getting people to look at me rather than him. What doesn't he want anyone to see?"

Eric sat back in his seat. "I know that look, Jen. Leave it alone. If you truly believe nobody's listening to him, you have no reason to interfere."

"You're right. Nobody who matters is paying any attention to him. But I want to know what he's hiding. He has a secret, and I think it relates to his wife's death. The only way to find out is to talk to him, which is exactly what I'm about to do."

"Not without me, you're not."

"No problem. Let's go."

His phone rang. "It's Havermayer. I have to take this."

Eric's side of the conversation was limited to a bunch of "uh-huhs" and "yes, ma'ams." When he returned his cell to his inside jacket pocket, he turned to me and said, "I have to go to work. I don't suppose you'd consider waiting for me to get off before you go over there?"

"The longer I wait, the more time he has to spread his lies. I have to put a stop to it now before people start to believe him."

"I wish you wouldn't go without me."

"I understand, but I have this feeling he'll be more reasonable if it's only the two of us. After all, he can just lie about what was said if there are no witnesses, so he has no reason to be hostile. You being there will put him on the defensive. Make him strut like you're a rogue rooster challenging him for his henhouse. Does that make sense?"

"It does, actually. I'd still feel better if you'd let me come along. Or better still, you didn't go at all."

"I know." But we both knew I wouldn't be able to do anything else until I spoke with Fredo. I had to go.

CHAPTER ELEVEN

I stood before Antonio's Ristorante's door, debating whether to go in and confront Fredo, who was rearranging tables in the dining room, wearing stained jeans and a near-translucent white T-shirt that had seen more than its share of use. Only two days after his wife was murdered, he'd returned to work as if nothing had happened. Was that the action of a guilty man or an innocent one? If I was honest with myself, I'd have to say innocent. A guilty man would go out of his way to demonstrate his grief in public.

No sign of Gil, however. Perhaps losing a sister caused him more pain than losing a wife did Alfredo. Without Gil, I'd have no buffer against Fredo's temper. And I had no way to defend myself against an attack. With luck, Gil was in the kitchen or my theory about Fredo having no reason to be hostile or antagonistic without an audience was correct. Either way, I'd have to risk it. I had to know why Fredo was so intent on convincing everyone I killed his wife.

After a few deep breaths to steady myself, I pulled open the heavy glass door. As soon as my feet crossed the threshold, he looked up, and his eyebrows dove for the bridge of his nose. "What do you want?" His voice betrayed his irritation.

Deep breath in, slow breath out.

I focused on speaking normally, more of a challenge than I'd thought it would be. "I only want to talk to you for a minute."

"About what? I have nothing to say to you."

"Look, I didn't kill Mara. You need to stop telling people I did and that I threatened you. You know that never happened."

He took a menacing step toward me. "It's happening right now. I feel threatened. You'd better leave before I call the cops or better yet, handle it myself."

Fear fired down my spine, quickly followed by anger. My hands curled into fists at my sides. "That's ridiculous. I haven't said or done anything the least bit threatening."

"You better get lost and let me finish cleaning up for my wife's memorial."

"You're holding it here?"

"That's none of your business."

I put my hands up. "Okay, no problem." I glanced toward the kitchen, hoping Gil might come out and play peacemaker now that I knew for sure Fredo wasn't putting on a show. No such luck. "Where's Gil?"

Fredo sneered. "He's over at the other place. Bawling his eyes out, probably."

121

Nice to know somebody in the family has a heart. Fredo sure didn't seem to. Time to break out my Daniel Davenport diplomacy. I relied on the social-butterfly twin when being my usual blunt self might be hazardous to my well-being. Like now. "Everyone grieves in their own way, Fredo."

He moved so close that aftershave mingled with sweat assaulted my nose. Better than the whiskey and bacon from yesterday, but not much. "If you're not out of here in two seconds, I'm gonna have you arrested for harassment."

While I didn't think he could make that charge stick, it seemed prudent to not take the chance. Too much to do today. And Havermayer wouldn't need much encouragement to bring me in on any trumped-up charge she could find. I refused to give her the satisfaction, so I smiled just to irritate him, waved, and ducked out the door.

I'd learned nothing about Fredo's secret, but I didn't expect to get anything from him, anyway. I'd only come over here to show him I knew what he was up to and tell him to knock it off. Learning anything else would've been a bonus. But really, Gil had all the answers. Maybe I'd have better success getting him to talk. As close as he and Mara were, he had to know Fredo's secrets. If nothing else, I'd have another look at the crime scene, as disturbing as that might be. There could be something the police missed in their search. Something that would lead me to the real killer.

I hung a right on Walnut Street and made the one-block trip to Second, where I took another right turn.

That gave me two blocks to consider what I'd say to Gil when I arrived at the almost-bookstore. How could I convince him to tell me what I wanted to know? He had to believe it was in his best interest to confide in me if he wanted to know who killed his sister. I had to make him see I was his best chance.

Diplomat Daniel's voice resounded in my head. Start with small talk and lead Gil into the conversation I wanted to have. His advice made perfect sense, but small talk wasn't my forte. I didn't care about the weather other than how it would affect me at any given moment. Sporting events held no interest, and I didn't share Angus's enthusiasm for gossip. What else did people talk about? Mental shrug. I had no idea.

I ran out of time before figuring it out. When I approached the building, my heart raced, and sweat popping up all over my body chilled me. My chest tightened, breaths coming in short gasps. Pain radiated down my arms. Was I having a heart attack? Impossible. I was only thirty. What was going on then? Why was this happening?

It had to be a panic attack. The last time I was here, I found Mara's body, and the police arrested me. That would be enough to send anyone into a panic. I needed to calm down.

Deep breath in, slow breath out.
Deep breath in, slow breath out.
The pain gradually subsided. My pulse slowed, and breaths became more regular. I wiped the perspiration off my forehead with my sweatshirt sleeve and dried my hands on my pants. A few more deep breaths brought

123

me back to myself. As close as I could be, anyway. Time to get this over with.

I reached for the doorknob. The door was unlocked, so I let myself in and searched the dim room. No sign of Gil. However, he had to be here unless the police left the place unsecured when they finished processing the crime scene the other day. Not likely that Havermayer would be that slipshod. Security was her business.

The main room was still empty of furnishings. No place for Gil to hide, so I peeked into the back room. The bookcases were lined up along one wall, and the boxes against the opposite. Funny, the police hadn't been that neat when they searched Ravenous Readers a few weeks ago after I found a dead man leaning against my back door. That reinforced my belief that the search was Havermayer's attempt to irritate me. And it worked.

Gil had to be in either the office or the bathroom. I chose the office. When I opened the door, he peered up from his seat behind the desk. He didn't smile, but at least he didn't scowl either. His hand went to his throat, where a scale pendant the same as the one Mara wore Saturday morning rested against his chest beneath the crisp white shirt he wore with three buttons open.

Perfect. He'd given me a conversation starter. "Hi, Gil. I stopped by to check if you needed anything."

He pushed perfectly manicured fingers under his glasses to rub his eyes and ran a hand over his pallid face as if to wipe away the dark circles. "Thank you." The tremor in his voice belied his calm demeanor. His chair squeaked as he leaned back. "It's been a trying time. Mara and I were very close. Now it's like a part of me is missing."

"I'm sorry." His Facebook page flashed into my mind. They certainly were close. "That's a nice necklace you're wearing. Wasn't Mara wearing one just like it Saturday?"

Gil flashed a sad smile and fingered the pendant again. A tear leaked from the corner of his coal-black eye. He wiped it away. "We were born one year and two days apart in October. Both Libras. One of the many things we had in common. I've always believed that's why we got along so well."

Although I wasn't a big believer in astrology, I went with his assumption to keep him feeling comfortable. "Could be. Being that close in age probably helped too. You were practically twins. Did you wear matching clothes?"

"No, we never went that far." He flashed a wistful smile. "But we did everything together. At least until Fredo came along. I don't know what I'm going to do now." He buried his face in his hands.

I sat in the folding chair beside the wooden desk and gave him a minute to pull himself together. Being an only child left me unable to imagine what he felt. And I was too young to understand what I'd lost when my father died. I only knew he wasn't there anymore.

After a minute, Gil sat up and wiped his eyes. "I'm sorry. I'm really struggling with this. My sister was everything to me. Our parents divorced when we were teenagers. My dad moved here, and my mom died a few years later. All we had was each other. Now I have nobody."

A twinge of empathy worked its way into my chest. I couldn't know what he felt, but his obvious distress sat in my heart like a stone. "What about Fredo? He's your family."

"Ha! Fredo always hated how close Mara and I were. He did anything he could to come between us. When our father died, we decided to run the restaurant together. Fredo got so angry at the prospect that Mara backed out and decided we should sell it instead. She was afraid of him. He has a violent temper."

A trait he made no effort to hide. "I've noticed he's hot-headed. He scared me pretty good yesterday."

Gil smiled. "Well, if it makes you feel any better, I couldn't tell."

"Thanks. I'd hate for Fredo to think I was weak. Bullies like him feed on weakness." I leaned toward the desk. "If you decided to sell, how did you end up moving here to reopen Antonio's instead?"

He tented his fingers, elbows resting on the desk. "Honestly, I'm not sure. We were in the process of finding a real estate agent to broker the sale when Fredo suddenly changed his mind. Mara said he came home one day and announced he and I would run the restaurant. She could join us or do anything else she wanted. She chose to do something else. I didn't blame her for that decision. I didn't really want to work with him either, but I felt like I had no choice."

Huh. If Angus had offered to buy the restaurant, why did they need a real estate broker? A lawyer, maybe, but not a broker. *Weird.* "And he never said why the change? It seems kind of sudden to me."

"Fredo never explained himself. Not to Mara, anyway. They were married, but his life was none of her business."

"You think it might've had something to do with the financial problems you mentioned yesterday? The loan he didn't repay?"

Gil reddened. "I was just guessing about that. From the way he reacted, I might've been right. He let me have it when we left your store. That's why I came back. I was afraid of what he might do to you if I didn't set you straight." He shook his head. "It didn't help, though. He's been spreading rumors about you all over town to destroy your credibility. I hope for your sake it isn't working."

"Not really. Not the way Fredo intended, anyway. Detective Havermayer wants to believe it, but she isn't that stupid. Although, she tried to use it to convince me she had more evidence against me than she does. It didn't work."

"Good. I'd hate for you to get in trouble over something I did."

I smiled at him. "Don't worry about me. I can take care of myself." My grin faded. "Gil, is it possible Fredo killed Mara? Did he have any reason to want her dead?"

He frowned. "No way. As much of a jerk as he can be, he was obsessed with her. She was the center of his world."

"Sounds like he was a bit possessive of her."

Gil chuckled. "More than a bit. He controlled her every move. She couldn't go to the bathroom without reporting to him first. He wouldn't allow her any friends. He *barely* tolerated me, but he knew she'd find the strength to leave him if he tried to cut me out of her life."

Hmmm. "Were those your observations, or did she tell you about their marital problems?"

"Absolutely. She tells me everything."

She used to, anyway. Maybe Mara had secrets of her own. Secrets that might've gotten her killed. "What about your theory that the guy Fredo borrowed money from sent someone to convince him to pay? Could a hitman have murdered Mara?"

He opened his mouth, closed it again, and inhaled deeply. "Anything's possible, I guess." He rubbed his temples, then his eyes. "If you don't mind, I don't want to discuss this anymore."

Poor guy. He just lost his sister, and I was badgering him about who might've killed her. Just to save my own butt. What would Daniel think of me now?

Way to make it all about you, Jen.

I rose to leave. "I'm sorry for being so insensitive. I don't think sometimes."

"It's all right. Some people believe you murdered her, but I'm not one of them. I'm sorry I said I did."

"Thank you." I had my answers, but I didn't want him to think I only stopped by to grill him about possible suspects. I had one more related question, though. "Gil, did Mara ever tell you why she was so sure I had something to do with your father's death?"

He sighed, sending dust motes in the sunbeam peeking through the blinds into a tizzy. "Not directly. All I know is she talked to my father, and he'd told her he was a suspect in a murder, but you were supposed to prove him innocent somehow. She didn't give me all the details, so I don't really know what she was talking about."

No way I would tell him, either. He had enough grief on his plate. "It was complicated. Too much to go into right now. Not that it matters anymore."

"Anyway, a couple days later, he was dead. In her mind, you were going to protect him and you didn't, therefore it was your fault."

"That seems a bit of a reach."

"She was a daddy's girl." He started to smile, then bit his lower lip. "Our father walked on water, as far as she was concerned. If something happened to him it had to be someone else's fault. It couldn't possibly be a result of the mess he'd gotten himself mixed up in. I'm sorry it had to be you she chose to blame. And I'm especially sorry about the way she chose to get her revenge."

If she hadn't planned to put me out of business because of her mistaken belief, I'd feel sorry for her. Actually, I did feel sorry for her. Being the prime suspect in her murder made it difficult to show it, though. "Me too."

He silently twirled a pen on his desk blotter, struggling to hold his emotions in check.

Time for a subject change. "Fredo mentioned he was cleaning up the restaurant for your sister's memorial. When's it going to be?"

He lost the battle, and tears filled his eyes again. He cleared them with his thumb and forefinger. "Friday at two. Will you come?"

I hadn't even considered attending since Fredo was convinced I'd killed Mara. "I don't think I'll be welcome under the circumstances."

"I would welcome you. I understand your reluctance, though, and I don't blame you. People can be cruel. Although in the short time I've been here, I've come to love the people of Riddleton. And the town itself. No matter what happens, I plan to stay here and make a life for myself. Riddleton has felt like home to me since we rolled over the town line. I've never felt anything like it. And I've met very few people who would actually consider you capable of killing someone."

A few like Havermayer. "I appreciate the invitation. Friday's four days away. If things calm down between now and then, I'll gladly come." I stepped toward the door, then turned back. "Is there anything you need before I go?"

Gil rose and came around the desk. "No, thank you." He reached for my arm. "Come, I'll walk you out."

We passed into the back room, and he stopped and scanned the area. "I don't know what I'm gonna do with all this stuff. I can't run a bookstore and work at the restaurant too."

I glanced at the bookcases, which were precisely what Lacey wanted for the kids' section expansion. "Well, if you're sure you don't need them, I can take a few bookcases off your hands. I don't have much money

130

to spend, though. You'd probably do better listing it all on Craigslist or someplace like that."

Gil rubbed his chin, thinking. "The landlord was nice enough to let us out of the lease, given the circumstances." He grimaced and studied the tops of his loafers to regain his equilibrium. "But we have to clean the place out by next weekend. If you can move it by Monday, I'll let you have it all for five hundred dollars. Books included. Can you swing that?"

My jaw fell. "Are you sure? You can get a lot more than that elsewhere. Those cases are brand new. They're worth triple that by themselves." But what would I do with all those used books? We only sold new ones in the store. For that price, though, we could keep them for online stock. We wouldn't make much on sales, but the value of the bookcases alone would more than cover the cost of what he had asked for the whole lot.

"I'm sure. I don't have the time or energy to deal with listing them or finding a buyer."

"Thank you. I very much appreciate it, but it feels terrible for me to benefit from your family's loss."

"You're helping me out, really. Besides, some good has to come from all of this. Just have it gone by Monday if you can."

"Thank you." I hustled back to the bookstore to tell Lacey and Charlie about our windfall. Lacey would be thrilled.

CHAPTER TWELVE

When I walked into the diner at ten 'til six, I found Eric, Marcus, Ingrid, and Angus camped out in our booth. Three other couples were spread out at booths and tables, cared for by Penelope, the server, and Jacob, the cook. I grabbed a chair from an empty table and joined my group. *My group.* Definitely a new concept to me. Strange how things could change while you're not paying attention.

I pulled my chair up to the end of the table. "Hey, guys. What's up?"

"Not much," Angus said. "Would you like to sit next to Eric?"

"Nah, I'm good. Relax and enjoy your break."

Marcus laughed. "Are you kidding? All he does anymore is take breaks."

Angus shot him a mock glare. "I don't see you working particularly hard, either."

"I'm on my dinner break. Man's gotta eat, don't he?"

"I suppose." Angus patted his rotund belly. "Guess I've done my share."

Penelope brought me a Mountain Dew. "Is anyone ready to order?"

I took a long pull on the straw, savoring the syrupy sweetness, knowing the kick would come later. "What's today's special?"

"Fried chicken, mashed potatoes and gravy, with green beans."

"Sounds good to me. I'll have one of those."

Ingrid agreed with me, Marcus ordered the meatloaf, and Eric chose fish and chips.

Angus squeezed out of the booth. "Guess I'd better get back to work since Marcus is going to goof off all night."

Marcus flashed his I'm-good-looking-and-I-know-it smile. "You got that right! My boss is really cool, though, so I can goof off if I want to. He doesn't mind."

Angus shook a finger at him. "Don't push your luck, buddy."

"Yes, sir!" Marcus snapped off a salute. "At your service, sir."

Ingrid elbowed him. "Stop playing silly buggers."

I glanced at Marcus for a translation. He shrugged and smiled at her as if she'd announced the secret to achieving world peace. From the look of it, spoken language wasn't their most important form of communication. He seemed happy, however, and that was all that mattered. He deserved some joy in his life.

Angus went to check on Jacob's progress, and I returned my chair to the table I'd borrowed it from and replaced him at the booth. "Have you heard any more about Angus's imaginary girlfriend?" I asked Eric.

"Not a word. I guess he's keeping it a secret for some reason."

Marcus leaned forward. "I asked him about it this morning, and he got a funny look on his face and walked away without answering. Pretty strange for him. Usually, he loves to talk."

"Perhaps they broke up," Ingrid said.

Eric sipped his drink. "Or maybe there's no girlfriend, and he thought Marcus was messing with him or something."

"Could be," I said. "But usually, Angus gives as good as he gets. He'd have gone along if he thought Marcus was playing around."

Penelope interrupted the speculation by laying our dinner plates before us. "Ya'll need anything else?"

Nobody spoke up, so I replied, "No, thank you. Looks like we're all set."

"Well, if you change your mind, you know where to find me." She hustled back to the counter to pick up her next round of orders.

I sank my teeth into a drumstick, and the perfect combination of seasonings, crunchy coating, and tender chicken mingled in my mouth. Angus's fried chicken was second only to my mother's. And a close second at that. Eric adored my mother's fried chicken. I should learn how to make it for him. Someday, when I had the time.

After swallowing, I turned to Eric. "Did you get a chance to talk to your buddy again?"

He responded with a quizzical expression and a mouthful of fish.

Men. Couldn't remember what they said from one day to the next. "About Fredo. You were going to try to get more information about him."

"Right. I spoke with him this morning, and he hadn't heard anything else. He did tell me Havermayer put a rush on the DNA samples from the scarf, though. We, I mean, they should know something in a couple of days, if not sooner."

I rolled my eyes. "It figures. DNA is the one thing that ties me to the murder. Of course, she wants *that* back in a hurry."

Eric squeezed my arm. "You've already explained why you touched the scarf. Nothing to worry about unless they find your DNA all over it."

"They shouldn't find it anywhere but the one spot in the way when I tried to check her pulse. I didn't touch it any place else."

He nodded. "Then you're okay."

Under any other circumstances, I'd believe him and be comforted. However, with Havermayer involved, I couldn't let my guard down for a minute. Boy, what I could do with all the extra time and energy I'd have if I wasn't constantly defending myself against Havermayer's frivolous accusations. I had to admit, though, the allegations weren't frivolous this time. I was a legitimate suspect, and she had a right to move forward accordingly.

"I can't believe Havermayer still doesn't know anything about Fredo's background," I said, wiping my greasy fingers on a napkin.

"Actually, she does," Ingrid said. "But I'm not sure if I should discuss it. Although, she never said it was confidential, and it's information anyone could find if they spent enough time on the internet."

"Of course, I don't want you to breach her confidence, but you know I'm just going to put Charlie to work on it. He'll find it eventually. He always does."

Ingrid laughed. "You would, wouldn't you?" She chewed on her lower lip, then seemed to make a decision. "I might as well save you the trouble. When I spoke to her about the autopsy results, she mentioned that Mara's husband had been in real estate in Chicago, but they hadn't found any properties in his name."

"There you go. Real estate transactions are a matter of public record. Even I know that. Havermayer couldn't have meant for that information to be confidential. If it was, she wouldn't have told you about it."

"Jen's right," Eric said. "As the ME, you had no need to know about his real estate dealings." He snapped his fingers. "You know, he might've been an agent. Then he could be in real estate without owning anything."

Ingrid twisted her lips in doubt. "That wasn't the impression I got. It sounded like he passed himself off as a tycoon, not an agent."

"He can't be a real estate tycoon without owning any property. How did he make money that way?" Eric pushed his empty plate away.

I retrieved a fresh napkin from the tabletop dispenser to wipe my mouth. "That could be why he had to get that loan he didn't repay."

"Could be," Marcus said, looking up when someone entered the restaurant. "Well, look who's here again."

I followed Marcus's gaze to our friend, the anonymous businessman, who settled into what had become his booth in the opposite corner from ours. "Did you ever have a chance to talk to him?"

Marcus nodded. "I introduced myself at breakfast. His name is Steve."

"Steve? What's his last name?"

"I don't know. That's all he said."

I used my fresh napkin to dab the crumbs off my lips. "What else did he say?"

"Not much. He gave one-word answers to every subject I tried without coming straight out and asking him what he was doing here."

Disappointing. I'd hoped for something that might give us a clue to whether he had anything to do with Mara's death. "I guess I'm just going to have to go over there and ask him what he's doing here then."

Eric grabbed my arm. "Oh no you're not. Leave him alone. What if you're right, and he's a hitman?"

"He won't do anything in a public place like this. Besides, I'm not on his list."

Ingrid grinned. "How do you know?"

"I don't, I guess. Who would want me dead?"

"Anyone who knows you!" they chorused and burst into laughter.

I faked a pout. "Ha-ha. Very funny. I thought you were my friends."

"We're just winding you up, luv."

"Gotcha." Of course I'd known they were only teasing. I'd hoped anyway.

Lacey and Charlie's ecstatic grins popped into my mind. "I almost forgot to tell you my exciting news."

"What's going on?" Eric asked.

"I spoke to Mara's brother, Gil, this afternoon. He'll let me have all the bookcases and books Mara'd accumulated really cheap."

Ingrid frowned. "He's moving fast, isn't he?"

"The landlord said he'd let them out of the lease if they could clear the place out by Monday. So, it's either get rid of the stuff quickly or pay a year's rent on a building he's not going to use. I'd probably do the same thing if I were him."

I watched Penelope bring the check to the businessman. Steve. I really wished he'd told Marcus his last name. Then we could get more information on him. I settled my gaze in his direction. "I'd love to know who that guy is and what he's doing here."

Marcus shrugged. "Nobody seems to know, and he's not talking."

I glanced at Eric. "We should follow him. See where he goes and what he does."

His eyebrows shot up. "Are you crazy? That's illegal."

"Only if we get caught."

"No, it's illegal regardless. If he spots us, we'll be charged for stalking."

"Guess we'd better not get spotted, then."

Eric placed his hands on the table. "No, Jen. Just plain no. I'm not doing that."

I took one of his hands. "What if he's the killer?"

"I'm sure Havermayer's looking into that possibility."

"Why? Did she tell you that?"

"Well, no, but she's thorough. I'm sure a stranger in town at the time of a murder would be high on her priority list."

Not if she has a chance to blame me. "I wish I shared your confidence. Last I heard, I was her prime suspect."

He pulled his hand away. "You were there, Jen. It's perfectly reasonable for her to suspect you."

I looked to Marcus and Ingrid for help. "What do you guys think?"

Ingrid put her hands up, palms out. "I'm staying out of this. I'm the medical examiner on the case. I can't be involved in deciding who the culprit is." She dropped her hands and leaned toward me. "However, hypothetically, I might consider the possibility that this guy had something to do with it. He's certainly a suspicious character. It could be worth a go, luv. Hypothetically speaking, of course."

A glance at Marcus produced a shrug and a headshake. "I think you're nuts. If the guy *is* the killer, and he catches you following him, you could end up dead the same way as that other lady did."

"No, I can't. I don't own a scarf."

Eye rolls all around.

Steven grabbed his check and headed for the cash register.

"It's now or never, Eric. Are you coming with me?"

He lowered his eyebrows and glared at me. "What choice do I have? Someone's gotta keep you from getting yourself killed." He dropped a twenty-dollar bill on the table and slid out of the booth behind me.

When we reached the sidewalk, Steven climbed into a late-model gold Mercedes parked on Main Street beside the diner, talking into his phone. We jumped into Eric's black Jeep Wrangler, sitting in front of the police station, and waited impatiently for Steven to get off the phone and make a move. After a minute of inaction, Eric started the car and eased out of his spot.

"Where are you going?" I asked.

"I'm gonna turn around on Pine, so we'll be in position to follow if he turns back toward Blackburn." He turned right on Pine Street and into the Riddleton Bank parking lot, coming out the other side.

When we reached the STOP sign at the corner, Steven was still sitting in his spot, immersed in his conversation. With luck, nobody would pull up behind us before he moved. Fortunately, little traffic cruised the streets of Riddleton on Monday evening.

I glanced toward the diner, and Angus watched us through the window with a puzzled expression. I waved, and he frowned and lifted his palms in a what-are-you-doing gesture. I gave him the okay sign with my fingers. He smiled and shook his head. I imagined nothing I did, at this point, would surprise him. Of course, he'd expect a full explanation the next time I saw him. I hoped I'd have something interesting to tell him.

Steven finally moved, making a U-turn toward Blackburn as Eric had anticipated. Eric turned left to follow, careful to stay back a few car lengths. We had no traffic to hide behind, but there was only one way to get to Blackburn from Riddleton unless you went to Sutton first to take the interstate. Our presence in Steve's rearview mirror shouldn't cause too much alarm.

We picked up some traffic as we approached Blackburn but stayed in touch with the Mercedes all the way to town, where Steven pulled into the Royal Place parking lot. Now we knew where he'd been staying, which made his presence in Riddleton all the more puzzling. It was a difficult commute in weekday traffic. He had to have a good reason.

Eric waited for two more vehicles to turn into the lot, then followed. Steven gave no indication that he was aware of us. So far, so good. We slid into a spot three spaces down from him and followed the sidewalk to the front entrance of the imposing structure. I glanced up and counted five floors of rooms above us. How many rooms per floor? Steven occupied one of them. We only had to establish which one.

Passing through the front doors, we entered a modern motif lobby with comfortable leather chairs augmented by wood-block tables. The elevator dinged, and Steven got in when the doors opened. I moved toward the desk, and Eric grabbed my arm.

"Wait," he said. "I want to see where he gets off."

The number above the elevator stopped on four and remained there. Eric released me. "Okay, he's on the fourth floor. What do you want to do now?"

"Let's try to find out something about him."

Eric lifted an eyebrow. "How do you propose to do that?"

"Can't you just flash your badge and ask the desk clerk?"

"No, I can't just flash my badge. This isn't my jurisdiction. Besides, they'll likely tell him when he comes down. Do we want him to know we're checking into him?"

Excellent question. "Not really." *Think, Jen.* "What if we tell them he's a potential witness, and we need to ask him some questions? We're not going to talk to him now, are we?"

Eric shook his head. "I have no standing in this case and no jurisdiction here. If I try to talk to him, I'll lose my job."

"So, we only need the desk clerk to give us his name and room number. Then we pretend to go up and interview him. The clerk will have no reason to tell Steven we were here because he'll assume Steven already knows."

"I can't do it, Jen. It's illegal and I'm a cop."

"I'm not. I'm going to try talking to the desk clerk. No law against that, is there?"

Eric shook his head. "I can't be here for this. I'll wait outside."

"Fine," I said to his retreating back.

I approached the desk. A baby-faced man wearing a name tag with L. Johnson printed on it smiled. "May I help you? Do you have a reservation?"

"I need to speak with the man who just went upstairs."

"I'm sorry, but I can't give out guest information."

"Please. My purse was stolen, and I think he might be a witness. My driver's license and credit cards were in it.

142

I have to get it back. Please help me. If I have his name and room number, I can tell the cops who he is and they can question him."

L. glanced toward a closed door marked *Manager*. "I'm sorry. My manager's on his dinner break. I don't feel comfortable giving you that information. Can you come back in about an hour?"

"I need to go to the police station and give my statement. It would be much better if I had all the information. And they'd have a better chance of getting my stuff back. Will you help me?" I batted my eyelashes at him, but he wasn't looking. Just as well. It probably wouldn't have worked anyway. "I guess, if I have to, I can just knock on all the doors on the fourth floor. I'm pretty sure that's where he got off the elevator."

Sweat broke out on L.'s forehead, indecision clouding his eyes. Finally, he sighed. "That won't be necessary." He tapped a few buttons on his computer and studied the screen. "His name is Steven Watkins, and he's in four oh seven. Is there anything else I can do for you?"

"No, thank you so much. You're a lifesaver."

"Good luck. I hope you get your purse back."

I smiled and met up with Eric in the parking lot.

The anonymous businessman had a name. Now we had only to figure out what he was doing in Riddleton.

CHAPTER THIRTEEN

The bookstore had four customers—two adults and two children—when I walked in Tuesday morning around eleven. Story Time had ended, and all but these two kids were gone. Assuming there were more than two to begin with. Charlie was rearranging the cookie trays to compensate for the ones he'd given the toddlers. Lacey had returned all the chairs to their proper places and now stood in the kids' section, scribbling notes.

Savannah charged toward her, almost bumping her off her feet. At least she'd finally learned not to jump on people, but her sheer size alone made an encounter with the excited German shepherd hazardous to the uninitiated. Lacey, however, was well prepared for the onslaught. Experience was an excellent teacher.

"Easy, girl!" She put a hand out to keep all four gargantuan paws on the floor. "I'm happy to see you too. Let's go get a treat."

Savannah pranced and bounced to the cash register, where the snacks were hidden. She sat, butt wriggling so much it barely maintained contact with the floor, while Lacey fished one out of the bag. She held it under the dog's nose, and Savannah gently nibbled it out of her hand. It took two months and a hundred puppy nips to teach her not to snatch. I suspect Lacey appreciated my putting in the time. Not so the adhesive bandage manufacturers, who saw a significant drop in sales.

"How's it going?" I asked as Lacey wiped the dog slobber off her fingers.

"Pretty good. We had ten kids this morning. Not bad for a Tuesday."

"Not bad at all. Almost Saturday numbers. I can live with that." I gestured toward the giraffes on the back wall. "What were you doing when I came in?"

She showed me her notebook. "I was figuring out what to do with all the new bookcases. They'll be perfect for the expansion. Just what we needed at a fraction of the price."

"If I can figure out how to get them over here. Do you know anyone with a truck we can use next weekend? They won't fit in my car or Eric's Jeep."

"I think Ben's brother might let us use his. I'll ask him."

"Thanks. Otherwise, I'll have to ask Zach. He's the only person I know with a pickup truck. I'd rather not, though. We're not exactly friends."

Zach Vick was the son of the former police chief who was murdered last summer. He'd been determined to find his father's killer, and I ran into him repeatedly while trying to prove Eric had nothing to do with it. Now he served as an RPD patrol officer, and my only encounters with him since involved my being accused of murder. Not exactly conducive to friendship.

"I'll see what I can do." She came out from behind the counter. "Let's talk about the changes we need to make."

I walked with her back to the kids' section. "You basically want to swap out all the two-shelf bookcases for the big ones, right?"

We turned when the door bells tinkled. Only our customers leaving empty-handed. Lacey sighed. "Oh well, maybe next time." She stopped near one of the two-shelf cases we had dotted around the floor. "I was thinking we could move these to the main sales area, use them for specials and sales, and line the full-sized cases around the walls. That will clear out floor space and give us a lot more room for books."

I cupped my chin in one hand, envisioning the new setup. "I see two problems with that. Number one: we'd have to elevate the small cases somehow, so people won't trip over them and sue us or ignore them because they're too low to easily see what's in them. Number two: the larger bookcases will cover up most of the giraffes. The kids love those giraffes."

Lacey spun toward the back wall, teetered, and grabbed the edge of the bookcase beside her to regain her balance. She closed her eyes and lowered her head.

"Are you all right?" I asked, brow furrowed. I pulled a chair out from under a tiny table. "Here, sit down for a minute."

She waved me off. "I'm fine. I just turned around too fast and got dizzy. I must be dehydrated or something."

Dehydrated? No way. Lacey drank more water in a day than I did in a month. "Possibly. Or you could be having a girl."

She gave me her you-must-be-out-of-your-mind, cocked-eyebrow look. "It's too early in the pregnancy to worry about anything like that. I'm okay. It's not my blood pressure."

I bit back my skepticism and nodded. "I'll take your word for it. For now. Just don't overdo it, okay?"

She maneuvered her fingers into an okay sign and turned back to the giraffes. "I think we can keep the smaller cases for the back wall so the kids don't lose the giraffes. It's only two sections. I'm pretty sure we can manage like that. We'll still have the extra space I'm after."

"And we can stack the smaller cases in the main room so they're visible. I'm sure there's a way to anchor them together so they don't topple over. I'll get Eric to take a look at it. He's pretty handy that way."

"That'll work. What do you think about using them for the used books instead of clearing one of the cases on the wall? Then, when we run out, people won't expect us to restock. Unless you want to get into the used book business?"

I rubbed the back of my neck. "I don't know. I go back and forth on it. It'll generate some sales, but we'll also lose new-book sales for people just looking for something to read and don't care what."

"What if we only offer used copies of books we don't already sell? Instead of losing business, we'll gain the customers who are just looking for something to read but aren't willing to pay publisher's retail."

Another great idea from Lacey. What would I do without her? I wasn't looking forward to finding out. "I like it. We can decide if we're going to continue selling used books after we see how it works out. And know the profit margin for books we actually have to pay for."

Poor, neglected Savannah trotted up for some attention. Lacey scratched her behind the ears, then took the stuffed bone out of her mouth and threw it. The dog sprinted toward the front of the store and screeched to a halt to snatch up the toy. Amazing she never had any rug burns on her pads. She trotted back and poked me with it. My turn.

"I guess we'll see how it goes," Lacey said over her shoulder as she moved to help a fortyish blonde who entered the store carrying an empty shopping bag I hoped she intended to fill with books.

Charlie hunched over his laptop perched on the pastry case, hunting for stuff I probably didn't want to imagine. He was wearing his uniform for the second day in a row. Perhaps I should take his temperature. There was definitely something wrong with him.

He eyed me when I planted my elbows on the case beside him.

"Hi, boss. What's up?"

I checked out his polo shirt and khakis. "I don't know, you tell me."

"I told you. I'm taking a break. I'm allowed to dress like a normal person, aren't I? I thought you'd be happy you hadn't wasted the money on these shirts altogether."

148

I poked him in the arm. "I don't care how you dress, Charlie. You'll never be normal. That's what I love about you."

He shot me an eye roll. "Glad to hear it." Then he gestured toward his computer. "I'm almost done with our seller's accounts. We should be up and running by the end of the week. If all goes well, we'll start generating some revenue. It won't solve our problems, but it'll help, right?"

His earnest expression tugged on my heart. "Absolutely. Thank you for working so hard on it. I knew I could count on you."

He threw his shoulders back. "Always! Speaking of which, how's your investigation going? Anything you need me to research for you?"

Yes, yes, yes! "Thanks for reminding me. Eric and I got the name of that guy hanging around town lately. It's Steven Watkins. Think you can do a deep dive on him? Find out what he's doing here?"

He posed with hands on hips, chest puffed out, and chin elevated, like a superhero. "You can count on me, boss."

I shook my head. No, Charlie would never be normal. No matter what he wore. "Also, see if you can find anything on the Di Roccas. Gil Scavuto too. Their lives in Chicago seem to be a big mystery to everybody but them."

The front door opening followed his double thumbs up. I looked over to check out our new visitor, who turned out to be Eric, in his crisp detective suit and shiny shoes. Havermayer must be rubbing off on him. I

149

smiled and went to greet him, but Savannah beat me to it. Waiting my turn while he gave her ear scratches and chest rubs, I realized it never occurred to me that I'd one day play second fiddle to my dog. Welcome to the New World.

I stood with my arms crossed, tapping my foot as if irritated. Eric knew better, of course. It was fun to mess with him, though. He paid no attention, throwing Savannah's toy into the stockroom for her to chase.

When she took off after it, he kissed my cheek. "Good morning."

"It was until you threw me over for my dog."

He scratched me under the chin. "There, is that better?"

I laughed and pushed his hand away. "Smart aleck."

He draped his arm around my waist, and we walked to the coffee bar, where I poured him a cup. Black, no sugar. Just the way he liked it. Or, as he put it, the way he'd become accustomed to drinking it because the police station break room always ran out of cream and sugar.

I filled my mug, and we wandered up to sit on the couch, where Savannah had made herself comfortable. I shooed her off, and she grumbled but obliged, trotting away to find someone who'd treat her with the dignity and respect she deserved.

Eric blew the steam off his cup and took a sip. "What's new and exciting around here this morning? Been busy?"

"Not much. We've been redecorating."

He surveyed the room, frowning. "It looks the same to me. What's changed?"

"Nothing, yet. Lacey's making plans for the new bookcases."

"Oh boy! I see a lot of heavy lifting in my future."

"And a little carpentry work if you're up for it. Lacey wants to put the small bookcases on the sales floor, and we have to hook them together so people don't trip over them." I squeezed his arm. "You don't have to help if you don't want to. We don't believe in making people work against their will around here." I ran my fingers through his hair and rested my chin on his shoulder. "Of course, I'm sure I can find a way to make you willing."

His entire head turned crimson. "I'll be happy to help."

"Awesome!" I kissed his heated cheek. "What's new and exciting at the RPD? Any fresh leads yet, or do I need to contact my lawyer?"

Eric narrowed his eyes. "Since when do you have a lawyer?"

"Since Veronica said she'd make Ted represent me if it turned out I needed one."

He set his cup on the table beside the couch. "Well, maybe it won't come to that."

"What does that mean?"

"Havermayer has a new suspect, but she won't tell me anything about him."

Hope popped its head up, teasing me. "Huh. I wonder who it could be?"

Eric shrugged. "Your guess is as good as mine."

"Wouldn't it be funny if it was Steven Watkins? Funny to us, anyway. She'd be mad as hell if she found out we were already looking into him, and she was just now catching up."

"So, she's not going to find out, right?" he said, meeting my eyes with his serious gaze.

"Right. I'd never do anything to get you in trouble."

Savannah trotted up and squeezed herself between us on the couch. I leaned around her to share a glance with Eric.

He laughed. "I hope the rest of our children aren't as clingy as this one."

The rest of our children? He's only kidding. Relax, Jen. "Really. We'd need the world's largest sectional and a bullhorn to converse."

"We could always text each other as some people do."

"No way. That's just silly."

He snapped his fingers. "I almost forgot. The DNA results came back on that skeleton you found in the tunnel."

"Cool. Anything interesting?"

"It's a Caucasian male, which we already knew from the medical examiner, of northern European descent, and he's not in the system, so no criminal history."

Not much, but it was new information, at least. "Okay. That's something to go on, anyway. Now all we need is his last hairbrush."

Eric's chuckle was interrupted by his phone going off. He fished it out of his pocket and showed me the screen. Havermayer. She either had a case for him or wanted him to arrest me while he was here. I chose door number one.

They chatted for a few minutes while I gave Savannah a belly rub with her stretched across both our laps. I could hear Eric worrying about the growing accumulation of dog hair on his pants while he watched. I grinned at his discomfort. He wanted to be a father. *Gotta take the good with the bad.*

He disconnected the call and shared a stunned expression.

"What's going on?" I asked.

"Fredo Di Rocca just phoned in a robbery at his house."

"Are you kidding? What did they take?"

Eric's phone dinged with a text. He glanced at it. "There's the address. I'll let you know when I find out."

We eased out from under the two-ton dog, and he brushed as much hair off his pants as possible. I retrieved the lint brush I kept for such occasions and helped him. Couldn't have him showing up at a crime scene looking like a Wookiee.

"I thought you weren't allowed to work on this case?"

"I can work the robbery, but not the homicide. Once I dig up a connection, if there is one, I have to turn it over to Havermayer."

"Sounds like she's just using you to do the grunt work."

"So, what else is new? I'm the trainee. That's my job."

CHAPTER FOURTEEN

I sat in my office staring at my laptop screen, the posters on the wall opposite staring at me. The more I reminded myself that I was on a deadline again, the less I wrote. It seemed that just the *word* deadline sent my brain into a deep freeze. It was book two all over again. Only this time, I couldn't be late, no matter what. The pressure built in my head like a balloon with too much air, and every instinct I had screamed, "Run!" But escape was out of the question. I'd accepted the offer.

The "Chapter Three" written in the middle of the top of the page taunted me.

Do something. Do something. Do something.

I had to get Daniel to Greek Week so he could pledge his fraternity. If he didn't pledge, he'd never go to the tunnels and consequently never find the dead kid. If he never found the dead kid, I had no story, and without a story, there'd be no book. I had to find the words somehow.

But in the back of my head lay the constant reminder I also had to find Mara's killer. If I didn't clear my name, I'd be on trial for my life when the book came out. Some people believed that any publicity was good publicity. In this instance, in particular, I strenuously disagreed.

And what about Lacey? Her dizzy spell this morning bothered me so much I chose to spend the afternoon at the store instead of going home to write uninterrupted in case something happened to her. Her pregnancy was only a few months along. Any problems she had would only get worse from here. I couldn't stay here every minute of every day, though. Not if I ever wanted to finish this book. But I had to protect my friend. Would I be forced to choose at some point?

Savannah lay sleeping in her bed beside my chair. Her eyebrows fluttered, and her paws and ears twitched in sync with her dream. I focused on the steady rise and fall of her ribcage, trying to clear my mind, but Ruth's voice on the phone telling me I had until the end of the year to write the next two books, and the publisher would tolerate no delays this time, ricocheted around my skull. No room for creativity with all that junk clogging up my brain.

I had another full-blown case of writer's block. How did I fix it last time? I moved back home to Riddleton. Not an option this time. Of course, the writer's block followed me here, so that's not what solved the problem back then, either. What was? What turned on my mental spigot so the ideas flowed freely again? If I could only remember, I might do it again.

After another ten minutes of typing and backspacing, I gave up and wandered onto the sales floor with Savannah yawning and stretching behind me. We had two customers, both middle-aged women, one perusing the Romance section, the other flipping through a mystery.

It'd been a while since the last time I read a book. Too busy writing them and solving murders. And when I had the time, I lacked the brain power. Writing and investigating were both exhausting endeavors. Especially since the investigations were usually necessary because I, or someone I cared about, had been accused of murder.

Perhaps I needed to do something about that. Reading might help jump-start my creativity again. After all, I'd have to use my imagination to immerse myself in the story. Maybe that energy would translate to my writing. It was worth a try. What I was doing now didn't work, that was for sure.

Charlie stood behind the pastry counter, studying his laptop screen like it held all the universe's secrets. Of course, as far as he was concerned, it did.

I leaned on the glass beside him. "Whatcha workin' on?"

"Hey, boss. I was actually digging through stuff on Steven Watkins, as you asked."

Maybe his computer *did* hold all the secrets of the universe. Riddleton's universe, anyway. "Any luck finding him?"

He chewed on his lower lip. "Not yet. At least not anyone who might be here right now. But I'll keep plugging away at it. Nothing escapes me."

"No kidding."

Lacey came out of the stockroom and carried a copy of Louise Penny's latest to the lady in the Mystery section.

I stopped her on the way back. "How are you feeling?"

She frowned. "I'm fine, Jen. Stop worrying about me."

"Can't help it. That's my job."

"Oh, it is not. Quit hovering. I'm not your child," she said with a laugh.

"Okay, okay. I'm just trying to help. I care about you, you know."

Her expression softened. "I know, and I appreciate your concern, but I can't spend the next seven months worrying about what might happen. That's not healthy for me or the baby."

I'd been so concerned about Lacey I hadn't considered the baby. What did I know about this stuff, anyway? Less than nothing. "I'm sorry. I'll quit bugging you."

"You're not bugging me. I'd rather not think about what might go wrong. If something happens later, we'll handle it then. For now, let's just be happy." She hugged me.

"You got it." I'd keep my concerns to myself, but that didn't mean I wouldn't have them.

The browsing women carried their choices to the register. One book each. While I'd hoped for more, it was certainly better than nothing at all.

Lacey rushed over to check them out. When the last one left, Steven Watkins came in, dressed for business in a gray pinstriped suit, white dress shirt, and solid black tie.

What does he want?

I strolled over to find out. "Hi, I'm Jen. Can I help you find something?"

"No, thanks. I'm just looking around," he replied without taking his eyes off the Art section. He seemed to be reading every single title.

I suddenly felt like a soldier standing inspection of my workstation. Regardless, I had to get him talking if I wanted to find out anything about him. "I've seen you around town lately. Do you have family here?"

"No."

"Are you planning a move to Riddleton?"

He met my gaze for the first time. "I don't know what my plans are at the moment."

The guy was a tough nut. *Come on, Daniel, whatcha got for me?* "It's a quaint little town. You'd like it here."

Watkins grunted noncommittally, stroking his close-clipped beard. "Seems like it, but I'm just here on business."

Business in Riddleton? Good luck with that. "Oh, anything interesting?"

"Not really."

I channeled Daniel Davenport again. Getting through to Chatty Stevie would be a challenge too great for my inadequate social skills. I desperately needed the help. "What line of work are you in?"

He moved on to the Biography section, again reading every title. "Whatever opportunities present themselves. I have many irons in the fire, as they say."

No help. I clenched my jaw, then released before he noticed my frustration. "Not too much fire in Riddleton, I'm afraid. That's why our fire department is all volunteer."

"You'd be surprised," he said, reaching for a book on the top shelf.

Under his suit jacket, a gun in a shoulder holster became visible for an instant. *Holy crap!* What kind of businessman carried a gun? No way he was a diamond merchant.

"Really? I love surprises. What's going on around here I don't know about?"

He gave me his full attention. "Miss, if you don't mind, I'd just like to see what you have here and be on my way."

Something in his muddy-brown eyes sent icy fingers down my spine. "Certainly. If you need some help, just let me know."

I retreated into the coffee bar and pretended to rearrange the pastry trays while watching Watkins mosey around my bookstore, randomly selecting books here and there and returning them to the shelf. He didn't strike me as an avid reader, though I'd been proved wrong before. It seemed he was more getting the lay of the land than searching for something to read.

Whatever. He wouldn't be the first window shopper we'd ever had. Only the most suspicious. Not from a shoplifting standpoint. I didn't think that was his goal, but he was definitely up to something. I only wished I knew what.

Charlie searched his computer while I played with his merchandise. He shot me a sideways glance once or twice but said nothing. Safe to say he knew I had my reasons, and I'd share them when ready. When Watkins did the circle around the coffee bar, I offered him a muffin. He shook his head and turned away. Maybe I should've tried a croissant or a cookie instead.

After an inch-by-inch exploration of Ravenous Readers, Watkins left without speaking to any of us again. I watched him cross the street to Antonio's through the front window. *Time to threaten Fredo again?* I'd have thought he'd made his point by now. Guess Fredo was a slow learner.

A few minutes later, Watkins came out, sauntering across the street with his hands in his trouser pockets. The only thing missing from his not-a-care-in-the-world pretense was a tuneless whistle. While I couldn't hear him from inside the store, I could see his lips weren't pursed. Fredo came flying out the door of his restaurant, flinging daggers at Watkins from his eyes. Watkins might not have a care in the world, but Fredo clearly did.

When Watkins cleared my field of view, I stepped outside to catch his destination. He climbed the steps to the town hall. Hmmm. What business could someone who didn't even live or work here have with our tiny town government? Could be that he intended to change one or both of those situations. As soon as he finished his business, I'd ask Veronica, our hands-on mayor, about it. She would know. She knew everything that went on in town. And not the way Angus did, either.

I loitered in front of my store for about fifteen minutes until Steven Watkins descended the town hall steps and crossed to the Dandy Diner. Must be time for his mid-afternoon snack. Or maybe it was Angus's turn for a once-over.

While trotting up the steps, I studied the brick facade of the only government building in town, erected in the 1940s when Riddleton was promoted to official town status. I entered through the double doors and walked past the clerk's office on the right, between the dark paneling and beige-painted walls—the paneling and paint separated by a brown-stained dado rail—to the mayor's office at the end of the hall.

I tapped on the doorframe.

Veronica looked up from the paperwork spread across her desk. "Hi, Jen. Come in."

"Are you busy?" I asked, settling into the chair across from her desk.

She waved a hand over the mess. "Always, but I have a few minutes for you. What can I help you with?"

"Steven Watkins, the guy who just left here, spent an hour examining every inch of my bookstore, then came over to see you. I was wondering what he wanted." I settled back, clasping my hands over my belly.

"Nothing too interesting. He asked about zoning laws in town. I got the impression he planned to open a business of some kind." She pushed her chair away from the desk and crossed her legs at the knees. "In fact, I spoke with Anne-Marie Vick the other day, and she told me he questioned her about real estate listings in town. Specifically, business property for sale."

Anne-Marie Vick was the wife of the former police chief who died. She now supported herself as a real estate agent. One of the best in town. "Did he mention what he intended to do with it?"

"Not to me. And Anne-Marie didn't say. Why all the questions?"

I forced back the anxiety creeping into my chest. "Well, the way he examined my place, I'm a little concerned he might pick up on Mara's idea of a used bookstore. I don't know if you've heard, but the contest keeping us going went bankrupt. We won't be receiving any more payments, and another bookstore in town would sink us."

She tapped a finger on her chin. "That explains why Detective Havermayer is so convinced you killed Mara Di Rocca. I knew it had to be more than just you being there."

"Yeah, she actually has a legitimate reason for suspecting me this time. But I didn't kill her. I wouldn't do that, even if it meant the end of Ravenous Readers. However, as upset as I am about Mara's death, I have to admit I'm still relieved we won't have to compete with her. Please don't tell Havermayer I said that."

Veronica cracked a smile. "I imagine she's already figured that out. But, if it makes you feel any better, Angus told me she has another suspect in her sights. Mara's ex-boyfriend. Apparently, he passed through town over the weekend. He was here when she died."

My chin hit my collarbone. "Eric mentioned she had another suspect, but he didn't know who. How did Angus find out?"

"How does Angus find out anything?"

I sat up straight. "The rumor mill. Got it. So, what's the deal with this guy? Was he seen with her or something? And what's his name?"

"I don't know his name or why Havermayer's interested in him." Veronica clasped her hands on the desk. "She must have a reason to think he might be involved, or she wouldn't be talking to him."

"True. The good news is, while she's chasing him around, she's not bothering me. I suspect that won't last, though, so have you had a chance to talk to Ted?"

"I did, and he said to tell you not to worry about it. He'll take care of you, and you can work something out on payment if necessary. He mentioned something about you covering expenses, but I'm sure I can talk him out of even that. Leave my husband to me."

"Thank you. I hope I don't need him at all, but it makes me feel better to know he'll be there if I do."

The phone rang, and Veronica reached for it. "Did you need anything else?"

"No, I'm okay. Thanks."

I left her to her work. When I reached the foot of the steps, I stood for a moment, enjoying the winter sun on my face. One of the many things I'd miss if I ended up in jail. I had to make sure that didn't happen, though. I'd lose everything I'd worked for all my life. And any hope for the future. I shook off the thought and headed back to the bookstore.

Knowing Ted Winslow would defend me should I need it eased my mind a bit. Now I had to figure out who Mara's ex-boyfriend was and what, if any, Steven Watkins's plans were. Maybe I'd luck out, and all he wanted was to stay close enough to keep Fredo in line until he repaid the loan. Or maybe I'd *really* luck out and prove he murdered Mara.

CHAPTER FIFTEEN

Ravenous Readers was empty of customers when I returned from meeting with Veronica. Lacey sat on the brown-and-gold-striped couch with Charlie hovering beside her, his face etched with concern. Savannah lay with her head in Lacey's lap while Lacey stroked her between the eyes.

"What's going on, guys?" I asked, dread bubbling into my chest.

"Lacey had another dizzy spell," Charlie replied. "She almost passed out this time."

"I did not!" She glared at him. "It's nothing. I stood up too fast, and Mother Hen here is making a big deal out of it."

I lowered myself onto the couch beside her, easing Savannah aside with my knee. "It's the second one today. That *is* a big deal. Perhaps you should see your doctor."

Lacey shook her head. "I'm only dehydrated. I've been busy and forgot to drink enough."

Charlie jumped up. "I'll go get you some water. Be right back." He trotted to the mini fridge we kept under the coffee bar and came back with a bottle.

After three quick swallows, Lacey nodded her thanks. "That's much better."

"Come on. Bottom's up." Charlie gestured toward the bottle.

She drank down to the halfway point and showed it to him. "There, you happy?"

I rested my hand on her shoulder. "Lacey, I think you should go home for the day."

"Nonsense." She stood and did a little tap dance. "See? I'm fine."

"And I'd like you to stay that way." I rose to meet her gaze. "Get some rest and see how you feel tomorrow."

Lacey shot me her stubborn-is-my-middle-name look. "I'll drink some more water, and I'll be fine. No reason for me to go home."

"Dehydration isn't good for the baby, either," Charlie pointed out.

"I know that, but who will close the store?"

He brightened. "We will." Patting me on the back, he continued, "Between the two of us, we'll get it done. Besides, you've been teaching me, remember?"

"Well, yeah, but . . ."

"No buts," I said. "You're going home to rest."

Lacey gave me a faux pout. "You can make me leave, but you can't make me go home and rest."

"True. I'd assumed *I* was the only immature one around here. Guess I was wrong," I replied with a smile.

"You know what happens when you assume." She gathered her purse and jacket from behind the register. "I wouldn't mind having an afternoon off, though. Lots of stuff going on. I have to—"

"Rest!" Charlie and I chorused.

"And drink water," he added.

"Got it. I'll see you in the morning."

"Only if you feel up to it." I waved her out the door. "Now, shoo!"

She flapped a hand at me and ducked out of the store.

I turned to Charlie. "So, what do we need to do to close this place up?"

"Other than break down the coffee bar? Hell if I know, but how hard can it be?"

The last time *I* said those words was when I offered to help Angus when the diner was shorthanded. The job turned out much more complicated than I'd expected. I suspected this one would as well. "I thought you said she'd been training you?"

He shrugged. "She has, just not on that."

I fired a glare at him. "Terrific. We're in trouble now."

"Relax, boss. We'll figure it out. It's only a few reports we never pay attention to, right? Worse comes to worst, we'll leave it for Lacey when she comes in tomorrow. Then she can show us both how to do it."

He made a good point. Except Lacey may not feel well enough to come in tomorrow. Either way, we'd have to muddle through. "I guess. Perhaps I can find the manual for the register. That should be some help."

"On *your* desk? Good luck with that."

I punched him lightly on the shoulder. "All right, smarty pants. I don't need any help from the peanut gallery."

The rest of the afternoon passed uneventfully. A few customers, a few book sales, a few minutes staring at my laptop screen to no avail while Charlie searched for information on my chief suspects: Steven Watkins, Fredo Di Rocca, and now, Mara's ex-boyfriend. Also, to no avail. It was as if none of them ever existed before showing up in Riddleton. I'd believe they might be figments of my imagination, except others had seen them too.

Charlie and my attempts to close out the register generated frustration and half a roll of blank register tape spewing out of the printer. I folded it up to use as scrap paper. Not that anyone wrote anything down anymore. Still, I could think of no other use for it, and it would take all night to roll it back up again. And I had no idea how to reload it into the machine when we were done. Of course, we could always chop it into confetti for the next parade. The town hall had a cross-cut shredder, and Riddleton loved parades. Something to keep in the back of my mind.

By the time Eric showed up to take me to dinner in Sutton, I'd reached my mental limit. Lacey could fix it in the morning. Lacey could solve any problem in the store. I needed to spend time with her, learning to do these things myself, while she was still available. I had a feeling fixing Lacey wouldn't be quite as easy.

We locked up and dropped Savannah off at home, leaving her happily munching kibble while we headed for my favorite Chinese restaurant. Nothing like an excellent all-you-can-eat buffet—including dessert bar and ice cream—to fill my belly and help empty my mind. I'd been working hard and accomplishing nothing for three days now. My brain needed a break.

"How did Fredo's robbery turn out?" I asked Eric as he negotiated the remains of rush hour traffic.

He glanced at me, then back out the windshield. "I don't know, Jen. Something seemed off about it."

"Off?" I turned in my seat as much as my seat belt would allow. "In what way?"

"Well, for starters, the entry point was supposedly a broken window, but most of the glass was littered on the ground outside the window. That means it was actually smashed from the inside and couldn't be how the burglar entered. And Fredo insisted he was at the funeral home making arrangements when it happened. So, who let the thief in?"

Interesting. "Did anyone else have a key to the house?"

"According to Fredo, only Mara and we found hers at the murder scene. Her keys are still in our evidence lockup. I checked."

"Huh. What did they take?"

Eric turned into the Golden Dragon parking lot. "That's the other weird thing. As far as we can tell, nothing of value was stolen. Big-screen TVs, laptops, jewelry were all accounted for. Of course, the place was ransacked, so if it were something small, Fredo would have to tell us about it."

I unbuckled my seat belt as the car rolled to a stop in

front of the brick building, topped by a dragon stretched from end to end. Painted red, not gold. Perhaps the gold paint cost more. I climbed out when Eric cut the engine. "Do you think the scene was staged?"

"Could be." He held the door for me to enter. "Either that or it wasn't your normal thief looking for something to sell. They could have been looking for something else."

A hostess showed us to a red-seated booth by the window.

"Something else like what?" I asked after we placed our drink orders.

Eric stood. "I don't know. Let's talk about this while we eat. I'm starving."

We each grabbed a plate from the stack at the end of a hot bar loaded with meat offerings. I worked my way to the other end, loading sesame and teriyaki chicken and beef with broccoli onto my plate. Then I came back up the other side, snagging a spare rib, sweet and sour chicken, and Mongolian beef.

After leaving my full plate on our table next to my drink, delivered in our absence, I returned to the hot bar with side dishes. The pork fried rice, lo mein, and crab Rangoon called my name. Not to mention the dumplings. I happily answered.

Eric returned with his two plates, and we ate silently until our dishes were almost empty and demanding stomachs satisfied. On our way back from the dessert bar, something occurred to me. "Eric, what if the ransacking was a reminder from Steven Watkins to Fredo that he was still in town and expected his payment?"

"I guess that's possible, but to what end?"

"Fear. Watkins can't kill Fredo, or he'll never get his or his boss's money. But he can sure make Fredo's life miserable. Maybe Mara was step one, and this is step two. Next step would be injuring Fredo or something like that."

"It didn't feel like that, though. It was more . . ." He set his plate of melon and orange slices down near his newly refilled glass. "I can't explain it. It didn't feel threatening. More like someone was searching for something."

I dove into my layer cake and ice cream. "Something like what?" The cool treat slid down my throat. "Wait a minute. Did Mara have life insurance? That could explain both the murder and the break-in."

"How do you figure?"

"Life insurance would be a terrific motive for either Fredo or Watkins to kill Mara. No matter which one did it, the loan shark would get his money back. And maybe the break-in was a search for the policy documents. Or better yet, a will."

Eric swallowed a bite of cantaloupe. "Okay, but only the beneficiary can collect on the insurance, so why would Watkins *or* Fredo bother trashing Fredo's house? Watkins still needs Fredo to collect, and Fredo can just call the insurance agent to file his claim."

"All right, what about Mara's will then? That might be worth trashing the place for."

"Her attorney would have a copy."

"Her attorney in Chicago. What if she'd recently changed it, and nobody knew who her local attorney was?"

He put down his fork. "What made you think of that? Did someone say something to you about a new will?"

"No, nobody's mentioned it. Why would anyone tell *me* about it?"

"I don't know. You sound pretty sure. I was wondering what you knew."

"I'm only throwing out possible explanations for the break-in. I have no idea what really happened. Maybe you could ask Havermayer. She might know. Checking on things like that should definitely be part of her investigation."

His eyebrows dropped. "Maybe, but she'll never tell me, either way."

The server delivered our check and fortune cookies. Eric handed me one and took the other. "The usual? Whoever has the best fortune pays?"

"Deal."

I tore off the cellophane, cracked open the cookie, and pulled out the slip of paper, cupping it in my palm so that Eric couldn't see.

Your Biggest Obstacle is You

Oh, brother. That was just silly. My bookstore was going under, the contest went bankrupt, and I'd been credibly accused of a murder I didn't commit. *My biggest obstacle is me. Yeah, right.* The only good thing about that fortune was that I probably wouldn't have to shell out for dinner this time.

Eric held his up and grinned. "Ready to switch?"

I held mine out, and he handed me his.

You Will Live a Long and Healthy Life

Totally lame, but I might convince him otherwise. Definitely a loser. "This one is absolutely the best. I think dinner's on you."

He cocked an eyebrow. "Are you kidding? Mine's nonsense. Yours, on the other hand . . ."

"Mine? No way, I'm my biggest obstacle. Give me a break. Given everything I'm up against, that can't possibly be true. But you could very well live a long and healthy life. That makes yours the best."

He handed me the check. "Give it up, Jen. You win, hands down."

I scowled at him. "Fine." I waved to the server and handed her the check and my credit card when she returned to our table. "Just for that, I'm getting more ice cream."

"Might as well. You're paying for it," he said with a grin.

I stuck my tongue out at him and headed for the soft-serve machine. A mixed swirl of chocolate and vanilla later, I came back to the table to find my credit card and the slip to sign. I left a generous tip and gave her my autograph. Too bad it wouldn't be worth anything until I died. I wouldn't tell her that, though. It might give her ideas.

When we settled in the car, I kissed him, relishing the way his soft lips melded with mine.

After a long minute, we broke apart and he asked, "What was that for?"

"That was for I love you. Do I need another reason?"

He grinned and shook his head. "Nope. That works for me."

I buckled up while he backed out of our parking spot. "Hey, did you ever get anything else on that person Havermayer was looking at? I heard he's Mara's ex-boyfriend."

"Where'd you hear that?"

"Angus told Veronica, and she told me."

"How did Angus . . . Never mind. I already know the answer."

I chuckled. "So, what do you know?"

"Not much."

"Not even his name?"

He sighed. "Frank Roselli. He's from Chicago and stopped to visit a friend on his way to Florida. That's all I know."

That was more than Charlie'd been able to find out. Now that I had a name to give him, he might be able to get more information.

We drove the rest of the way home in silence, too stuffed to make intelligent conversation. And my brain was filled with theories about Fredo's break-in. Theories he wouldn't want to hear. When we arrived at my building, we spotted a patrol car parked crosswise, blocking three available spaces.

I regarded Eric. "I wonder what's going on. I hope there hasn't been a break-in here."

"I don't know." He glanced around, then pointed. "Hey, isn't that Havermayer's Suburban? What's she doing here?"

The detective got out of her SUV and approached my side. "Step out of the car, please."

Two patrol officers slid into position behind her.

What the hell? I opened my door and stepped onto the pavement. "What's going on, Detective?"

"Turn around and place your hands on the roof of the car."

Eric came to where we stood. "What are you doing?"

She moved him out of the way. "I'm arresting your girlfriend. Now step back and don't interfere."

He put up his hands and took two steps back. "On what charges?"

Havermayer gestured to the patrol officers. One of them came forward and patted me down for weapons. The other pulled my hands down behind my back and handcuffed me while my dinner crept up into my throat.

I swallowed hard. "Why are you doing this?"

"Jennifer Dawson, you are under arrest for the murder of Mara Di Rocca. You have the right to remain silent. Should you give up this right, anything you say . . ."

Panic squeezed my belly, and I threw up on her detective oxfords. Havermayer jumped back, but it was too late. At least something good would come of this.

When I finished emptying my stomach, I said, "Eric, call Ted Winslow. And take care of Savannah for me, please."

His face crumpled into a mix of anger and distress. "Don't worry about anything. I'll take care of it."

The cop hauled me away before I could respond.

CHAPTER SIXTEEN

The interview room hadn't changed since the last time I was here five days ago. The same uncomfortable chair sat in front of the same scratched table, watched over by the same camera in the corner near the ceiling. What was I doing here again? What new information had they found that led them to be so convinced I'd murdered Mara that they arrested me?

I sat with my elbows on the table, my head in my hands, dread spreading through me like lava, destroying everything in its path. Exhaustion added a hundred pounds to my legs, and I rested my head on my arms, giving in to the fatigue barreling through my body.

The door opened, and I sat up. Ted Winslow came in wearing a polo shirt and jeans, carrying a leather briefcase. His thinning brown hair was mussed as if he'd used his fingers for a comb on his way out the door. I'd interrupted his evening with his family.

I smoothed my unruly locks and failed an attempt at a smile. "Hi, Ted. I'm so sorry to drag you out like this. I didn't know what else to do."

He settled into the chair beside me. "No problem, Jen. It's one of the drawbacks of being a defense attorney. I'm used to it. And happy to help." He patted me on the back. "We'll straighten this out, don't worry. Why don't you tell me what's been going on? Start at the beginning, tell me everything, and don't leave anything out, no matter how bad you think it might make you look. If you hold something back, I can't help you, and I don't like being blindsided in court. Okay?"

Don't worry? Easy for him to say. I nodded and filled him in on everything that'd happened since my first argument with Mara, finishing with: "And I have no idea why they've arrested me again." The words alone brought bile back into my esophagus. Lucky for Ted, my stomach was pretty much empty.

"I'm assuming we'll find that out when Detective Havermayer questions you again, but I'll be right here with you this time. And don't say anything without checking with me first."

He pulled a yellow legal pad and a pen from his briefcase. I found comfort in his calm, relaxed demeanor, and my stomach settled. Whatever Havermayer thought she had on me would easily be explained away. It had to be. I wasn't guilty of anything but being in the wrong place at the wrong time. Although, I suspected plenty of people in prison right now would say the same thing. Never dreamed I might someday be one of them, though.

He asked me a few questions—mostly about my state of mind when I went back to see Mara and found her dead—and then went to summon Havermayer.

Ready or not, here she comes.

When he sat back down, he said, "Just let me do all the talking. I don't want you to say *anything* unless I tell you to. Understand?"

"Yes, I understand." It must be important for me to keep my mouth shut for him to tell me twice. I hoped Havermayer wouldn't push the wrong buttons and draw out an uncontrolled reaction. She was adept at making me say things without thinking. Her goal in life was to make me incriminate myself.

Havermayer came in carrying a manila folder, perched on the chair across from us, and stared for a minute. From the smug expression on her face, it was clear she was enjoying this moment. My experience with her told me she'd looked forward to having me in this position since we met. I'd always sworn I'd never let it happen. Another mission not accomplished.

Ted broke the silence. "Why are we here, Detective? Why have you arrested my client?"

My client. Two words I'd never expected to apply to me. But I was grateful I had someone of Ted's caliber on my side to say them.

The detective leaned back in her chair. "We have evidence your *client* murdered Mara Di Rocca because she was opening a competing business, and I'm going to put her away for the rest of her life. That's what we do with murderers around here."

Murderer? Me? My already sour stomach filled with lemons.

My attorney smirked. "Let's have a look at that evidence, shall we?"

"I'm sure the assistant district attorney will happily show it to you during discovery."

Ted masked his frustration with the best poker face I'd ever seen. "All right, so, once again, why are we here?"

"Honestly? Because I wanted to see the look on her face when she learned that stupid mutt she loves so much is about to get her convicted." She opened the folder, removed a photograph, and slid it across the table toward me. "You know what that is?"

I leaned over and studied the picture, which showed a thin black and brown line on a white background. I had no idea what it was. I glanced at Ted, who gave me the okay. "The Great Wall of China from outer space?"

She smiled and crossed her arms. "It's a dog hair, Ms. Dawson. From a German shepherd, to be exact. One of several we found on Mara Di Rocca's scarf. Care to explain how it got there?"

Her satisfied smile made me want to climb over the table and rip her throat out. However, I was in enough trouble already, so I balled my fists in my lap instead.

Ted chuckled. "Have you ever had a dog, Detective? Their hair gets on everything. The owner carries it everywhere with them. This is a simple case of transfer. My client admits she was at the scene. The hair got on the scarf when she moved it to check the victim's pulse."

"That's true, Counselor, but that doesn't explain how it ended up on the underside, lodged in a crease far from where we found Ms. Dawson's DNA."

My stomach threatened to eject the little left in it. I pressed my lips together.

"Come on, Detective. Get serious. Ms. Dawson takes that dog everywhere with her. It's been a warm January, and she's likely shedding up a storm. Leaving hair in every building in town. Anyone could have picked up a few hairs on their clothes and carried them to the crime scene. This doesn't mean anything."

"That's certainly possible. Good luck proving that's what happened, though."

"I don't have to prove it. I only have to create reasonable doubt. And there's plenty of that to go around. I think you've made a mistake, and you're going to end up regretting it. The smart thing to do would be to release my client now. If you take this to a judge, you'll embarrass the ADA, and he won't like that very much." Ted stood and closed his briefcase. "So, what's it going to be?"

Havermayer's haughtiness faltered slightly. "We'll see, Mr. Winslow. We'll see." She collected her photo and scooted her chair back. "But either way, your client's not going anywhere until she's arraigned and the judge grants bail. *If* the judge grants bail."

Ted placed his hand on my shoulder. "I'll see you in the morning, Jen. Don't worry about anything. I'll have this nonsense thrown out."

Don't worry about anything.

Yeah, right.

They parked me in a six-by-eight room with white concrete walls, a steel door, and a tiny window. At the far end was a pair of bunk beds not quite wide enough to fit an average-size man. And nothing else. At least I had a few feet to pace in, but I'd have to watch my speed lest I get dizzy. I sat on the lower bunk's edge, then bounced back up again, ducking my head to avoid slamming it into the upper bunk frame.

How had I come to this? *Beats me.* I fought for my bookstore, and now I might lose everything, including my freedom. Would a jury convict me based on the flimsy evidence Havermayer had? I had a good reason for being on the scene, and anyone who's ever had a dog knows their hair becomes a wardrobe staple. I wouldn't vote to convict someone without a lot more than that. But I wouldn't be on the jury. Those choices were in the hands of the ADA and Ted. Another of the many things over which I had no control.

I'd spent my entire life feeling like a balloon in the wind. Buffeting back and forth, up and down, with no say in what happened to me. Did everyone feel that way? Some people seemed to think they made their own luck. Determined their own future. I'd never been one of those and truly believed they were deluding themselves. But what if they weren't?

Sure, there would be things we couldn't control. But I didn't even do well with the things I could. Peter Pan had been my favorite fictional character. Growing up was overrated, I'd always said. And look at where it had gotten me. Sitting in a jail cell with my future out of my hands, a failing bookstore, and another novel I couldn't write.

Perhaps it was time to take charge of my own life. To stop flying around willy-nilly on the breeze with no true destination in mind.

Time to grow up, Jen.

I stretched out on the thin, lumpy mattress, barely long enough to accommodate my five-foot-six frame. How did the big guys handle it? Maybe they weren't supposed to be comfortable. Part of the you-don't-want-to-go-to-jail-because-you'll-be-miserable theory of law enforcement. Well, it was working for me. I wanted nothing more than to go home, take a long, hot bath, and fall into my bed with Savannah tucked in beside me. Dog hair and all.

Unfortunately, my ability to do that was solely in the hands of the judge I'd see in the morning. Someone I'd never met and who didn't know me at all. He or she would decide whether to let me out of here. Whether to let me go on with my life.

Talk about out of my control.

The smug look on Havermayer's face planted itself firmly in my mind. She was so sure she had me where she wanted me. All because of some dog hair. How did the hair get on the scarf, anyway? I never touched the scarf where Havermayer said she found the hair. Someone else had to have picked up the hair, probably in the bookstore, and transferred it to the scarf.

That widened the suspect pool to anyone in the store that day. Or in the diner. Or in Mara's store after I made my first visit. It could be almost anyone in Riddleton. There were only a few folks in town with motives, however. Few people had ever even met Mara. I had to focus on the ones who had.

I eventually drifted into a light sleep battered by dreams of Mara's body slumped over her desk and Savannah's hair falling out and suffocating me. I was grateful when an officer brought me a breakfast tray at . . . I had no idea what time. The holding cell was like a fallout shelter. No contact with the outside world whatsoever. But unlike a normal shelter, all the bad stuff was on the inside.

The tray had a Dandy Diner to-go box loaded with eggs over medium, bacon, grits, and toast. A sizable Styrofoam cup of coffee with cream and sugar sat beside it. *Thank you, Angus.* I hadn't realized the diner supplied the food for RPD's detainees. Then again, I'd never thought about it. Or had reason to.

The delectable smells triggered my appetite, though I'd never have believed I could eat in this situation. On the other hand, I'd disgorged most of my dinner onto Havermayer's shoes last night. I smiled as I dunked the corner of a slice of toast into an egg yolk. Had to take my victories where I could find them.

I'd just downed the last of my coffee when they collected me for the ride to Sutton. We made a pit stop at the facilities, where I did my business and splashed some water on my face. Nothing else I could do besides running my fingers through my spiky hair, making it even spikier. Hopefully, the judge wouldn't decide based on my appearance. Although, I was sure he or she'd seen worse.

They handcuffed and loaded me into the back of a patrol car. Havermayer was nowhere around. A surprise, considering with her absence, she'd passed on another opportunity to gloat. I was certain she'd be at the courthouse, though. No way she'd miss that spectacle. It'd been her dream to put me in front of a judge, even if it was for a crime I didn't commit.

I stared out the window at the sunrise, breaking over the drugstore across the street. At least I finally had an idea of the time. Not that it mattered much. I was at the mercy of the justice system for the next few hours, if not longer. Ted would get the case thrown out for lack of evidence. Or, at the very least, convince the judge to let me out on bail. He had to. I refused to think about what might happen if he couldn't.

My driver climbed into the car, and I recognized the profile of Zach Vick. I blew out a lungful of air. It was someone I knew, at any rate. Chatting with him might take my mind off my cramping shoulders and relieve some of the tension zinging through my muscles.

When we crossed the town limits, I broke the silence. "How've you been, Zach? I haven't seen you in a while."

"Fine."

Great. Monosyllabic answers would do nothing to help keep my mind off anything. Maybe if I kept trying, he'd come around. "How's your mom? I hear she's been busy lately."

"Fine."

So much for that theory. "Why won't you talk to me? We've been through a lot together."

The nape of his neck turned red, but his voice remained gruff. "I don't talk to prisoners. They try to distract you while planning their escape."

I sent him an eye roll he obviously couldn't see. "Seriously? You think I'm trying to escape? You know me better than that. Besides, where would I go?"

"I'm not taking any chances, so just shut up, okay?"

Okeydokey.

Note to self: never commit a crime. Being a prisoner stinks.

CHAPTER SEVENTEEN

A deputy sheriff led me into the courthouse through the basement door. No metal detector to walk through this time. No keys to put in the bowl, either. I was on the wrong side of this process. A place I never dreamed I'd be. My fate was in others' hands, and I didn't like that at all. But nobody cared what I liked or didn't. I was a prisoner.

They settled me in a holding cell two floors up, which had to be near the courtroom. Moving someone like me, a detainee, from one place to another was the most dangerous part of the process. They'd want to make the distance from point A to point B—the cell to the courtroom—as short as possible. Once inside, I was surrounded by cinder-block walls ending at a wire-mesh gate with an opening precisely the right size for my wrists.

Three men and one woman had already claimed benches lining the cinder block, and a toilet and stainless-steel sink occupied the back corner. I snagged a spot on the back-wall bench, avoiding eye contact with anyone else. Not in the mood for any what-are-you-in-for conversations, mostly because I didn't want to know with whom I shared space this morning. For some strange reason, I didn't see this as an opportunity to make new friends.

I leaned against the wall and closed my eyes, wishing I felt safe enough to nap. Not a chance, though. As things stood, every time someone moved, my eyes flew open, and I went on high alert. No real reason for it. They all seemed as demoralized and subdued as I was. Perhaps I'd seen too many movies to relax.

An hour or so that seemed like months later, they led us into the courtroom through the door beside the jury box and lined us up against the wall. Nameless, faceless, barely humans caught up in a system with only one purpose: to get justice.

The judge, Peter McCall, according to the nameplate on the desk in front of him, was talking to Ted Winslow and another man in a business suit. I could hear nothing they said, but I hoped Ted was negotiating for my release.

Judge McCall waved the men back to their tables, then whispered something to the clerk at a small desk beside the bench.

She shuffled papers and nodded. Then she stood and announced, "The state of South Carolina versus Jennifer Marie Dawson. Murder in the first degree."

My heart flipped, and my stomach threatened to return Angus's breakfast when the bailiff took my arm, and I spotted Havermayer in the gallery. She grinned like a Cheshire cat as I was led to the defense table. Ted squeezed my arm in reassurance, but my knees buckled, all the blood sustaining them having rushed to my suddenly throbbing head.

"Are you all right?" Ted asked. "Have they been treating you well?"

I nodded, not trusting myself to speak.

The judge brought my attention to him. "Ms. Dawson, you have been charged with murder in the first degree for the willful murder of Mara Di Rocca. How do you plead?"

After a deep breath and a throat-clear, I responded, "Not guilty, Your Honor." He had to believe me. I didn't do this.

"Very well. I'll hear the people on bail."

The well-dressed man at the table across the aisle from me responded, "Your Honor, given the particularly heinous nature of this crime, committed solely for financial gain, the people request remand."

Remand? They want to keep me in jail until my trial? Oh, God . . .

The judge turned to Ted. "Mr. Winslow?"

Ted skimmed a paper in his briefcase. "Your Honor, my client is an upstanding, well-respected member of the community. She's a business owner with family ties and not a flight risk. In addition, the assistant district attorney's case is completely circumstantial. We request she be released on her own recognizance."

My palms dripped sweat as the judge glanced from one attorney to the other, then flipped through some papers on his desk. If he kept me in jail awaiting trial, I'd never have the opportunity to find Mara's real killer. And what about the bookstore? It might take years

188

before my case came up. Lacey's maternity leave was only months away. No way Charlie could do it all by himself. They'd have to close the store.

Deep breath in, slow breath out.

Finally, the judge made his decision. "Let's split the baby, gentlemen. Bail is set at one hundred fifty thousand dollars, cash or bond." He banged his gavel. "Next case."

A hundred and fifty thousand dollars? Where would I possibly find that kind of money?

Ted leaned toward me and whispered, "Don't worry. We only need ten percent for the bail bondsman. It's already taken care of. We'll have you out in no time."

The bailiff grabbed my arm and led me back to the door before I could respond. What did he mean? How could it be already taken care of? No one I knew could afford that, even if it was only fifteen thousand. Ted must have me confused with someone else.

Once back in the holding cell, I headed straight for the toilet to throw up my breakfast. I felt better afterward, though my stomach still churned. At least I was alone and able to relax for a minute. I stretched out on the bench along the back wall and closed my eyes, but my mind whirled too much for me to sleep.

Ted seemed confident I'd make bail, so I shouldn't worry about it. That was what he said. He had to be right. I'd never make it in the county jail for a year or more. And my whole life would be gone. Just being arrested might destroy my writing career. Even if I were exonerated, I'd lose readers who didn't believe I was innocent. Assuming I didn't lose my publisher first.

Did I have a morals clause in my contract? I couldn't remember one, but it'd been years since I read the first agreement, and I hadn't seen the new one yet. Actually, I didn't even have a contract yet. Only an offer, which my publisher might withdraw if they learned of my situation. It wasn't like I was writing a tell-all memoir they would be happy to wait for. It was just another mystery in my series. There were thousands of writers waiting to take my place.

One of the men came back next, and I sat up. The others would return shortly, and I wasn't interested in being hassled for taking up too much room. I only had to keep my head down and mind my own business long enough to get out. I could do that. No problem.

The last prisoner had come back when a deputy called my name. I stood and approached the wire-mesh gate he opened for me to step through, then led me to a room where my personal items—phone, purse, and keys—were returned. I checked to ensure everything was accounted for and signed the receipt. Then I thanked the clerk, who pointed to a door opposite the one I'd entered through and wished me luck. No doubt I needed it.

Eric waited for me on the other side. He enfolded me in his arms, and tears filled my eyes, leaving a wet spot on his red-and-blue-striped tie. I tried to move away, but he pulled me closer, resting his chin on my head. I felt more loved than I had since my father died. My mother was right. He was a keeper. I only hoped I didn't drive him away like all the others.

Finally, he released me and gazed into my eyes. "Are you okay?"

I wiped the tears off my face and sniffled. "I'm fine. Happy to see you."

"Me too." He threw an arm around my shoulders and eased me toward the exit. "Come on. There's someone else who wants to see you too."

When we stepped outside, Brittany ran over and hugged me, then examined me all over like she had to decide whether to buy me and for how much. "How are you? Did they hurt you?"

"No, I'm fine. Just a bit shaken up by it all." Fine might've been a bit of an exaggeration, though. Fear, anxiety, and dread whirled through me like a tornado on the plains. I didn't have to tell her that, though. She knew me so well I couldn't possibly hide it from her if I wanted to.

"I'll bet. Let's go get some coffee, and we'll make a game plan."

"A game plan?"

She slipped her arm through mine and led me to Eric's Jeep. "Yeah, to get you out of this mess. I'm not visiting you in prison every week for the rest of your life, so we must prove your innocence. Convince the ADA to drop the charges."

I nodded, gratitude momentarily paralyzing my voice box. "Speaking of getting me out, who posted my bail?"

Eric replied, "Don't worry about that right now. You're out. That's all that matters."

My mouth fell open. "You did? How? You don't have that kind of money."

His cheeks reddened. "Actually, I do. My father had a life insurance policy. When he died, my sister and I were the beneficiaries. I invested my half in a long-term CD that I could borrow against. It wasn't much, but enough to pay the bondsman to bail you out."

He has a sister? I'd had no idea. He never talked about his family. Of course, I'd never asked either. I figured he'd tell me when he was ready. What did that say about me? Was I really that self-centered? It seemed so. No wonder he became frustrated with me. I was a terrible girlfriend. He deserved better. Tears welled up again.

"Thank you. I promise I'll show up for court."

He kissed my cheek. "I know that, silly. Of course, if you'd rather, I have enough left to fly you to Armenia. No extradition treaty with the US. You'd have to fend for yourself once you got there, though."

"Sorry, but my Armenian is a little rusty. I'll just stay here and fight it out."

He squeezed my arm. "I was hoping you'd say that."

"I'll bet."

We went to Starbucks and commandeered a table in the corner. Surrounded by well-dressed, well-groomed men and women on break from their well-heeled jobs, I felt like the jailbird I was. The tornado had swept up embarrassment as well. I still wore my clothes from yesterday and needed a shower with a steel-wool scrub brush. Coming here was a mistake I'd rectify as soon as possible.

When Eric returned with my latte, I wrapped both hands around the cup and sipped until I was almost human again. The hot liquid bathed away the chill that'd enveloped me the moment I entered the courthouse. I set the cup down and rubbed my wrists where the handcuffs had been without thinking about it.

Brittany watched me, her eyes oozing concern. "Are you sure you're all right, Jen?"

No. "I'm okay. I'll be better after a shower, clean clothes, and a nap. In that order."

"I don't blame you. I just wanted to spend a few minutes with you before we head back to town. Everyone is buzzing about your arrest, and I don't think you'll have much privacy for a few days."

I lifted my cup in her direction. "Here's to the Riddleton rumor mill. I gave them enough fodder to keep them going for a week at least."

She smiled. "Well, a good while, at any rate. I'm not sure about a whole week, though."

My head was heavy with fatigue, and I held it in my hands. "So, what did you want to talk about?"

"The investigation into Mara's murder. Olinski hasn't told me much, but they wouldn't have arrested you if they'd found anyone else to pin it on."

Eric focused on Brittany. "They're following the evidence. There doesn't seem to be any against anyone else. Or so I've been told, anyway."

Brittany's eyes flashed. "Are they even looking?"

I laid a hand on her arm. "There isn't anyone. Everything points to me as the killer. *I* can't even think of any other viable suspects. All I have right now is unfounded suspicions."

"Who've you considered so far?" she asked.

"Mara's husband, Fredo, and Steven Watkins, the strange guy hanging around town since the day before

193

the murder. Oh yeah, and I heard Havermayer is looking at Mara's ex-boyfriend too."

Brittany chuckled. "Is that all you got?"

"Some little stuff has come up, too, which I don't put much stock in. Like Angus buying a scarf identical to the one that strangled Mara and offering to buy Antonio's and being turned down. Theoretically, that could be a motive for murder, but I don't believe for a minute he had anything to do with it."

Eric shook his head. "No, I can't imagine it. That doesn't seem like enough of a motive to me. I'd need more than that to even consider it."

"Well there's a rumor that Angus has a married mystery girlfriend, and that's why he won't talk about her. Marcus said he asked Angus about her, and he walked away without responding. That seemed strange to me. And yes, I know, I sound just like Angus right now." I took a swallow of cool latte, swirling it around in my mouth first to relish the creamy flavor. "Maybe they had a bad breakup? I can't think of any other possible motive he might have."

After a sip of her own, Brittany studied me with a steady gaze. "What can I do to help?"

"I don't know if there's anything we *can* do. I have no idea how to proceed. I'm stuck."

"What do we know about Fredo Di Rocca and Steven Watkins?"

"Not much. Charlie's been working on it for a few days, and last I heard, he hadn't had much luck. Fredo was supposedly a big real estate guy in Chicago, and

Charlie found nothing at all on Watkins. It's like the guy's invisible or something."

"I'll see what I can find out," Eric said, then lifted his eyebrows. "What if he's in witness protection? He wouldn't have a background then."

"That's true. Gil insinuated he had mob ties," I said. "Can you call the US Marshals? They're the only ones who would know whether he's in the program."

"I don't know any, but I'll mention it to Olinski and see what he says. We'd need some proof he's involved in Mara's death before they'd tell us anything, though. And probably not even then. They're pretty serious about protecting their witnesses."

"It's worth a shot," Brittany said. "Especially since we don't have any other leads."

I rubbed my gritty eyes with the heels of my hands. It felt like I was battling a Sahara Desert sandstorm with no idea where I was or which way to go. Blinded by my own ignorance.

Eric reached across and stroked my arm. "You're tired. Let's get you home so you can rest. We can talk about all this later."

"And don't worry about anything," Brittany added. "I'll dig into those two guys and see what I can learn. Maybe Charlie and I can work together on it. Between the two of us, we'll come up with something. I promise."

"Thank you. And thanks for being here. Both of you."

A warm bubble grew in my chest. The two people I loved most in the world stood beside me. I didn't have to face this situation alone. And that made all the difference.

CHAPTER EIGHTEEN

I peeled my eyes open around three in the afternoon, not quite ready to get up, but knowing I'd never sleep tonight if I didn't. Savannah pressed herself against me, resting her head on my chest. She hadn't left my side since Eric dropped me off, as if she knew something terrible had happened. I stroked her between the eyes and kissed her wet nose. I'd missed her too.

After a glance in my bathroom mirror at the disaster sleeping on wet hair had created, I threw on an "I Heart SC" baseball cap and sweats to take her for a walk around the block. The air had chilled as the sun lowered toward the horizon, bathing the street in a deceptively warm orange glow. Winter couldn't end soon enough for me.

We passed a couple of people coming out of the Goodwill. One waved, and the other turned away. I suspected they might be a general representative of the town's feelings about me. One half might believe I'd murdered Mara; the other half never would, no matter what. As much as I'd love to win over everyone, the residents of Riddleton never agreed on anything. Veronica had won her mayoral election by only twenty-three votes, and all her opponent had to offer was amazing donuts. Fifty-fifty was the norm in this place.

When we returned, I grabbed a drink from the fridge and fired up my laptop. Savannah took up her usual position on the couch, watching me with her head resting on her paws. My guardian angel. What would happen to her if I went to prison? My mother would likely take her in. She and Gary adored her almost as much as I did. Would Savannah remember me when I got out? Probably. Dogs never forgot a smell. Assuming I got out in her lifetime. Or at all.

I wiped my face with one hand and struggled to concentrate. I had to write while I still could. Unfortunately, the more pressure I put on myself, the more my brain refused to cooperate. I could do nothing about my looming deadline. Other than miss it, of course, which was out of the question.

I might be able to do something about all the distractions, though. The bookstore's financial problems would remain in limbo. There were no solutions I could see right now. I hadn't made it to the bank yet, but what would be the point? There was no way they'd give a loan to someone under indictment for murder. My only hope was to find the person who killed Mara. Now that I'd been arrested and charged, the police search for an alternate suspect would end. It was up to me now.

I brought up Mara's Facebook page and clicked on some of the vacation photos. They were all tagged with the location and date. As far as I could tell, Mara and her brother had traveled together regularly, without escort, since their late teens. Once or twice a year, they'd taken a cruise or some other reasonably priced jaunt to a single destination. Until their father died. After Tony's death last summer, the number and extravagance of their trips exploded.

First, they did a grand tour of Europe, including England, France, and Spain. Then, off to the Caribbean for visits to the Bahamas, Jamaica, and the Cayman Islands. They spent the month before they moved to Riddleton in Central and South America, adding stamps from Mexico, Bolivia, and Colombia to their passports. Tony must've had a tremendous life insurance policy with his children as joint beneficiaries. Where else would they get that kind of money? And why wasn't Fredo with the siblings on any of them? Maybe he really didn't like having his picture taken. He could be a modern-day Howard Hughes in the making. *Who knows?*

And now they'd come to Riddleton to reopen their father's restaurant and a new bookstore to put mine out of business. I scrolled through the rest of Mara's posts, looking for something that showed she truly believed I'd killed her father. Or at least had something to do with his death. I found nothing. Even though she wasn't the type to post photos of her every meal, something that important surely would've made it into her social media. Wouldn't it?

The only mention of Tony was his obituary, and there were no references to me at all. If Mara believed what she told me, she would've plastered it all over her social media pages. Isn't that what people did now? Made stuff up and broadcasted it to the world as if it was true? As Shakespeare once wrote, "Something is rotten in the state of Denmark." Riddleton, too.

I massaged my temples, desperate to find some way to approach this investigation. The only person I hadn't directly spoken with was Steven Watkins. And, frankly, he scared me. Especially now that I knew he carried a gun. I'd have to approach him in a public place, but even that guaranteed nothing. He could come after me later when I was alone. Maybe even hurt Savannah to make his point. I couldn't risk that.

On the other hand, if he was Mara's killer, he'd want me alive to stand trial. If the state convicted me, he would be free and clear. And even if acquitted, the police wouldn't reopen the investigation because they'd believe I did it and got away with it. They wouldn't waste their time unless new evidence turned up. And so far, there *was* no other evidence.

I had to take the risk. Whoever Steven Watkins might be, there was bad blood between him and Fredo. Whether he was a mob enforcer here to make sure Fredo paid his debts or just some guy who didn't like Fredo, I didn't know. But it was time to find out. I had no other options. Better to do something than go to prison waiting for another choice to present itself.

Savannah popped her head up when I went into the bedroom to change my clothes. I couldn't approach Watkins dressed like a bum. I had to appear at least civilized, or he probably wouldn't even speak with me.

While I had limited hopes for my mission's success, that would leave me with no options at all.

I chose jeans—a clean pair out of the drawer, not ones from the can-be-worn-again pile—a baby-blue silk blouse, and the black leather jacket Eric had given me for Christmas. He must've grown tired of hearing me complain about having lost my old one. A pair of black leather oxfords made my ensemble complete. Not too dressy, not too sloppy. Precisely what I was going for. Now it had to work.

Having no idea where Watkins might be, I leashed Savannah so I could wander around town looking for him without being too conspicuous. I'd never realized how often having a dog could come in handy. I could hunt for murder suspects, even have whole conversations with myself on the street, and nobody thought anything of it. Plus, she was a friend, companion, and decoy whenever I needed one. What's not to love about that?

Savannah led me down the steps, excited about the excursion. She didn't seem to care where she went as long as she got to go. Fortunately for both of us, my current lifestyle let her accompany me more often than not. We ambled past the Goodwill to peek in the Dandy Diner's window, looking for Watkins. No luck. Too late for lunch and too early for dinner.

I didn't see his Mercedes parked anywhere on Main Street, so we crossed to head down Pine toward Second. No sign of his vehicle near the library, the bakery, or the gas station. We turned right on Second, past the abandoned used bookstore and the vet, without encountering Watkins or his vehicle. A right on Oak Street, past the Snip & Clip and, a block later, the Feed and Seed, produced the same result. He was either on foot and inside a building or already on his way back to Blackburn for the day.

Not ready to give up, we took a left on Riddleton Road to clear the Catholic church and the doctor's office, then headed back up Park Street to the park. No Mercedes and nobody in sight but a lone jogger making his way slowly around the track. Savannah strained toward the wrought-iron gate, but I wasn't dressed for squirrel chasing today. And I was on a mission.

We retraced our steps down Second Street, adding the empty Bannister's Bar and Grill to my no-sign-of-Watkins list. Left on Walnut took us back toward the bookstore. Might as well poke my head in there and let Lacey and Charlie know I was all right. Steven Watkins was no longer in Riddleton. Whether just for today or for good, I had no way of knowing.

Savannah charged through the door the instant I opened it, searching for her automatic bacon snack feeder, Aunt Lacey. The store was quiet, although books abandoned on various tables, and Charlie wiping down the coffee bar, told me it hadn't been that way for long. Perhaps my arrest was as good for business as my solving another murder. A depressing idea.

Lacey came out of the stockroom with an armload of books to shelve. A broad smile crossed her face when she saw me. "Hi, Jen. Recovered from your trip to the pokey?"

Never. "Good news travels fast, I see."

She popped a copy of *The Rise of Theodore Roosevelt* into Biography and worked her way down the wall.

"Busy day?" I asked while my German shepherd prodded Lacey for a treat.

"Hang on, little girl. Let me get my hands free; then I'll take care of you," Lacey told her, laughing. "You know, you really should consider feeding this dog occasionally."

"Sorry, I don't have a house to take out a second mortgage on. She'll just have to make do with food remains on the street and treats from you."

"Yeah, right. I'll bet you spend more feeding her than you do on yourself."

"Only because Eric and I take turns paying for our meals."

Lacey worked around the store to the other side, shelving her last book in the Graphic Novels section. She fished the bag of bacon treats out from under the counter by the cash register. "Here you go, kid." She handed one to the starving dog.

Savannah swallowed it whole and begged for another. I smiled and shook my head. How did she get so spoiled so fast? I didn't mind, though. For what she gave me, she deserved every special thing she received. And a whole lot more I couldn't afford.

I wandered over to help Charlie while Lacey lavished affection on my little girl, who wasn't so little anymore. At full-grown and eighty-five pounds, she consumed almost a pound of kibble per day. Plus, treats and my leftovers. Prewashing the dishes was her favorite chore. I never had to remind her.

Charlie poured what remained in the coffee urn into an air pot and carried the urn to the sink to wash. I collected the utensils and empty pastry trays and followed.

He smiled his thanks and took them from me. "How are you feeling?"

"I'm all right. A little tired. I didn't get much sleep last night."

"Does our jail not provide five-star accommodations?"

"More like one. But they did offer room service and a complimentary breakfast."

He scrubbed melted chocolate off the muffin tray. "Well, if you want, I can file a complaint for you. The mayor is a friend."

"Nah, it's okay. I'd rather know what you've found on Fredo and Watkins, so I don't have to worry about going back there again. Also, I found out the ex-boyfriend's name is Frank Roselli. That should help."

"It will, thanks. I haven't learned much more about Fredo. He was in real estate, and had a pile of money that appeared out of nowhere, then disappeared just as fast." He rinsed the soap off the tray. "And Steven Watkins is a phantom. I'm beginning to think that's not his real name."

I'd never thought of that. He could be using an alias. Then again, maybe *he* was the one in witness protection instead of Fredo. If so, we might never learn anything about him. "How can we find out who he really is?"

"I'm not sure I can. If we had the resources, we could snap a picture, run him through facial recognition, and see what comes up, but I don't have access to any of those databases. The State Law Enforcement Division could probably find him. Do you know anyone in SLED?"

I handed him another tray. "No, but I bet Olinski does. Now that I've been charged with Mara's murder, I can't imagine him refusing to help me clear my name. He has to know there's no way I killed someone just to keep her from opening a competing business."

"I would hope. Maybe you should ask him about it. We have nothing to lose at this point. I don't know where else to look or even who to look for."

"Thank you, Charlie. I think I will."

Lacey finished overfeeding my dog or, more likely, ran out of treats and joined us. "You will what?"

"Charlie thinks Watkins might be using an assumed name. I'm going to ask Olinski if he has any contacts at SLED who might help us figure out who he really is."

"Good idea. Do you think he'll help you?"

"I hope so. He has no reason to bar me from investigating because they no longer have an active investigation. They've arrested the culprit as far as they're concerned."

"That's true."

"I think I'll run next door and ask him about it now. Do you mind keeping Savannah? She should be stuffed enough to take a nap by now."

Lacey laughed. "Of course not. I'll watch her anytime."

"Thanks." I headed for the door and, when I opened it, found myself face-to-face with Steven Watkins.

CHAPTER NINETEEN

I stepped back and allowed him into the store. "Good evening, Mr. Watkins. How are you doing today?"

If he was surprised I knew his name, he didn't show it. "Fine, thank you. And you?"

"Very well, thanks. Funny that you should show up here. I'd hoped for an opportunity to speak with you."

His eyebrows lifted. "Oh? What about?"

How to answer that question? If I told him the truth, that I wanted to know if he murdered Mara, I might expose myself to danger. At the very least, I'd offend him, and he wouldn't tell me anything.

What would Daniel say? He'd tell me to play the writer card. "I'm basing a character in my next book on Fredo Di Rocca, and I wonder if you'd consider giving me some insights into him since you two are friends." I gestured toward the coffee bar. "Would you like some coffee?"

"No, thank you. It's a little late in the day for me."

He frowned. "What makes you think Mr. Di Rocca and I are friends? We hardly know each other."

"I'm sorry. I've seen you together a few times and just assumed. My mistake."

Watkins studied me with his lips pressed together.

I hurried to fill the silence. "The two of you seemed to be arguing the other day. Would you mind telling me what that was about?"

"I don't see how that's any of your business."

I sat at the nearest table. "You're right; it's not. It might give me a look into his personality, though. That would be very helpful in my character development."

He settled in the seat opposite. "Why don't you ask him then?"

My cheeks heated. "He won't talk to me. He thinks I killed his wife."

Watkins smirked. "So does the entire judicial system, from what I hear."

"You're old enough to know you can't believe everything you hear. I'm innocent, and I intend to prove it. Until then, I have a book to write." I said those words as if I could finish it before blowing away the cloud hanging over my head. However, he didn't have to know that.

"I see. How can I help you?"

"What were you and Fredo arguing about?"

"We had a business disagreement. I made a proposal, and he wasn't interested. Things got a little intense."

A proposal or a threat? "What did you propose?"

He shook his head. "I'm not able to disclose that information at this time."

"Why do you think he became so upset?"

"Again, you'd have to ask him that." He shrugged. "As a writer, you should know by now that sometimes people act in strange and unexpected ways."

Touché. I smiled. "Yes, I've noticed."

Lacey walked by, tapping her watch.

I glanced at my phone—6:05. Past time for us to close. "Thanks for your time, Mr. Watkins. My manager is not so subtly reminding me that it's closing time. I'm sorry you didn't get the opportunity to do what you came in for."

He stood. "No problem. I can come back tomorrow." He moved toward the door, then turned back. "I hope you find what you're looking for."

"Thank you." I did too.

I collected Savannah and headed toward home. It was too late to talk to Olinski. The police station was one place my dog couldn't go in town. By the time I took her home and returned, he'd be gone for the day. Perhaps he had a date with Brittany tonight, and I could catch him there. I texted Brittany asking if they were going to see each other.

A minute later, she replied: No date tonight. What's up? Charlie thinks Watkins might be a fake name.

My phone rang. Brittany had no patience for texting complex conversations.

I answered. "Hey."

"Where are you?"

"On my way home."

"Great. Come by my place."

"Okay, but just for a minute. I'm pooped."

"All right," she replied and disconnected the call.

Savannah dawdled her way home, giving me a rest stop every few feet until we reached the oak tree at the foot of the steps. She claimed her spot, then trotted up. I followed as quickly as my leaden legs would carry me, Savannah cheering me on from the top.

Brittany opened her door when I reached the halfway mark. I waved, and she laughed.

"What's so funny?"

"You look like you're a hundred years old."

Close, but not quite. "You only look as good as you feel, right? And I feel like I'm a hundred and ten."

She gave me two thumbs up. "I guess you nailed it, then."

When I reached the landing, she threw her arm across my shoulders and led me to the couch. "Just get comfortable, and I'll bring the wine. Are you hungry? I have some leftovers I can heat up."

"I'm too tired to eat."

She laughed again. "That'll be the day. How about a roast beef sandwich? My mother sent me home with a ton of stuff when we had lunch with them Sunday."

My stomach rumbled, finally figuring out how little I had eaten today. "Sounds great. I'll run over and get Savannah's dinner, so she won't drool all over our shoes while we eat."

"Yeah, like that's going to stop her."

"I can dream, can't I?"

I heaved myself back to my feet and went across the hall, returning with a dog bowl full of kibble and another with water. Savannah dove in when they hit the floor, not bothering to wait for us. Guess I needed to teach her some manners.

"Anything I can do to help?" I asked Brittany.

"No, thanks. I got it. You can pour the wine if you'd like."

I retrieved a bottle from the refrigerator and two glasses from the cabinet beside it. Brittany decorated our plates with potato chips while I poured, took a large swallow, and poured again. Should I be drinking wine in my current condition? Probably not, but I really didn't care at this point.

I likely wouldn't stay awake long enough to finish the glass anyway. And it wouldn't be the first time I'd fallen asleep while talking to Brittany. I'd always been a lightweight when drinking alcohol. Plus, I was already exhausted. She'd understand, though. She never took things like that personally.

"So, what's all this about Watkins being an alias?" Brittany asked, carrying our plates to the coffee table.

"Charlie says he can't find anything on a Steven Watkins who might be our guy in South Carolina or Chicago. The closest he could find was a congressman from Kansas. And why would he come to Riddleton? We're not exactly in his district." I bit into my sandwich and the robust beef flavor bathed my taste buds.

She sipped her wine. "No kidding. I haven't found anything, either, but I don't search in the same places he does. Usually, he can find things I can't."

The meat hit my empty stomach with a thud. "Usually, but not this time. Charlie says the guy's a ghost. Maybe he came back to haunt us."

Brittany snickered. "He must be the ghost of Riddleton past."

"Nah, I'll bet he's the ghost from the future, showing us the error of our ways." I drained my glass and refilled it.

"Well, he'd better start talking if he expects us to learn anything. We're a bit too thick-headed to figure it out on our own."

I lifted my wineglass. "I'll drink to that." A wave of dizziness hit me. I should slow down, but the alcohol had given me a sense of well-being I hadn't had in days. My eyelids grew heavier with each mouthful, though. I fought against it, wanting to enjoy the feeling a little longer. The sun would bring harsh reality back in the morning.

"You know what I wonder, though?" Brittany studied me over the rim of her glass. "How did he get a hotel room without showing ID?"

"If he's who we think he is, I'm sure he had no trouble getting a fake ID. He probably has a whole stash of them for when he has to go on the run. Along with a bazillion dollars in cash."

"A bazillion? How many zeros is that?" She giggled, showing the effects of the wine, too. Another good reason for me to stay awake. Brittany was a hoot when she drank. I needed a few good laughs tonight. Something to help me feel like myself again.

My phone rang before I could reply. Eric's academy picture filled the screen. I swiped.

"Hey, baby, what's up? You having a good day?" I slurred my words. *Oops.*

"Not as good as you, I see," he said with merriment in his voice. "Where are you?"

"Brittany's. She's getting me drunk to take advantage of me." I winked at her.

"Sure she is."

"What're you doing? Come over and play with us."

"I can't right now. I'm still working on Fredo's break-in."

"Fine. Be that way." I pouted. "Find anything interesting?"

"Possibly. We found a set of fingerprints in Fredo's house that we couldn't identify. Could be anyone, though. Could even be left over from Tony's time there."

Another large swallow of wine went down my throat. "What about our local stranger, Steven Watkins? Think they could match his?"

Eric cleared his throat. "Possibly, if we had his prints to compare them to."

"I might be able to help with that. He's supposed to come to the bookstore tomorrow. I'll give him a cup of coffee. Then we'll have his prints." I giggled at my brilliance. They really should let me help with their investigations.

"It's a nice thought, but I'm not sure your cardboard cup will retain legible fingerprints. It has a grainy finish. To get a clear print, the surface needs to be smooth."

"Well, I guess I'll just have to get him to touch something else, then." I hiccuped. "Don't you worry. I'll figure it out."

211

"If you even remember this conversation tomorrow." He took a breath. "Frankly, I'd just as soon you stayed out of it, Jen. You're in enough trouble already."

"Yeah, but if Watkins ransacked Fredo's house, we might tie him to Mara's murder. Then I wouldn't be in trouble anymore."

He sighed. "All right. If he happens to touch something, save it for us. But don't do anything stupid trying to get his fingerprints. I don't want to lift them off your dead body, okay?"

"Okay. I'll behave."

"That'll be the day."

We planned to speak again in the morning, then said our goodbyes.

I tried to help Brittany with cleanup but tripped over my own feet and landed on my butt. Savannah squeezed in beside me and poked me in the nose with her snout. Brittany sent me back to the couch, where I stretched out and closed my eyes. The dog took my place on cleanup duty.

When I next opened them, darkness and silence muffled my senses, disorienting me. Brittany had removed my shoes, socks, and jeans and covered me with a blanket before going to bed herself. I sat up and rubbed my stiff neck. Brittany's couch cushions had to be stuffed with rocks instead of foam. No way I could spend the night on it and still be functional in the morning. I had to go home.

The room whirled around me like a carousel, minus the flashing lights and music. When the contents of my stomach lurched into my throat, I sealed my lips and swallowed hard. I'd vomited more in the past week than I had in the decade before it.

Enough is enough.

I reached for Savannah, but the couch was too small for both of us, so I felt around on the floor beside me. No sign of her. Did she go to bed with Brittany? I'd be surprised if she did, but I wouldn't risk waking Brittany looking for her. She'd be fine for the rest of the night, and I could pick her up in the morning.

My eyes adjusted to the darkness, and I found the neat stack of clothing Brittany'd left on the coffee table. I dressed while still seated, fearing I'd fall over when I tried to stand. But I couldn't sit there indefinitely so, gripping the couch's arm, I gingerly rose and swayed in place. Eventually, I released my grip long enough to pull my pants up, somehow managing to remain upright. Now I only had to get to my apartment without waking up the whole building or falling down the steps.

I trailed my fingers along the wall until I reached the door. When I opened it, a sliver of light from the streetlamps illuminated the landing, and I slipped out and closed the door behind me. I'd left my door unlocked when I retrieved Savannah's supplies. No need to hunt for keys. A good thing because I'd left them on Brittany's coffee table with my phone. No biggie. I'd pick them up in the morning when I collected Savannah.

When I flipped the light switch beside my front door, an uneasy sensation hit my gut. I shook it off. Everything seemed exactly as I'd left it. Probably a reaction to the alcohol. I didn't drink to excess often, but when I did, it always hit me hard. I should know better by now.

Whatever. Time to brush my teeth and go to sleep. According to the old saying, everything would look better in the morning. Unless I had a wicked hangover, that is.

I took care of business and headed for the bedroom. When I stepped through the doorway, someone slipped a black hood over my head. At the same time, I felt a sharp jab in my upper arm. I lost consciousness.

CHAPTER TWENTY

I awakened lying on a thin mat under a musty blanket in a dank room illuminated only by a battery-powered lamp. When I sat up, the hurricane in my head leaped to category five. My fuzzy, arid eyes blinked rapidly, and I rubbed them with my fingers. I still couldn't see enough of anything to give me a hint about my surroundings.

A wave of fear surfed through my belly. Where was I? Back in the tunnels? No, the smell and feel of the air were different somehow. I didn't have that closed-in feeling I had down there. And the wall behind me was Sheetrock, not dirt. Too bad. At least I knew how to get out of the tunnels. This place was a mystery. And not the good kind with a guaranteed satisfying ending.

I picked up the lamp and shined it around, the light only radiating a few feet in any direction before disappearing into the black. Beside my mat sat a case of bottled water, a box of protein bars, and an empty five-gallon bucket accompanied by a roll of cheap toilet paper. Someone expected me to be here for a while. I had to find a way to disappoint them, despite the snowball forming in my chest.

My head ached, and I cracked open a water bottle, downing it to help with the alcohol-induced dehydration. Although, that shot in my arm might have something to do with it too. I had no idea what they'd injected me with or how long I'd been out. Or how to counteract the effects. The snowball grew, chilling me in a way no amount of tepid water could warm up again.

Deep breath in, slow breath out.

Using the wall for support, I climbed to my feet, grimacing against the pain shooting through my skull. I'd give anything for a bottle of acetaminophen right now. Whatever drug they'd used, it offered no residual pain relief.

When I bent to retrieve the lamp, agony knocked me back to the mat. I lay on my side, hugging my knees until it passed, taking comfort from the fetal position. The illusion of safety threatened to paralyze me, but I had to find a way out of here.

Suck it up, Jen.

Easing back into a sitting position, I grabbed the lamp and climbed the wall again, gritting my teeth against the ensuing storm. When it subsided, I moved a few feet along the concrete floor and lifted the light to eye level for a better view of my surroundings.

Cardboard boxes lined the opposite wall, and to my left, I found windows near the ceiling too small to squeeze my chocolate-chip-muffin-enhanced butt through. If I ever got out of this, I'd go on a diet, although to be honest, I probably wouldn't have fit through them anyway.

To my right, stairs climbed to the floor above and abandoned furniture occupied the space beside them. Overhead, a light fixture with no bulb hung from the ceiling. I was in somebody's basement. Why would someone kidnap me and trap me in their cellar?

I listened for signs of the house's occupants but heard nothing. No footsteps. No voices. I shuffled to the stairs and froze at the bottom, ears straining for any hint of a sound. Still nothing. Had I been abandoned here? There had to be somebody watching to ensure I didn't escape. Perhaps there was no escape route, so they didn't have to worry about it. A flash of fear grew the snowball into a full-fledged snowman. The light vibrated and my feet seemed rooted to the floor.

Deep breath in, slow breath out.

I'd use their overconfidence against them. The steps seemed firm, and I started up, careful to keep to the sides so they'd be less likely to creak. No noises of any kind. They must be relatively new. At the top, I encountered a solid wooden door. I turned the knob and pushed, but the door didn't budge. Not even a little. It had to be bolted from the outside. I shined the lamp around the edges but saw no spaces, and the hinges were on the other side. No way out.

My heart raced, and sweat appeared on my forehead and under my arms. Another hint of fear crept into my belly. I was in trouble with no idea how to get out of it. I slipped back down the stairs to my mat and turned off the lamp to save the battery.

I needed to think for a minute. There had to be a way out of this place. I chugged another bottle of water. If I could eliminate the headache, or at least reduce it to a tropical storm, I might focus better. Come up with a solution to my problem. Or at least the beginnings of one.

I leaned my head back against the wall and stretched out my legs before me, letting my brain free-associate. The answer hovered on the edge of my consciousness. I only had to wait until it waded through the muck. The supplies at my side told me I had plenty of time. Not that I intended to stick around here that long. I wasn't crazy about protein bars.

Focusing on my breathing emptied my mind of extraneous thoughts. For a few seconds at a time, anyway. I pushed away anything irrelevant to the issue at hand. I hadn't been in many basements—most houses in this area didn't have them because of flooding—but a suspicion that something here wasn't quite right irked me.

I inhaled to force oxygen into my brain. My headache ebbed to a tolerable level. The water was doing its job. It shouldn't be long now until I could think lucidly again.

The layout I'd observed in the lantern's dim glow floated in my head. I ran through the panorama, one scene at a time. I had a used furniture store in one section, a wall full of cardboard boxes, an empty wall with narrow windows along the top, and the stairs. And my mat and supplies, of course.

Despite my efforts to focus, I had begun to doze when loud male voices sounded on the floor above. I couldn't make out the words, but it seemed like an argument. They went back and forth until suddenly, it was quiet. Had they left again? Without checking on me? They had to figure I'd be awake by now.

Then I heard one man say, "We have to get rid of her. It's too risky." And that man sounded suspiciously like Fredo Di Rocca, but I couldn't be sure. The one thing I knew was that they were talking about me unless they had another female hostage stashed somewhere else in the house. Perhaps my time was shorter than I'd originally believed.

Either way, I had to find some form of defense if one of them came down here. I hoisted myself off the mat, picked up the lamp, and moved toward the boxes. There might be something in one of them I could use as a weapon. Or a clue as to why I'd been kidnapped.

The first carton I tried was full of clothing. No help now, but it might come in handy after I'd been here for a week or so. I set it aside. Box number two contained papers and old photographs. I flipped through some photos, trying to establish whose house I was in. They were mostly scenic landscapes, a few with an older couple I didn't recognize. I closed it up and moved on to the next one in the stack.

I went through the boxes one at a time, finding little of use in my situation. I opened one with decorator's swatches and brochures for doors and window treatments. Somebody was planning a remodel. No help for me, though. As I closed the carton, the niggle in the back of my mind came to life again. What was I missing? What was this room missing?

219

And then I had it. Most basements had a door that led to the outside. This one didn't. Unusual but not unheard of. But what if it did? What if the owner had it covered up during the reconstruction? If I could find it, I might be able to access it and get away. Whoever left me here wouldn't have taken the trouble to secure the door because they knew I couldn't see it from inside. I couldn't escape through an exit I didn't know existed.

Carrying the lantern, I hustled to the window wall. It was smooth all the way across. No seams or cracks to give away the door's location. Assuming there was a door. I had to know for sure, though, and I had nothing to lose but time by searching for it. I suspected time was one thing I had plenty of. For now, anyway.

I rapped on the wall with my knuckles, listening intently, and worked across the room. It all sounded the same unless I hit a stud. However, I had no idea if the sound in front of a door was supposed to differ from the sound in front of the outer wall. There was only one thing left to do. Chop holes in the wall and see what lay behind them.

Scrambling back to the box wall, I picked up where I left off. Only this time, I dumped them on the floor and rifled through the contents, no longer taking care to repack them. I needed a large and sturdy tool to punch through the Sheetrock. I'd settle for a hammer and screwdriver if I had to. And I could use the hammer for defense if necessary.

Carton after carton lay empty on the floor, covered with clothing, knickknacks, and miscellaneous junk, and despair brought me back to the brink of immobility.

This was a waste of time, but I had only one stack left. Might as well finish up. Who knew what treasures might be found in one of the last three cartons? It depended on my definition of treasure.

In the very last box, I hit pay dirt. Carpentry tools. I dug through saws and hammers and boxes of nails. At the bottom, I found what I needed. A one-foot bar with a hooked claw on one end and a straight edge with a notch on the other. A nail puller. I could use a hammer and the straight end to punch the hole and the claw end to pull away the drywall.

Footsteps sounded through the ceiling, and I froze. Had I made too much noise? I snatched a hammer out of the box and turned off the lamp. Squatting beside the stairs, I held my breath, waiting for someone to come down. The hammer was heavy in my hand, but adrenaline would help me use it if necessary. My heart pounded in my ears, muffling the footfalls. I held my breath.

The sounds receded, and I released the air from my lungs. My slick hand dropped the hammer, but I caught it with my other hand before it clattered against the concrete floor. Sweat dripped into my eyes. I wiped my face on my shoulder. That was close.

I retrieved the nail puller from the tool carton and carried it, along with the hammer and the lamp, to the outer wall. Where would the door be? Most likely in one end or the other, but it could easily be in the middle too. No way to know, so I'd have to start on one side and punch holes down the wall without attracting the attention of anyone on the floor above. *Piece of cake.*

Where to begin? I only needed to expose enough of the area to see if a door or the outer wall lay behind it. So, a two- or three-inch opening every few feet at eye level should do it. I picked a spot about a foot in from the side wall and set the straight end of the nail puller against it. When I tapped the claw end with the hammer, the bar broke through the drywall, but the clash of metal on metal reverberated in my ears like a marching band in a cemetery.

I froze once again and listened for footsteps. The clank probably wasn't nearly as loud as it seemed up close, and it was unlikely anyone upstairs could hear it. However, my nerves couldn't take the stress of wondering after every hit. I fished through the clothing box, found a thick wool sock, and wrapped it around the end of the hammer. That should take care of the problem.

Setting the bar at the edge of the previous cut, I tapped it again, producing a muffled thud, and widening the slit another inch. Then I turned the nail puller around and used the claw to yank enough Sheetrock away for me to see the insulation between the inner and outer walls. No door. I slid down the wall to my right a few feet and tried again. Same result.

Two tries later, I had reason to hope. When I cleared the drywall from the tiny opening, I saw nothing. No door, but no insulation, either. A surge of adrenaline shook my hands, and the nail puller clattered onto the floor at my feet. I held my breath.

Please don't come down here. Please don't come down here.

Deep breath in, slow breath out.

I was so close. I only needed a little more time. Blood rushing through my ears deafened me, and I turned to watch the door at the top of the stairs. I'd been down here for hours. Why didn't anyone ever come to check on me? Maybe they didn't want to risk me seeing who they were, which probably meant they didn't intend to kill me. However, I didn't plan on waiting around to find out.

Little by little, I enlarged the hole until I could hold the lamp up to the opening and still see what was inside. I took a deep breath, crossed my fingers, and peered in. Impenetrable darkness greeted me.

I pushed my hand through and reached around in the empty space, praying a mouse wouldn't mistake my fingers for lunch. A minute later, my fingertips contacted a cool, smooth surface about a foot to my right. It had to be window glass. I'd found my way out.

It would take forever to use the claw to pull away little bits of Sheetrock at a time. I needed a better plan to clear a large enough area for me to fit through and pry open the door. I used the straight edge of the bar to cut a six-inch line leading directly across from the bottom of the hole. Then I did the same at the top of the hole and connected the lines vertically. A quick tap of the hammer and the entire block fell out. Joy surged into my feet, and I did a little dance. My plan had worked. I'd be out of here in no time.

I cut vertical lines from the edges of the open block to just above the floor, then cut a horizontal line to connect them. When I grabbed the top of the cut drywall, it came right out. A three-foot-square section all in one piece. I squeezed into the space between the wall and the door, which was secured only by the doorknob lock.

After inserting the straight edge of the nail puller into the space between the doorframe and the door, I shoved it in while slamming my shoulder against the door. It gave, and the door swung open. I was free.

I stepped through and ran as fast as I could away from the house into the woods. Safely undercover, I stopped behind a tree to get my bearings and catch my breath. The house was surrounded by trees except for a dirt driveway with two vehicles parked on it. A black SUV and a dark gray sedan. I couldn't tell what models. The easiest thing to do would be to follow the drive to the main road and flag down a passing car. Except I didn't dare expose myself. I had to stay in the trees where I couldn't be seen.

Darting from pine to pine, I stayed as close to the road as possible while remaining out of sight. No sign of pursuit yet. My kidnappers hadn't noticed me missing, or they didn't care. I still thought it strange they'd assume I couldn't escape, though. They had to be amateurs. No professional would be so careless. They would hear no complaints from me, however.

The dirt driveway ended at an unlit gravel road I didn't recognize. I squinted into the darkness, searching for any recognizable landmark. Nothing but trees all around. Nausea attacked my belly. I swallowed hard and followed it with deep breaths until it passed.

Where the hell am I?

CHAPTER TWENTY-ONE

After slipping into the woods to assess my situation, I rubbed my arms to combat the chill. I'd left my jacket lying draped across the arm of Brittany's couch. The gravel stretched in both directions with no landmarks in sight. I knew nothing about navigating by starlight; even if I did, I had no idea what direction to go. My kidnappers had to be affiliated with someone involved in Mara's death, so I could safely assume I wasn't that far from Riddleton. Maybe.

Calling on my friends Eenie, Meenie, Miney, and Moe sent me to the right. I stayed far enough in the trees that I could still see the road but couldn't easily be seen by anyone on it. The half-moon low in the sky provided enough light to see obvious obstacles like trees, but sticks, pine cones, and fallen branches tripped me whenever I encountered them. I was quickly covered in dirt and scratches, but adrenaline kept my legs moving at a decent pace.

The gravel ended at a field, and a dirt road branched off to the left. A driveway? Could only be an abandoned farm road that led nowhere. I had two options: take a chance the road that cut between two fields, which offered no cover, led to a house where I could call for help, or go back the way I came. Headlights approaching slowly, gravel crunching beneath tires, interrupted my deliberations. I found a pine wide enough to conceal me and hid behind it. They couldn't see me. I peeked around the tree to track their progress.

The vehicle, most likely the black SUV that had been parked near the house, crept past. A light from the passenger-side window played off the trees. I turned sideways and pressed against the pine, shaking and sweating despite the mid-winter evening air. It had to be the kidnappers. Nobody else would have a reason to search the woods with a flashlight. It figured they'd pick the moment I escaped to check on my condition. Bad luck haunted me like the phantom of Murphy's Law.

When the SUV turned down the dirt road, my decision was made for me. I sprinted back the way I'd come, slipping on pine needles and tripping over branches. I saw another hot bath in my future. Maybe a few Band-Aids. Assuming I got out of this alive. The trees ended at the drive to the house I'd escaped from.

Now I had another decision to make. Should I go back to the house and find a phone to call for help? It was too dark to see how many people were in the SUV when it passed. There were at least two, though. One to drive and the other to handle the flashlight. I had to assume if there were more people involved, they'd left them behind in case I returned. Better to forge ahead and hope for the best.

I scuttled across the driveway into the shelter of the trees on the other side. My legs ached with fatigue and the sting from numerous pine-cone-induced scratches, but I couldn't stop. I had to get help. Darting between the pines, I stayed within sight of the road. The last thing I needed was to get lost in here.

My limbs demanded a rest break, however. I stopped far enough away from the house that I couldn't tell if the kidnappers in the SUV had returned. I imagined they had the same plan I did: try one direction, and if they didn't find me, try the other way. I caught my breath and went back on the move again. This gravel road had to lead to a paved one somewhere. I only had to keep going until I found it.

I had no sense of how far I'd traveled when I spotted headlights ahead of me near what I could see of the horizon. How did the abductors pass by without me noticing? They couldn't have. It had to be someone else. A good Samaritan for me or reinforcements for them? No way for me to know, so I stayed out of sight in the woods, doing my share to close the distance between us.

When the vehicle was almost upon me, I hid behind a tree and peeked out, as I'd successfully done before. The driver was in no hurry, creeping along below any possible speed limit, and I had a clear view of the car. It almost seemed like Eric's Jeep, but it couldn't be. How would he know where to look for me?

Suddenly, the interior light came on, framing the person in the passenger seat, who held up a cell phone.

It was Brittany. Somehow, they'd found me. I bolted through the trees to the road, waving my arms and shouting. Red brake lights interrupted the darkness.

I ran to the Wrangler and jumped in the back seat. "Get out of here. Hurry! They'll be back any minute."

Eric did a quick K-turn and stomped on the gas pedal, tires spewing gravel behind the car.

Brittany turned and leaned over the seat. "Jen! I'm so glad we found you. What happened?"

After relaying the abridged version of my kidnapping and escape, I asked, "How did you figure out where I was?"

Eric grinned into the rearview mirror. "I loaded a phone tracking app onto my phone and punched in all the numbers of people who might be involved in the case—Fredo Di Rocca, Gil Scavuto, Steven Watkins, even Frank Roselli, the ex-boyfriend. All the phones were in Riddleton, with no indication the owners had anything to do with your disappearance, except Fredo Di Rocca's. We tracked him to the house I assume you were held in."

So, it *was* Fredo's voice I'd heard. "Thank you."

Brittany reached for my hand. "I'm thankful it worked. I was so scared when I couldn't find you this morning. I knew you'd never leave Savannah without telling anyone where you were going."

"I wouldn't leave you two, either, you know."

They glanced at each other and laughed. "Sure, you wouldn't," Eric said.

I crossed my arms. "Hey! That's not true. I love you guys." The adrenaline that had fueled my escape ebbed away, and my body grew heavy with fatigue, making me chilly again. "Eric, would you turn up the heat, please?"

"Sure." He reached over and turned the dial farther into the red. "If you're cold, there's a blanket in the back."

"Would you like my sweater?" Brittany asked.

"No, thanks. I'll be fine in a minute. I'm just winding down, that's all."

I glanced out the window, knowing I'd just lied to my best friend. I wasn't fine at all and wouldn't be in a week, let alone a minute. But if I told Brittany about the fear that lingered in my psyche, even though I knew I was safe now, she'd worry. Hover over me, and I couldn't handle that. The sanctity of my home had been violated. I'd been violated. Not physically, but psychologically and emotionally. I needed some space to adjust.

Brittany peered at me over the seat, concern etched on her face. "You've had a rough couple of days. A good night's sleep will help."

"She's going to have to give a statement," Eric said.

"Can't it wait 'til tomorrow?" Brittany asked.

"Possibly. I'll call Havermayer when we get back." He rubbed the nape of his neck. "She should be okay with waiting until morning. But you'll have to get over there first thing."

"No problem," I said.

Eric glanced at me in the mirror. "Do you have any idea whose house that was, Jen?"

"Not really. I flipped through some photos in a box in the basement where I was held but didn't see anyone I recognized."

"Besides Fredo, who else was there?"

"I don't know. I never saw anyone. I don't think they intended for me to see them. They locked me in with a few days' worth of supplies." I rubbed my hands together for warmth. "I took that as a good sign. Like they didn't want to have to kill me."

"Any idea why they took you in the first place?"

"None at all. I did hear one of them say they should get rid of me, but I got the impression he was voted down. Nobody showed up to follow through anyway."

"I'm glad he was," Brittany said.

"Me too."

"Of course, getting rid of you is like trying to get gum off your shoe. Practically impossible." She grinned at me over the seat.

"And yet you came looking for me." I stuck my tongue out at her.

Dots of light appeared here and there through the windshield. My muscles relaxed a tiny bit as we returned to civilization. The skyline, if you could call it that, of Sutton came into view.

I tapped Eric on the shoulder. "Where are we going? I want to go home."

"I'm taking you to the hospital to get you checked out."

"I'm fine. A little banged up and extremely tired, but fine. Please take me home."

He shook his head. "You were drugged. We have to find out what they used. It's evidence, and we have to make sure there won't be any lasting effects."

"I'll ask Ingrid to draw my blood in the morning. I don't want to go to the hospital. Again. If I show up there one more time, they're going to name a wing after me."

He met my gaze in the rearview mirror. "The morning will be too late. You've been gone almost twenty-four hours. The drug might be out of your system by then. It may already be too late, but we have to try."

I knew all that, but the adrenaline had worn off, and I could barely keep my eyes open. All I wanted to do was sleep. Well, take a bath, then sleep. "Fine. They can draw my blood, then we leave. I don't need a doctor to kiss my booboos. They're only scratches. Deal?"

After a moment, he reluctantly replied, "Deal."

Closing my eyes against the harsh street lights flying past at regular intervals, I laid my head back until the Jeep slowed for the turn into the hospital parking lot.

Here we go again.

Once inside, Eric flashed his badge and relayed his request to a woman at the desk. Fifteen minutes later, someone led me to a small room where a female vampire, otherwise known as a lab tech, waited for me. She smiled and directed me to sit in the chair beside the desk, holding a tray with a tourniquet, an alcohol wipe, an empty tube with a royal-blue top, a gauze pad, and a strip of paper tape stuck to the edge. I had to give her credit. The vampire came prepared.

Fifteen minutes later, we were back on the road. I curled up in the back seat for a nap, waking only when Eric slipped the Jeep into a parking space in front of my building, then came around to help me out of the car. With his arm around my waist, we navigated the steps. Brittany used her key to let us into my apartment, and Savannah leaped at our entrance as if her back legs doubled as industrial springs.

I put my hand out to calm her. "Easy, girl. I missed you too." I eased past her to the couch. "Just let me get settled, and I'll pet you."

Savannah ran circles around me as I negotiated the distance with Eric's help, then leaped the final three feet onto the couch so she could greet me on arrival. As soon as I sat down, she stretched across my lap and showered me with doggie kisses. We'd only been separated for a day, but she acted as though it'd been a year. Of course, she did that when I ran down to check the mail, too, so I probably shouldn't read too much into it.

Eric sat beside me while Brittany puttered in the bathroom, running water for a bath. I leaned my head on his shoulder and closed my gritty eyes. He kissed the top of my head. For the first time in two days, including my day at the courthouse, I felt safe.

When Brittany came to collect me for my soak, Eric went outside to call Havermayer. With luck, she'd agree to a morning meeting rather than interrogating me tonight. It was after midnight, and I'd had almost no sleep since Tuesday night. It was now officially Friday, and it felt like I hadn't slept for a month.

My future sixty-year-old self stared back at me in the bathroom mirror. Dark-blue half-moons supported light-blue eyes nestled in a puffy red face. Sheetrock dust coated my black hair, which added credence to the idea

I'd aged overnight, and I had dirt and scratches all over my arms and legs. It snowed drywall and soil when I removed my clothing, and I debated whether to put it in the hamper or just throw it away. Unable to decide, I dropped it on the floor and stepped into the tub. I channeled Scarlett O'Hara.

I'll think about that tomorrow.

The hot water stung when I eased into it, but my muscles began to relax almost immediately, making the pain worthwhile. Relaxing my mind proved the more significant challenge, however. Now that I was safe, determining who had kidnapped me and why dominated my thoughts.

Fredo had to be involved, or Eric wouldn't have tracked his phone to the house. Was Steven Watkins there too? I'd heard no other voices, but I'd only spoken to him twice, so would I recognize his voice anyway? Maybe, but I couldn't count on that. And who was the man Fredo was talking to? My first thought after Watkins was Gil, but he hated his brother-in-law. I couldn't imagine him helping Fredo commit a felony. Unless he had no choice.

Which still brought me back to why I was kidnapped in the first place. What did Fredo have to gain? If he murdered Mara, my arrest for the crime left him in the clear. Of course, my disappearance would direct all law enforcement energy toward finding me, leaving them no time or motivation to continue investigating anyone else. Still, he'd have been better off leaving me alone because once I was arraigned, the police considered the case closed.

My eyelids grew heavy as the water cooled. I needed to get moving before I fell asleep and drowned. I soaped and gently scrubbed, then ducked my head under the water to rinse out the dust before reaching for the shampoo. I'd need a shower in the morning to wash properly, but I could at least get some of the crud out of my hair before climbing into bed.

I let the water out and toweled off, dabbing at the scratches. Brittany had left clean shorts and a T-shirt on the counter next to the sink. I slipped them on, feeling almost like myself again. When I opened the bathroom door, a fresh coffee aroma filled my nostrils. Brittany had been busy. She handed me a cup and directed me to the table, where she'd left a plate of scrambled eggs and toast.

"You never mentioned actually eating any of those protein bars, so I fixed you something light to eat."

I sipped my coffee, then settled into the chair. "Thank you. I never thought about being hungry. I guess overwhelming stress is the best diet plan of all."

She sat beside me and drank from her cup. "Perhaps, but I wouldn't recommend it."

"Darn. And I was going to write a book about it." I wiped toast crumbs off my lips. "It would've been a best seller, too."

"Perhaps, but the follow-up book would be a real bear to write. Quit while you're ahead."

"Good idea."

Eric came back in and joined us at the table.

"What did she say?" I asked him.

"You need to be at the station at nine. She'll take your statement then."

Goodie. Another interview with Havermayer. A perfect way to start the day. "How mad is she?"

He chuckled. "She's not mad, just concerned. She's even giving you around-the-clock protection. There's a unit parked outside right now."

"Huh. I guess she doesn't want me killed before she can get me convicted and sentenced to death."

He chuckled at the irony. "Actually, I think she might be second-guessing herself." He laid his hand on my arm. "Don't get me wrong, she still thinks you did it, but she's willing to consider other possibilities now. I'd say that's progress."

"That's big of her. Let's hope it's not too late."

CHAPTER TWENTY-TWO

When "Born in the USA" blared out of my clock radio Friday morning, I vowed to move to Canada. Would they let me carry Savannah over the border? No matter. It was way too cold up there for me. I wouldn't make it through one winter. Maybe Mexico instead.

I shoved my little girl aside and draped my feet over the side of the bed. She scooted around to rest her chin in my lap. I stroked the top of her head. "Why so clingy today? I'm right here, and everything's fine." *Terrific.* I just lied to my dog.

Urging my stiff, sore legs into motion, I shambled to the bathroom, then hit the kitchen for coffee. Savannah pulled her leash off the doorknob and brought it to me. I poured my coffee into a to-go cup, threw on my Nikes, and followed her out the door. A Riddleton patrol car sat in the parking lot. I'd forgotten about my protective detail.

Officer Zach Vick exited the passenger side. "Where are you going?"

"I have to walk the dog. It'll only take a few minutes."

He reached into the car for his hat. "I'll come with you."

"That really isn't necessary. I doubt anyone will bother me in public during the day."

"Sorry, Jen. You're our responsibility. I go, or you don't."

I smirked and gestured for him to join us. He'd come a long way from the little boy he was last summer. And at least he was speaking to me again. "If you insist."

Zach fell into step beside me, alert eyes darting everywhere, resting nowhere.

"So, how've you been? We haven't talked in a while." I gave him a sideways glance. "And don't you dare say fine."

He hooked his thumbs in his duty belt as we waited for Savannah to finish christening her oak tree. "Fine."

Oh no, he's not getting away with that this time. "Are you enjoying being a police officer? Is it everything you thought it would be?"

He checked the doorway of the Dollar General as we approached. "It's not quite as exciting as my father made it out to be, but I like it."

"Yeah, Eric loves to talk about the interesting parts of his job. He hates all the paperwork, though. And in a small town like Riddleton, that's probably ninety percent of what he does."

"I don't know," Zach said. "We've had more than our share of murders lately." He gave me a side-eye.

My face heated. Was he taking a shot at me? *Pissant.* "True. Things have been hopping around here. It's unfortunate."

237

We completed the rest of the circuit in silence, Zach checking every doorway and behind every tree. Savannah ignored him and did her thing—scratching, sniffing, and squatting her way around the block. When we safely returned to the steps, he tipped his hat and got back in the car.

Oh, brother.

After providing coffee to my sentries, I took a quick shower to properly wash my hair, then checked the time. I had less than an hour left before my next meeting with Havermayer. Facing her again worried me, as it would be my third grilling in less than a week. About as much fun as swimming in a pool full of piranhas.

The face in the mirror appeared a little more recognizable than last night, but not much. I still had shadows under my eyes, but it no longer looked as if I'd been in a prize fight. After wrestling with my hair, I headed into my bedroom to dress.

Savannah lay in the middle of the bed, watching me with her head on her paws. She knew I was getting ready to leave, and I could see the hope in her expressive brown eyes.

"Sorry, kid, not this time. I have to get filleted by Havermayer again."

Her eyebrows twitched. I sat beside her and scratched behind her ears. She loved that, but she loved getting to go with me even more. I hated leaving her behind, but I could see the just-sucked-a-lemon expression on Havermayer's face if I showed up with my dog at my side. It could be fun, though. But not worth it. She'd take her irritation out on Eric.

I stalled as long as I could, but by eight fifty-five, I had to leave. I gave Savannah a chew stick for a consolation prize, closed the door behind me, and trudged down the steps. My sentries offered me a ride. It seemed more like a command than an offer, however. Not in the mood to argue, I sat locked in the back of a patrol car again. At least I wasn't handcuffed this time.

Havermayer, red-eyed and haggard from lack of sleep, sipped coffee in the interview room and even provided a cup for me. I checked the back of her neck to ensure she hadn't been invaded by a body snatcher. Nothing unusual. It must be her. I dropped into the chair opposite and clasped my hands on the table.

"Good morning, Jen. How are you feeling?"

Like she really cares. "I could use a little more sleep, but other than that, I'm okay."

"Glad to hear it." She set her coffee down and held my gaze. "Tell me what happened."

I told her the whole story, beginning with the hood over my head and ending with me leaping into Eric's Wrangler. My coffee had cooled by then, but I took a sip anyway. Nothing like cold, burnt cop coffee to get you going in the morning. It was all I could do to keep the taste from reflecting on my face.

"I'm impressed. Not many people would've thought to look for a hidden door."

"I got lucky. Things worked out for me."

She smiled. "That happens a lot, doesn't it?"

Had I ever seen her smile before? Not that I could remember. "If you say so."

"Why do you think you were taken?"

"I have no idea. If I knew who it was, I might be able to guess, but I don't."

"Eric told me he found you by tracking Alfredo Di Rocca's phone. Doesn't that tell you anything? He was likely involved."

I bought time by swallowing more coffee, the grimace uncontrollable this time. No wonder Havermayer was always so grumpy. "Possibly, but I can't fathom why."

"Is he on your suspect list?"

Uh-oh. Wasn't expecting that one. "What suspect list?"

Havermayer cocked her head and stared at me. "Come on. You're not fooling me. We both know you've been trying to find Mara's killer since we released you the first time."

Busted. "I haven't done anything wrong. Besides, if you were the prime suspect in a murder, wouldn't you try to do something about it?"

She nodded. "I probably would. So, what have you come up with? Why do you think Di Rocca's involved?"

Was she really asking for my help? I resisted the urge to check the back of her neck again. Maybe she was high on something. "It's always the spouse, isn't it? He has the most to gain. Mara's half of the restaurant. The remaining money from Tony's life insurance. Whatever's left of it. She spent a bunch traveling with Gil. And who knows what kind of relationship they had. Mara seemed more interested in her brother than her husband."

She pinched her dark eyebrows and studied me.

Why was she looking at me like that? "What?"

240

"Tony didn't have any life insurance. He let the policy lapse to save money when Antonio's took a downturn last year."

Huh. "She must have gotten money from somewhere. She and Gil traveled all over the world after Tony died."

"How do you know all this?"

I shrugged. How did anyone learn anything these days? "Facebook. They both posted pictures from everywhere they went. Mara's were tagged with the location and date."

"Interesting." She rolled her empty cup between her hands.

I'd never seen Havermayer unsure of herself before. She seemed truly bumfuzzled. "Now that you know I'm a target, will you ask the ADA to drop the charges against me? I didn't kidnap myself. And I didn't kill Mara."

She ran a hand through her sandy-blond hair, then smoothed it back down. "We're not quite there yet. After all, you could've staged this whole thing to fool us into thinking you're innocent. People do things like that all the time."

And she's back. I pressed my lips together, measuring my words carefully. "I understand why you have to consider that possibility, but can't you see how absurd that is? Go out to that house yourself. Eric can tell you where it is. You'll see the setup and what I had to do to escape. Why would I go to all that trouble? I'm sure if I gave it some thought, I could come up with a whole lot easier way to trick you into believing in my innocence."

"We have people out there right now. The house is empty, and there's no indication that anyone's been there in quite a while."

A chill ran down my spine and spread through all my nerve endings. I clenched my tingling fingers. "What? How is that possible? I dumped all those boxes on the floor, and the wall is all torn up."

Havermayer shook her head. "The basement is empty except for some old furniture and neatly stacked boxes of junk."

How could that be? "And the wall?"

"Completely torn down. But there are slabs of drywall and paint cans as if the owner is remodeling. It all looks perfectly normal."

I swallowed the lump of panic that had appeared in my throat. "None of that was there when I left. It has to be staged."

"Maybe. Or maybe you made the whole thing up to convince us you're innocent." She leaned her elbows on the table. "I'm not saying I believe that, but it's what the assistant district attorney will say."

Panic crept into my mind. As much as I hated to admit it, she was right. They had only my word to go on. Wait. Not only me. "What about Eric? He's the one who found me. Are you saying he's involved too?"

"No, of course not. But he didn't actually see anything, either. He picked you up on the road, right?"

I nodded.

"He never went to the house or saw Di Rocca and his partner or partners. The only thing he can attest to is that you were stumbling down the road, and he picked

242

you up. And Di Rocca's phone was at that house. And since we didn't find evidence of your confinement . . ." She shrugged. "There's not much to go on."

Frustration pushed my fingernails into my palms. I shook out my hands. "You think I made the whole thing up. And the Ms. Nice Guy routine you've been handing me this whole time has been to trick me into saying something incriminating." I jumped to my feet, almost knocking my chair over. "I'm done talking without my attorney present."

"Sit down, Jen."

My whole body vibrated, and I curled my hands into fists again. *How dare she?*

Anger flashed at me from her eyes. "Sit!"

I sat. "I'm not making this up."

"I never said I didn't believe you. I'm only telling you what the ADA will say."

A hint of relief pushed at the panic and frustration, but caution was always necessary where Havermayer was concerned. "So, what now?"

"Go home and get some rest. You look like hell."

I laughed in spite of myself. "Well, you're no beauty queen at the moment, either."

Her lips twitched. "This has been a tough case. Believe it or not, I *did* try to find another suspect. There was just too much evidence against you."

"No luck with Frank Roselli?"

She glanced at me in surprise, then gave a barely perceptible headshake. "He has a solid alibi. He was at a party with about thirty other people, and he's in enough of the pictures that he had to be there all night."

Despair joined my frustration. I was running out of options. "Have you considered that strange guy who's been hanging around town all week? His name is Steven Watkins, and that's all we've learned about him. That, and he's staying in an expensive hotel in Blackburn. Either the name is an alias, he's in witness protection, or he's completely off the grid."

"What makes you think he's involved?"

"Gil Scavuto told me that Fredo had borrowed money from a shady character in Chicago, then left town. He insinuated that the guy may have sent an enforcer to make Fredo pay up. Maybe Watkins is that guy, and he killed Mara to frighten Fredo into repaying the loan."

She stared at me as if trying to decide whether I was serious or not. "And maybe the guy is Santa Claus updating his Naughty and Nice list. This is pure speculation. I can't do anything with that."

"At least find out who he is and what he's doing here. He seemed to have an argument with Fredo the other day. That has to mean something." I took a deep breath. "Run him through facial recognition and find out who he really is."

She snickered. "This is Riddleton, Jen. We don't have those kinds of tools."

"SLED does."

"The man hasn't done anything wrong that we know of. I can't just make a request without some kind of evidence that he's involved. I'm sorry. There's nothing illegal about hanging around town. Besides, unless he's been caught on camera someplace, what would SLED use for comparison?"

I blew out a frustrated lungful. Nothing I said made any difference. "Fine. Do you need anything else from me? Am I free to go?"

She gestured toward the door. "Go. But stay out of trouble, or the court will revoke your bail. And be careful. Since we didn't find any evidence at the house, we can't maintain your security detail."

It figures. "Understood. I didn't particularly like having babysitters anyway."

I left the station, not one bit closer to clearing my name than I'd been yesterday.

CHAPTER TWENTY-THREE

As I entered Ravenous Readers, Charlie was reading *Spacebot* to a half-dozen toddlers. He was dressed in his khaki and red uniform once again. And doing a pretty good job of it, to my surprise. But where was Lacey? In the year and a half I'd owned the store, she'd never once missed a day of work. All the potential pregnancy-related disorders I knew of flew through my mind, and I fervently wished her issue was minor. Especially since the problems I was familiar with were anything but.

I watched from the outskirts of the group as Charlie slapped the book closed and said, "The End" with a flourish. The little ones cheered and waved their crowns. Perhaps I should consider allowing him to entertain the kids more often. I didn't want to hurt Lacey's feelings, though, so I'd let her decide.

Charlie descended his throne and made his way toward me. "Hi, boss. How'd I do?"

"I didn't come in until the end, but what I saw was

terrific!" I patted him on the back. "We'll have to put you to work more often. The kids love you."

He beamed as if he'd just been awarded the Nobel Prize for picture book reading. "Thanks. I had fun."

"Where's Lacey? Is everything okay?"

He lowered his head, then looked back up at me. "She wasn't feeling well. I think it's her blood pressure again, although she wouldn't say."

"You should've called me. I'd have helped you."

"I thought about it, but after all the excitement you've had lately, I figured you could use the rest. I handled it." Concern clouded his brown eyes. "How are you, by the way? I was worried when I heard what happened."

"I'm all right. Tired and sore, but no major injuries."

"That's great, but I'm still glad I didn't call you. You need to take it easy for a while."

"Thank you, but you shouldn't have to take care of everything by yourself."

"I didn't mind. I love this place. I want to help any way I can."

"I appreciate all you do around here. I know I don't say it enough, but I do." I squeezed his shoulder.

His cheeks turned red. "I know, boss."

I texted Lacey to make sure she was okay, then rushed to the cash register to check out a mother whose child wanted their own copy of today's selection. My phone buzzed as I handed her the book and receipt. It was Lacey, assuring me she'd be in by this afternoon. I told her not to worry about it. Charlie and I could manage, and I wanted her to take a well-deserved day off.

Charlie rearranged the pastries on their respective trays while I poured myself a cup of coffee. I broke down and asked the question that'd been on my mind for days. "Okay, Charlie, what gives with the uniform? I'm not buying that people-are-tired-of-the-same-old-outfits story you gave me the other day."

His whole head turned red this time, ears, neck, and all. "Well, I've been talking to this girl online, and she mentioned something about coming by here to meet me in person. I didn't want her to think I'm some kind of freak."

Hmmm. How would Daniel respond? "First of all, you're not a freak. You're unique, and you should own that. Be proud of who you are and how far you've come."

"I am, but what about all the old sayings about putting your best foot forward and first impressions are lasting impressions? Shouldn't I try to impress her first?"

I sipped my coffee—a thousand times more palatable than the cup I had at the police station—to give me time to consider my response. "I think about it this way. If I pretend to be something I'm not just to impress a guy I meet, eventually I have to be myself, or I'll be miserable. Then what if he doesn't like the real me? Maybe he sticks around for a while, but sooner or later, the relationship will end because now *he's* miserable. So, I've invested all this time and energy into a relationship doomed to fail from the start. I would've been better off just being myself from the outset."

Charlie shook his head. "My mother would have a stroke if she heard you say that. I'm pretty sure she pretended with my dad for a long time. She was one of those get-up-at-four-in-the-morning-so-he-never-sees-me-without-my-makeup kinds of women. She finally got over it a couple of years ago."

"My mother was too. In my opinion, you should be yourself. If she doesn't like you, you part as friends and look for someone else. And if she does, you know it's because of who you are, not who you're pretending to be. That's my two cents, for what it's worth. I wish you luck no matter what you decide."

"Thanks, but she hasn't shown up yet, so it's likely a moot point anyway."

"Give her time. She probably doesn't want to look too anxious."

"We'll see."

My phone rang, interrupting my unsolicited-advice session. My heart skipped a beat when Eric's picture appeared on the screen. My knight in shining armor, calling to check on me.

I swiped. "Good morning. How are you?"

"Busy, but I thought I'd take a minute to see how it went with Havermayer."

Sweet guy. "She was actually cordial, for a change. I wondered if the body snatchers had gotten to her."

He laughed. "That's a blast from the past."

"True, but if the clone fits . . ."

"She can be nice when she wants to be."

I shuffled my feet and leaned on the counter. "So you keep telling me. She's never chosen to be nice to me before, however. It worries me."

"Maybe she's warming up to you."

"Yeah, like a blowtorch. She told me they didn't find anything when they searched the house. She said she believed my story, but the assistant district attorney would say I made it up to convince them I was innocent."

Eric cleared his throat. "It's possible. I ran a check to see who owns the house, but it's a shell corporation. I'll try to get more information later. Maybe I can find out who owns the company, but I'm not holding out much hope."

I'd hope enough for both of us. My future might depend on it. "Have you figured out what the deal is with Fredo's robbery yet?"

"No, but I don't have much to work with. It looks more like vandals than thieves since nothing was taken."

"Nothing Fredo was willing to admit he had in the first place, you mean."

"Possibly, but then why would he have reported it to begin with? He could've just gone after the people himself instead of involving us."

I shrugged, even though I knew he couldn't see it. "That's a question you'd have to ask him, I guess."

"True."

We listened to each other breathe for a minute. Eric broke the silence. "How are you feeling? You've had a tough time of it."

"I'm all right. A little tired."

"You should go home and take a nap."

"I can't. Lacey's out sick today. I have to help Charlie. Which stinks because I wanted to go back out to that house this afternoon."

"In that case, I'm glad you have to work. That would be a really stupid thing to do. If Fredo was involved in your kidnapping, you'd be walking right back into his arms."

"He'll be at Mara's memorial this afternoon, and Havermayer said the house was empty. Besides, I can handle myself."

Eric groaned. "I hate when you turn what I say into a personal attack. That's not what I meant, and you know it."

Good going, Jen. "I'm sorry. I'm not trying to start a fight. I'm tired and cranky. Forgive me?"

"You know I will. I always do." He hesitated, then said, "I better get back to work. Havermayer's going to be looking for me."

"Better you than me. I'll talk to you later."

I ended the call, but before I could put the phone back in my pocket, it rang again. Brittany this time.

"Hey, bestie, what's up?"

"Nothing much. Just checking on you. How are you?"

Ready for people to stop asking me that. "I'm okay. I survived Havermayer, although she said some crazy stuff."

"Like what?"

I told her what the detective said about there being no evidence in the house. "I need to go back and find proof I was there."

"No. No, you don't. That would be insane."

"You're always telling me I'm crazy. So, this must be normal for me."

"True, but that doesn't mean it's smart." She sighed. "You're going to talk me into coming with you, aren't you?"

My first grin of the day appeared. "I'm gonna try. Will it work?"

"Probably. When did you want to go?"

"I'm stuck at the store today, and you have to work in the morning, so how about tomorrow afternoon?"

"It's a date. Try not to get us both kidnapped this time."

"I'll do my best." I hung up, satisfied I finally had a game plan. Perhaps I might win this one after all.

Charlie reached under the counter for the glass cleaner and paper towels. Tiny handprints decorated the display case in front of the chocolate chip cookies. No surprise. They were the little ones' favorite choice.

I retrieved the feather duster from under the register and worked my way around the wall. "Hey, Charlie, did you ever have any luck finding out who Steven Watkins really is?"

"Not yet. There isn't much to go on, but I'm trying everything I can think of."

"I talked to Havermayer about it this morning, and she said there wasn't anything she could do, either. He had to break the law or be a suspect for her to make a request to SLED for facial recognition."

"I was afraid of that. I'm not sure what our options are. We might just have to wait for him to reveal himself. He must have a reason for being here, right?"

"You'd think. But if he's a mob enforcer, he won't tell anyone his true identity. Hopefully, Havermayer will check him out. She seems open to finding another suspect now, at least. I'm not sure how much good it will do me, though." I dusted a couple of shelves in the Biography section, then remembered something. "Hey, Charlie. Don't worry about trying to find info on Mara's ex-boyfriend. Havermayer told me he has an alibi."

He flashed me an okay sign.

When I ran the duster down the side of the bookcase nearest the stockroom, I noticed something wedged between the last book on the bottom shelf and the case. I squatted to take a closer look but still couldn't tell what it was. I stuck my fingers in, hoping it wasn't a mouse carcass or something similar. It turned out to be a flash drive. No markings, though, so I had no idea who it might belong to.

I held it up. "Is this your flash drive, Charlie?"

He came out of the coffee bar and took it from me. After turning it over in his hand a couple of times, he said, "No, I don't think so. I hardly ever use these things. I save most of my stuff to the cloud. Not much I want to save anyway. The wrong people might see it. Where did you find it?"

I pointed to the spot. "I guess we'll have to plug it in and see if the owner put their name on whatever's on it."

Charlie twisted his lips to one side. "I don't know, Jen. The drive could have a virus or malware on it. Maybe we should just hold it and wait for someone to ask about it."

I sighed. "You're probably right, but my gut tells me Watkins dropped the thing. He's the only one who's been in here not shopping for books. And he squatted to examine all the bottom shelves. How else could a flash drive have ended up wedged down there?"

"I think you've got another case of wishful thinking. Anyone could've brought that in and dropped it. Probably a student."

"They email or upload all their stuff now, don't they?"

"I don't know. I've been out of school almost as long as you have. Could be." His face brightened. "I have an old laptop and I wouldn't care if it got compromised. If you want, I can run home and get it."

"Would you mind? I'm dying to know what's on this. I guess I've been hanging around Angus, the Gossip King, too long."

"Definitely. I'll be right back."

Three customers came in as soon as he walked out the door as if they'd been waiting for him to leave. Not likely, however. Everyone loved Charlie. I made two lattes and fetched a copy of Colleen Hoover's *Ugly Love* from the stockroom for a brunette wearing thick glasses. The twenty-something latte drinkers settled on the couch, surfing on their phones.

The brunette checked out about the time Charlie returned. He set up the computer on the pastry case, and I joined him.

He plugged in the flash drive. "All right. Let's see what we've got."

One file came up, and he clicked on it. An Excel spreadsheet with no identifying information opened. It contained a list of Riddleton businesses, in alphabetical order, with numbers beside them.

I reached over Charlie's shoulder and scrolled down to Ravenous Readers. It had the number fifty beside it. Bob's Bakery had forty, and the Piggly Wiggly, two-fifty. I had no idea what it meant.

"What do you think?" I asked him.

"I don't know. It definitely wasn't dropped by a student, though."

"Probably not. But if it does belong to Watkins, what could all this mean?"

He shrugged. "For starters, I think it means he might not be a hitman after all. Other than that, it beats me."

My stomach twisted into a pretzel. If that was true, the suspect pool in Mara's murder was reduced by a third, leaving me treading water in the deep end. And I didn't swim very well.

CHAPTER TWENTY-FOUR

Charlie and I cleared the lunch rush, functioning in tandem as a team. Not many people actually worked in Riddleton, but many of those who did stopped by to browse before heading back to work. We managed to make a few sales, and so far, I considered our day without Lacey a success. Although I still had some doubts about our ability to manage without her during her maternity leave, they were starting to fade away. I hoped they'd disappear altogether by the time *she* did.

I had no time to consider whether Charlie had learned how to close the store out when Lacey came in a little after one. It turned out she had the same trouble following instructions I did. Must be why we got along so well.

"Why are you here?" I asked as she stowed her purse under the cash register.

"I told you I'd be in this afternoon."

"And I told you to take the day off. We're okay."

She set her hands on her hips. "And so am I. Stop being a Nervous Nellie."

"Well, excuse me for caring about you," I said in faux irritation.

"You're excused. Don't let it happen again." She smiled. "Besides, don't you have a book to write?"

"I do, but there's no way I can concentrate with so much other stuff going on. If I go on trial for murder, I'll be too busy to write anyway."

"It'll take at least a year for your trial date to come up. Your deadline's in six months, right? You'll have plenty of time."

I laughed. "In my dreams. Besides, if it's all the same to you, I'd just as soon not have a trial. I fully intend to get myself off the hook long before then."

"I hope you're right. Good luck."

"Thanks. Since you're here, there *is* something I can do toward that end. Are you sure you want to stay? I really don't mind working for you."

"Positive." Lacey gestured toward the door. "Go do what you need to do. I want you to be around to work for me next time."

"Next time? Uh-uh. You're never allowed to get sick again." I pulled out my cell phone and pressed the icon beside Brittany's photo. She answered on the second ring.

"What are you doing right now?" I asked after we exchanged greetings.

"Nothing important. Why?"

"Lacey's here, so I thought we could run up to the house this afternoon instead of waiting until tomorrow.

Everyone will be at the memorial, so we won't have to worry about getting caught."

"I thought you wanted to go to the memorial."

I worried my lower lip. "I'd be walking right back into Fredo's clutches. Let's go out to the house and look around instead."

She blew air into the phone. "I'm still not convinced it's such a smart choice, Jen."

"I know, but if the police didn't find any evidence I was there, they had to have missed something. Havermayer says she believes me. However, I'm still out on bail for the murder. She said the ADA won't drop the charges without proof. I need to locate something to prove my story isn't made up."

"Okay. Give me an hour, and I'll be ready to go."

"Great. That'll allow me time to take care of Savannah. Poor baby's been cooped up in the apartment all morning."

"See you then."

I hung up and glanced out the window toward Antonio's. The memorial started at two, but a few cars were already parked in front of the restaurant. Gil had asked me to attend, but being in the same room with Fredo, the man who may have kidnapped me, probably wasn't a wise thing to do. He might take advantage of the opportunity to try again. Or worse.

My German shepherd bounded toward me as I walked through the door, smacking everything within reach with her tail. She was the only one in my life who loved me no matter what. And I had only to show up.

My heart filled as I kissed her between the eyes, and she rewarded me with a sloppy lick on the cheek.

I wiped away the drool and reached for her leash. "Come on, kid, let's go for a walk."

We negotiated the steps and made our obligatory stop at the oak tree. If they ever cut that thing down, my dog would never relieve herself again. Fortunately, it had been there for a hundred years and would likely stand for a hundred more. Riddleton wasn't known for making changes. Too much push-back from the residents for whom change was a crime that should be punishable by death. I wondered once if I wasn't becoming one of them, then immediately put it out of my mind. I probably was, though.

The rest of the trip around the block was tedious but uneventful. Every tree, fire hydrant, and blade of grass had to be examined, or Savannah's life was incomplete. Still, it made her happy, and I had the time, so why not? I still had a half hour to spare before picking up Brittany when we returned to the apartment.

When we got back I slapped a peanut butter sandwich together, washing it down with cold coffee left in my cup from this morning. A quick stick-to-your-ribs meal topped off with an energy boost. Perfect for an afternoon of evidence gathering. Assuming there'd be evidence left to gather. There had to be. I couldn't have the police believing I'd devised a story to fool them into thinking I was innocent. Especially since I *was* innocent.

Leaving a bowl full of kibble, fresh water, and a rawhide chew for Savannah behind, I tapped on Brittany's door, then let myself in. "You ready?"

She replied from the bathroom. "Almost. Just let me finish brushing my teeth."

"Brushing your teeth? You meeting someone there I don't know about?"

She came out, wiping her mouth on a towel. "You never know. My mother taught me to always be prepared."

"She also taught you to wear makeup and fix your hair just to go to the mailbox, and I don't see you doing that either."

"Yeah, well, you can't have everything." She threw a yellow cardigan on over her floral-print blouse. "Okay, I'm ready. Let's go."

"Yes, ma'am. Do you remember how to get there? I slept through the trip there and was a little too rattled to keep track on the drive back."

"I can't imagine why," she said with a grin. "I think I can find it. You want me to drive?"

"Might as well. It's either that or listen to you complain the whole way."

"I only complain because you're such a lousy driver."

We trotted down the steps to her blue Chevy Cruze, parked beside my Dodge. "I am not. You just can't stand that I refuse to creep along at five miles an hour below the speed limit."

"No, I complain because my arms get tired from being braced against the dashboard the whole way."

I slid into the passenger seat and buckled up while Brittany started the car. The trip seemed shorter than I'd expected, even with a couple of wrong turns included. Within thirty minutes, we stopped in front of a gray clapboard building in the middle of nowhere. The basement door, through which I'd escaped, was easy to see as we pulled up. Too bad I was unconscious the first time. It would've saved a lot of time searching.

Brittany cut the engine and turned to face me. "Okay, what now?"

"Now, we go inside and find proof that I've been here before." I released my seatbelt and jumped out of the vehicle.

She did the same, and we climbed a half-dozen wooden steps to the front door. I knocked and waited for a response. Just because we assumed nobody would be there didn't make it true. Although, what I'd say if someone answered, I hadn't considered. Fortunately, I didn't have to come up with anything. Nobody did.

I tried the knob, but it refused to turn. "It's locked."

A flower pot with no flowers sat on the wraparound porch beside the entrance. "Maybe there's a spare key around somewhere." Brittany dug through the plant-free dirt. When she came up empty, she lifted it to look underneath. Nothing there or on top of the doorframe either. "Is there a back door?"

"I have no idea. I didn't exactly memorize the layout the other night. I was a little preoccupied with getting as far away from here as possible, as quickly as possible."

"Why? Didn't you like it here?" Brittany laughed and took my hand. "Come on, let's check in the back."

We trotted down the steps and turned the corner. I tried the basement door as we passed, but it too was locked. We continued to the rear entrance, which faced a grassy yard surrounded by trees. Whoever owned this place clearly enjoyed their privacy.

Brittany tried the door while I peered through a window into a kitchen with appliances left from when a refrigerator was still called a Frigidaire.

"Any luck?" I asked.

"Nope. This house is buttoned up tight."

"Maybe, but I'm not ready to give up yet." No flower pots rested on the back porch, so I slid my hand across the top of the doorjamb, hoping for a key. Not this time. "Let's check the windows. We could luck out and find an open one. If not, we might just have to break one."

"Oh, no. I'm not breaking into this house." Brittany folded her arms across her chest. "Orange isn't my best color, either."

"I look terrible in orange, which is why we have to do this." I pushed up on the window I'd just been looking in. It didn't budge.

Brittany tried the one on the other side of the door. The window moved an inch, then stopped. "Hey, I think this one is open. It's just stuck."

"Maybe if we work together, we can get it." I joined her and placed both hands on my side of the top. "You ready?"

She did the same and nodded. Together we pushed up as hard as we could without success. The window was stuck fast.

I wiped gray paint flecks off my palms onto my jeans. "We need something to pry it open," I said, resting my hands on my hips. "Maybe a big stick or something."

"We could just try the other windows," Brittany said.

"They're too high off the ground. It's this one or nothing. And nothing isn't an option."

We searched the porch for any object we could use for leverage without finding anything. I ventured down into the yard and checked beneath the porch. A Sixties-era foot-brake bicycle, a lawn mower, and a rusted wheelbarrow with no wheel greeted me. I duck-walked underneath, hoping something useful would present itself. No such luck.

I then scoured the grass to the other end of the porch but still saw nothing we could use to raise the window. When I came out the other side, I stood and examined the side of the house to confirm my suspicion that the windows were too high for us to reach. Unfortunately, I was right. However, my gaze fell on a shovel propped against the clapboard about halfway down, which we could use to our advantage.

Brittany hung over the rail, watching, and I said, "I think I have something," and sprinted to the shovel we might use as a lever. I grabbed it, careful to avoid splinters, and carried it back to the steps. "Think this'll work?"

"It's worth a try."

Just enough space remained between the window and the sill for the shovel's blade. Once in position, I leaned all my weight on the handle. The window moved about another inch and stuck again. We had to get this thing open. It was our only way in.

I pounded on the sides of the wooden window frame and tried again. This time, we gained three more inches, which maxed out our leverage. I refused to give up.

I gripped the bottom of the window and pulled with all my strength. The window shot up the frame, glass rattling. I covered my head, expecting it to shatter into a million pieces, but it didn't break. We were in.

I swung my leg over the window sill and said, "Wait here. I'll let you in the door."

Brittany nodded, looking around nervously. "I hope nobody heard that."

"Nobody like who? I don't think there's another soul around here for miles."

"I hope you're right."

I dropped to the yellowed linoleum floor and unlocked the back door for Brittany. She closed it behind her. "Where to now?"

"I'm not sure." I pictured the basement layout in my mind. The stairs leading to this floor had been to my right when I sat on the mat. The outside door was on the left in the center of the wall. Since the kitchen was in the back middle of the first floor, the door to the stairs had to be on the left side of the room.

The sink behind us led to a counter, which ended at the stove beside the circa 1950s refrigerator. On the other side of the fridge was a deadbolted door. That had to be it. I strode across the room, slid the deadbolt open, and turned the knob. The door opened onto stairs leading down. I flipped the light switch on the wall inside the kitchen next to the door, illuminating the staircase.

I waved Brittany over and headed down. "This was where they kept me." When we reached the bottom, I pointed out where the mat and supplies had been. The Sheetrock I'd damaged had all been removed, and the boxes were stacked against the opposite wall again. The furniture store was still there too. The floor had been swept, and all signs of my presence had disappeared. Havermayer hadn't exaggerated. No evidence of my kidnapping remained.

"What do you think?" Brittany asked.

"I think we need to dump out those boxes again. My only hope of proving I'm not a raving lunatic or a liar lies in the box with the tools I used to rip open the drywall."

"Unless they took the tools with them."

"If they did, I'm finished. I can't think of any other way to prove I was held captive here. However, I'm hoping they didn't recognize the significance and just loaded the nail puller and hammer into a box with all the other junk."

"I hope you're right." Brittany pulled down the first carton on the right and rifled through old clothing and miscellaneous papers.

I took the first box on the left and emptied it. "Don't worry about making a mess. We must find something with my fingerprints on it and get out of here as soon as possible."

The one I'd dumped had photographs and frames mixed with clothing. Moving on to the next one, I continued until Brittany upended a carton of assorted items, including a clothing item that hit the floor with a thud.

I instinctively grabbed her arm. "Hold on a second. There's something wrapped in that T-shirt." I started to unroll it, then stopped. "Video this, so Havermayer can't accuse us of planting it."

Brittany pulled out her phone and began recording.

I unrolled the shirt and revealed the contents. It was the nail puller. I held it out toward Brittany, touching only the T-shirt. I didn't want Havermayer accusing me of planting my fingerprints either. "This is what I used to break through the wall. It's exactly what we need to prove I was here. I only hope they didn't wipe it clean of prints before they hid it away."

I carefully wrapped the tool in the T-shirt as we'd found it. "Let's go see Detective Havermayer."

CHAPTER TWENTY-FIVE

Savannah and I waited by the Riddleton Park gate for the rest of the runners to arrive Saturday morning. I stretched out on the stone bench and dozed while she lay on the ground beneath. A restless night filled with bizarre dreams of being entombed woke me early but not early enough to do anything else. Not that I could focus on much anyway.

How much longer would I be free to hang out on a bench by the park? A year, perhaps, as long as I showed up for all my court dates. Which meant I had a year to finish the next two books in my series and fulfill my obligation. Assuming I could break the writer's block. Would anyone buy the books after I'd been convicted of murder? Probably. It wasn't like this case would make national news. And some might buy them *because* I'd been convicted.

However, I also had a year to find an alternate suspect for Mara's murder. If I wanted this mind-numbing cloud hanging over me until then. An impossible situation. I'd made no progress toward solidifying the bookstore's future and hadn't written a word since my initial arrest. What made me think I could finish the books under these conditions? I couldn't continue living this way. I couldn't even really call it living.

Ingrid and Eric arrived simultaneously and strolled up from the parking lot together. I sat up, and Ingrid slid in beside me. "How are you feeling, luv?"

Savannah rested her head in Ingrid's lap, tail whipping back and forth. Ingrid stroked her neck while awaiting my response.

"I'm fine. Exhausted but having trouble sleeping. And when I do finally fall asleep, I have all kinds of weird nightmares. It's driving me crazy."

Eric kissed me on top of my head and dangled his white neck towel for Savannah to play tug. She happily obliged, grabbing the end and dropping into a bow.

Over her playful growls, Ingrid said, "I'll bet. If you want, I can give you something to help you sleep."

"No, thanks. Not yet, anyway. I've had enough drugs in my system lately. I don't need any more."

"Have they established what you were drugged with?"

I peered at Eric.

He squeezed my knee. "You were injected with GHB. There were trace amounts left in your bloodstream. A few more hours and it would've been completely gone. I'm glad we didn't wait to go to the hospital."

"The date rape drug? But I wasn't raped. I'm sure of it."

Ingrid smiled. "You weren't on a date, either, luv. It seems they used the drug to make it easier to transport and confine you."

"Super. Eric, has Havermayer arrested Fredo yet?"

He presented the towel for Savannah to grab again. "Not yet. She arranged for him to come in for questioning, but he never showed. She tried to pick him up after the memorial, but he disappeared sometime between his eulogy and her arrival. We can't find him anywhere. We're monitoring his credit cards, the airport, and the train and bus stations. He won't get far, don't worry."

Ingrid touched Eric's arm to halt the battle for towel supremacy. "What about his mobile phone? Can you track that the way you did to find Jen?"

"It's turned off. He probably trashed it after he realized that's how we found him in the first place. Assuming he figured it out, of course."

I rubbed Savannah's neck to ease her disappointment at the war being cut short. "I'd love to know what he hoped to gain by kidnapping me. He obviously planned to keep me for a while. But why?"

Eric stared into the park, then back at me. "I guess it's okay to tell you this. We think he wanted to hold you until you missed a court appearance. Then the judge would issue a bench warrant and revoke your bail. It's the only thing that makes any sense."

"And I wouldn't be able to investigate him anymore."

"Exactly."

"But Ted hasn't told me about any other scheduled court appearances. How long was he planning to hold me?"

Eric took my hand. "The next appearance probably hasn't been scheduled yet, but there will be more coming up soon. And you'll have to be there for all of them. Either way, I'm glad you got away and we found you."

"Me too." I smiled at him. "If you believe he might be guilty, shouldn't they drop the charges against me?"

"Havermayer won't consider recommending it until she has enough evidence to convince the prosecutor. He's in charge now."

I lifted the corner of my mouth into a half-smile. "At least I've finally convinced your boss I'm innocent."

"I wouldn't go that far, but she's considering the possibility. I call that progress."

Ingrid stood and began stretching her upper body. "Does this mean you're allowed to work the case, Eric?"

"Some aspects of it. I can work the kidnapping but not the murder. I probably shouldn't even be working that, but our department is so small we have to sidestep the rules sometimes. There just aren't enough detectives to go around. Working the kidnapping is something, anyway. I don't feel so helpless anymore."

Angus and Lacey arrived at eight on the dot, and we moved into the park for our stretching session. *Ugh*. Even after all this time, my muscles still rebelled. Some people just weren't meant to be flexible. I firmly believed that.

When I completed my fifteen minutes of torture—made much more interesting by Savannah's insistence on moving in the opposite direction no matter which way I needed to go—I corralled Lacey. "Are you sure you should be here this morning?"

"Why not? Pregnant women are encouraged to continue their normal activities for as long as possible. Especially exercise."

"What about your dizzy spells?"

She smiled. "Well, if nothing else, running will keep my blood pressure up. At least while I'm doing it. Besides, I'm fine. I had a rough run of morning sickness yesterday, not dizzy spells. I didn't think our customers would appreciate my sprinting away to vomit every ten minutes, so I didn't come in until I felt better."

I held her gaze, trying to come up with a relevant argument. My brain came up blank. As usual. "I'm worried about you, that's all. I don't want anything to happen to you or the baby."

"Thank you." She stepped away, then turned back. "Almost forgot. Ben is picking up his brother's truck and dropping it by the store later, so we can collect the stuff Gil's giving us."

Stuff? Right. Bookcases and books. I'd forgotten all about it. "Awesome! Thank him for me. I'll call Gil and make the arrangements."

She nodded and took off down the path with Eric and Ingrid.

Angus, Savannah, and I jogged side-by-side-by-side, competing for the trophy labeled: slowest pace that could still be considered running. Actually, my German shepherd barely achieved a good trot beside me at the end of her leash. Poor thing couldn't count on me for a good workout. She didn't seem to mind, though.

When we achieved our normal rhythm, Angus said,

"I heard they arrested you the other day. I'm sorry. What evidence do they have?"

I curled my hands into fists, then shook them out. "Other than the fact that I was there, left my fingerprints and DNA on her neck, and dog hair on her scarf? Nothing. And what's my motive? According to Havermayer, I killed her because she was opening a competing bookstore. I mean really, what kind of reason is that for a regular person to commit murder? A sociopath or a psycho, maybe. But me? Come on. It's ridiculous."

Angus said nothing.

I sighed. "Yes, I know. They have more than enough to prosecute, but I didn't do it."

"I believe that. But how do you prove a negative? It's almost impossible to prove you didn't do something unless somebody sees you doing something else. Which I assume nobody did?"

"Nope. I have no alibi for the time of the murder."

"Sounds like there's too much evidence against you. Are you having any luck finding an alternate suspect?"

"Yes and no. I have a few ideas but can't find any proof to back them up. Or a motive. The most obvious choice is the husband, Fredo. But why would he kill his wife?"

Angus counted on his fingers. "Money, jealousy, hatred. All three? Maybe he wanted her share of the restaurant. Or she was having an affair."

"Speaking of affairs, word on the street is you have a secret girlfriend, possibly married. What's up with that?"

He stopped running to stare at me, slack-jawed. "What are you talking about?"

Savannah poked my hand. I started up again, and he followed. "You can tell me. I won't say anything. Who is she?"

"There is no *she*. I don't have a girlfriend, married or otherwise."

Defensive much, Angus? "So, who did you buy that scarf for? It was just like the one Mara wore the day she died."

"I know you don't believe it, but some things really are coincidental. I sent that scarf to my niece in New Hampshire. You can check with Brianna, the post office clerk, Nancy Drew. I mailed it out last Monday."

"Okay, don't get snippy. I was only teasing you."

His face reddened. Something I didn't think possible since the exertion needed to run usually took care of that pretty well. "Sorry. I was shocked that you would ask me something like that. I'd never be involved with a married woman. Nobody's ever even accused me of it, and people ask me about my love life all the time. It's irritating."

"I get it. Before Eric came along, I had the same problem. Between that and questions about my next book, I'm surprised I never hurt anyone."

"You could never hurt anyone."

"Tell that to Detective Havermayer."

"She'll figure it out one of these days."

I didn't bother to reply. My feelings on the subject were well documented.

My activities the past few days caught up with me at the one-lap mark, and somebody dropped a load of bricks on my back. Pushing my leaden legs forward required more energy than I could muster. Brain fog rolled in. "Angus, I think I'm going to call it a day."

"Are you okay?"

"Yeah, I'm just tired. Everything's catching up with me."

"I'm not surprised. Honestly, I didn't expect to see you today. Do you want me to drive you home?"

The prospect of dozing in his front seat seemed much more appealing than the two-block walk back to my apartment, but he loved his Saturday morning run. It would be unfair of me to cut it short. "No, thanks. I'll be okay."

I dropped off at the gate and waited for the rest of the gang to catch up, so I could say my goodbyes. If I'd left without explanation, Eric would be upset, assuming the worst. I'd worked hard at learning to consider his feelings. Our relationship had improved because of it, and I didn't want to risk messing up again.

Eric stopped when he spotted me standing there and wiped the sweat off his forehead with his towel. "Are you okay?"

I nodded. "I'm going home. I guess I wasn't ready for this yet."

"I wondered about that when I saw you here this morning, but I didn't want to say anything." He grinned. "Trying to keep the peace."

"I appreciate that. I'm trying too, you know."

"I've noticed. Go on home and get some rest. I'll call you later."

My ringing phone pried me out of a deep, dreamless sleep. I rolled over to grab it off the nightstand and discovered the hard way Savannah had pushed me to the edge of the bed. I landed on the floor with a thud, and when I glanced up, my dog peered at me with a "What are you doing down there, Mom?" expression on her face. I glared at her and answered the call.

"Tell me you love me."

Huh? I checked the phone screen. Charlie Nichols was printed across it. "What are you talking about, Charlie?"

"I just did something great. Tell me you love me!" His excitement rushed through the phone like a kid who'd found a pony under the Christmas tree.

I sat up and rubbed my eyes with my free hand. "Okay, I love you. What's going on?"

"I found Steven Watkins, only his real name is Simeon Kirby, and he's not a hitman from Chicago. He's a real estate developer from Spartanburg, specializing in building tourist areas. He wants to turn Riddleton into the next Myrtle Beach! Isn't that exciting?"

Exciting? Not the word I'd use. "What are you talking about? And how do you know all this? Did you hack into his emails or something?"

He giggled. "A magician never reveals his secrets. Besides, you don't want to know. Call it plausible deniability."

I suspected he was right. I didn't want to know. "What's his fascination with Riddleton? We're a sleepy little town. Tourists aren't interested in us."

"Not right now, but they will be if he has his way. He's been buying up property on Lake Destin. I think he wants to build a resort on it. Tourists will be interested in that."

"So, why all the secrecy?"

"If his plan got out, the property values would go up, and he'd have to pay more for the land. This way, people think he's buying for personal use and will sell at the current rate. It's the same thing Disney did in Florida when he needed land to build Disney World."

Savannah jumped off the bed and squeezed into my lap. I switched the phone to my other hand and scratched her chest, allowing my brain time to absorb the new information. I didn't share Charlie's enthusiasm for the planned development. I loved my sleepy little town. "Why are you so excited?"

"Don't you see? More people means more business for the bookstore. All we have to do is hang on until the tourists come. We're going to make it!"

I'd been to Myrtle Beach in the summer. Visions of packed sidewalks and bumper-to-bumper traffic zoomed through my head. I didn't enjoy the visit, and I certainly didn't want to live that way. But more important, I'd lost one of my suspects in Mara's murder.

I told Charlie I'd see him later and wrapped my arms around Savannah, burying my nose in her fur.

"What're we gonna do now, little girl?"

CHAPTER TWENTY-SIX

After I finished my shower and dressed, I found Savannah prancing in the living room, swinging her leash around her face. I turned my head to the side and reached into the combat zone to take it away from her. The flying clip on the end had come too close to her eye for my comfort. The vet, Dr. Felton, didn't work on Saturday, and I wasn't up to an emergency trip to Blackburn. My bank account wasn't either.

My legs had lost ten pounds each while I napped, and I skipped down the steps behind my dog. While Savannah made her oak-tree stop, I noticed the dark clouds gathering on the horizon, and the air had cooled ten degrees since this morning. We were in for a nasty afternoon. I suspected our bookcase-moving operation might be rained out. With luck, Ben's brother wouldn't need that truck back today.

The spring in my step abated in the gloom, which now matched my mood. Charlie's news sliced through me like a double-edged sword. Not only was Simeon

Kirby about to upend my world, but he also had nothing to do with Mara's murder. How much time had I spent investigating him that I could've used to find another suspect? In my defense, there *were* no other apparent options. There had to be someone, though. What did I miss?

One thing that kept nagging at me was the other man with Fredo the night he kidnapped me. Who was he? Fredo was the one who said they should get rid of me. I was almost sure of that. So, Fredo must have the most to lose if I continued to investigate. There could only be one reason. When the police found Fredo, they'd have Mara's killer in custody. Then they'd have to let me go. It was the only thing that made sense.

Obviously, Fredo didn't get his way that night. I was still here. Of course, I might've escaped before they could finish the job. Either way, the other guy delayed the operation long enough for me to get away. Except the supplies they left indicated they had no intention of getting rid of me when they nabbed me. What changed?

Maybe nothing changed. Maybe the two men had competing intentions to begin with. Fredo needed help to control me. Perhaps his accomplice refused to participate if it meant killing me, so Fredo told him what he wanted to hear to gain his cooperation. The truth came out, and they argued, giving me time to escape. So, who was the other guy?

Fredo hadn't lived here very long. Who would he know well enough to ask for help committing a felony after such a short time? Riddleton wasn't rife with criminals. In fact, the crime rate was negligible. A shoplifter or an occasional spat between neighbors constituted the bulk of what kept our patrol officers busy. We didn't even have a noticeable drug problem. Sure, some people probably indulged in private, but I'd never seen a dealer on any street corner in town. Or anywhere else, for that matter.

It made more sense for the second man to be someone Fredo brought with him to Riddleton. Since the only people who accompanied him that I was aware of were Mara and Gil, and Mara was dead, it had to be Gil. His sensitivity had shown through every time I'd spoken with him. It made sense that he provided the supplies meant to keep me alive and relatively comfortable given the circumstances.

But how to prove it? I couldn't go to Havermayer pointing a finger at him without evidence. Food, water, and toilet paper wouldn't be enough to convince her. The overheard half of a conversation wouldn't work either, since it was Fredo's voice I recognized, not Gil's.

I had to talk to Gil. Convince him to confess.

By the time we trotted back up the steps, I'd regained some of my earlier optimism. Even the darkening sky couldn't detract from my belief that I'd finally cracked the case. Come Monday, this would all be over, and I could get back to working on solutions to Ravenous Readers' problems and writing my book. If I could convince Gil to confess to participating in the kidnapping, I could put this whole ordeal behind me.

In a perfect scenario, Gil would plead guilty to kidnapping charges, and then the prosecutor could offer him a lighter sentence for testifying against Fredo for Mara's murder. I had to make Havermayer see the logic. Then she could lay it out for the assistant district attorney, who would make the deal. It wasn't a perfect solution, but it closed both cases. A win for everyone. Except Mara, of course.

If I can convince him to confess.

I gave Savannah a chew stick and her stuffed monkey and told her I'd be back in a few hours. Most people would tell me she couldn't understand what I said, but I knew better. She might not comprehend each individual word but always got the general idea. That's all that mattered. She was my buddy, and I never lied to my buddy. Well, almost never.

Zipping up my jacket, I stuffed my hands in my pockets and ducked my head against the wind, which had picked up since a little while ago. The black sky hovered low enough that it seemed I could almost touch it. Lightning crackled in the distance, and I picked up my pace. This wasn't the kind of storm I wanted to get caught in. It would come in fast and hard, but maybe it would blow over soon enough for me to pick up the bookcases this afternoon.

I called Gil and arranged to meet him at his store at one, then hustled down the deserted street, determined to reach the bookstore before the first drop of rain fell. Not that I cared about getting wet, but one drop would quickly be followed by a thousand more, along with thunder, lightning, and possibly hail. Being pounded by miniature ice balls wasn't my idea of a fun way to spend the afternoon. More like torture, second only to waterboarding, and I had no secrets to tell to make it stop.

Ravenous Readers had no customers, which didn't surprise me. I wouldn't have risked being caught in the storm if I didn't have to. I'd much rather be curled up on the couch in my warm, cozy apartment, reading a good book. Or better yet, writing one. My book-three deadline grew nearer every day, and I was no closer to finishing it than I was four days ago.

Lacey knelt behind the showcase beside the cash register. I leaned on the top, watching her through the glass. "What're you doing?"

She looked up with a stack of bookmarks in each hand. "I'm rearranging this case. People seem to buy the ones closest to the register more often, so I'm moving the ones in the back forward. Then I'll know if they're buying the others because they like them best or only because they're the ones they see while checking out. Make sense?"

"Absolutely. That's a great idea." One I'd never have thought of in a million years. As a manager, Lacey brought little things to the table that I couldn't. Even if I learned all the details of running the store, the little things made the difference between success and mediocrity or, even worse, downright failure. The things I'd have to work here for years to learn. I dreaded the prospect of her maternity leave. However, I dreaded the possibility of not being here for it even more. No bookmarks in a jail cell. Probably not even in the prison library.

A thunderclap rattled the windows, and buckets of rain fell out of the sky. I moved toward the front of the store. The raindrops bounced a foot off the sidewalk before settling into puddles blocking the door. At this rate, I might have to swim to the truck when it subsided. And I'd have to dry out the bed before I could load it. If the cartons got wet, it would ruin the books inside. Not to mention the bookcases warping when they dried. Or worse, falling apart if Mara hadn't purchased high-quality equipment.

I wandered back to the coffee bar and filled my "Writer in Residence" cup. After doctoring the brew with cream and sugar, I watched the rain fall so hard I could barely see Antonio's across the street. Nothing like a January thunderstorm to brighten my day.

Charlie, still wearing his uniform, was in his usual position: hunched over his laptop. He glanced up and turned the screen so I could see it. "I've been looking at the spreadsheet from the flash drive, and I think I know what it is."

The mysterious list of business names and numbers covered the screen. "Oh yeah?"

"Maybe. I'm only guessing, but since Kirby's a real estate developer, these numbers might be the value of each business. Or what he's willing to pay for them, anyway."

My eyebrows shot up. "You think he wants to buy up the whole town? Why?"

"I've been looking at some of the other places he's worked in, and he might tear down the buildings and use the land for hotels and the kinds of unique shops tourists like. He's done it before. Why not here too?"

"Holy crap. You think he wants to turn Riddleton into Kirbyville?"

"It's possible. And as Steven Watkins, he could buy everything on the down-low. Nobody would ever realize what was happening until it's too late."

My stomach did a handstand. "We can't let that happen."

"How would we stop it?"

Any way we can! "By making sure everybody knows what he's doing."

He closed the computer. "But why would they believe us? We don't have any proof."

It always came down to proof. Something I almost never had. "I don't know. We'll figure something out."

"Speaking of figuring things out, have you come up with anything to keep us afloat yet?"

The million-dollar question. "Honestly, with everything that's going on right now, I haven't thought about it. I didn't even make it to the bank to ask for a loan. It would've been a waste of time anyway. They won't lend money to someone awaiting a murder trial."

"That's never gonna happen, Jen. You'll find the real killer long before then. I have faith in you."

I blew on my coffee to cool it. "Thanks, but even if I think I know who it is, I still have to prove it. And the evidence has to be irrefutable, or the ADA won't consider it."

"How can I help?"

I wished I knew. "If I think of something, I'll let you know."

The rain slowed to a drizzle, then finally stopped. The clouds parted, and a sliver of sunlight peeked through. I might be able to salvage something of this afternoon, after all. I walked outside to assess the damage. Leaves and twigs floated in the sidewalk puddles, and a river rushed along the curb into the storm drain. The aroma of petrichor drifted in the air.

Ben's brother's truck had collected about an inch of rain in the bed. I lowered the tailgate and climbed in, looking for the drainage plugs. When I pulled the black plastic caps, it had little effect. The truck was parked on level ground. Gravity was no help.

"You want to try this?"

I turned to find Lacey holding the squeegee she used to clean the windows. "Good idea, thanks." I took it from her and went to work. "We'll get you another one if I mess it up."

"No problem. I hate washing the windows anyway."

With the squeegee pushing the water toward the drains and the opening between the tailgate and the truck bed, it only took a few minutes to clear the bulk of it. I wiped my wet hands on my jeans and jumped down. "Now, I only need a towel to sop up the rest. I'll swing by home on my way to meet Gil."

Lacey put up her hand. "Hold on. I might have one in the car."

I cocked an eyebrow. "You carry extra towels in your car?"

"I have two kids. I carry everything."

She returned a minute later with a red, white, and blue striped beach towel, which had Myrtle Beach emblazoned on it. "Here you go. I shook it out, but it probably still has some sand in it."

"I'll clean out the truck before I bring it back. I don't want to end up on your brother-in-law's hit list too."

Lacey laughed and waved her hand. "Nah. Don't worry about that. He's a pussy cat, just like Ben."

"Glad to hear it." I checked my phone for the time—12:55. "I need to go meet Gil. I can load the book cartons myself, but I might need Charlie's help with the bookcases if you can spare him. We'll see when I bring back the first load."

She grabbed my sleeve. "Are you sure Gil's still okay with you taking this stuff? You hadn't been accused of murdering his sister when he made the offer."

"He seemed all right when I spoke with him on the phone."

"Yeah, but what if it's a ruse to get you there so he can take his revenge or something? Mara tried to put you out of business because she believed you had something to do with Tony's death. You said yourself the two of them were very close. Now his father and sister are both dead, and you're in the middle of it."

"I'll be careful. If he makes me uncomfortable in any way, I'll leave."

"I don't know, Jen." She rested her top teeth on her lower lip. "Maybe you should take Charlie with you just in case."

The picture of Charlie in a Superman suit with his chest puffed out and hands on his hips flashed into my mind. I smiled. "If anything seems the least bit off, I'll come back and get him. I promise I won't do anything foolish."

She nodded. "I can see nothing I say will change your mind, so I'll just have to trust you. See you in a bit."

I climbed in the pickup and drove toward Mara's store.

CHAPTER TWENTY-SEVEN

I eased to a stop in front of the almost empty building once meant to be a used bookstore. My slick hand slid on the shifter as I moved it into the park position, and my heart did a somersault. Maybe Lacey was right. I should've brought Charlie along. If Gil really was the second kidnapper, I could be walking into a trap. He sounded fine on the phone, but maybe that was just to lure me in. To make me feel comfortable enough to be alone with him. And he didn't know I suspected him. Too bad I didn't think of all this before.

Deep breath in, slow breath out.

My pulse slowed, and I stepped out of the truck, lowered the tailgate, and headed for the door. After another deep breath, I turned the knob and went inside. As soon as I crossed the threshold, my heart hammered in my ears. But the front room was empty, the same as during my previous visit.

I walked through the doorway into the back room. Eight six-shelf oak bookcases were stacked against one wall with roughly two dozen medium-sized cartons piled in front of them. The lacquered oak wouldn't match the cherry bookcases we had on the main sales floor, but since they were all going in the kids' section, it shouldn't matter much. We could always paint them the same color if customers found the difference jarring. I doubted anyone would care, though.

I called out, "Gil?"

"In here," he replied from the office.

When I entered, he was sitting at the desk, holding a framed photograph against his pinstriped oxford shirt. He turned his tear-stained face toward me. "Hi, Jen. I guess you're here to pick up your stuff."

"I am, but if it's not a good time . . ."

He put the photo into the center desk drawer and clasped his hands on the cluttered blotter. "No, it's fine. I was just looking at some old pictures. The memories got to me. Besides, all this stuff has to be out of here by Monday, so today is perfect."

Gil had taken his sister's death hard, and I struggled to match the guy in front of me to the man who helped kidnap me the other night. Could I be wrong about him? Anything was possible, but I still couldn't fathom who else that second person could be. Who else would believe I was relevant enough to kidnap? And it had to be someone Fredo was subservient to.

Granted, I knew nothing about Fredo's friends. Maybe he *did* meet someone here he convinced to help him. The other person involved seemed in charge, though. Fredo had to ask permission to get rid of me. Did Gil strike me as someone who could orchestrate a kidnapping and murder? No way. Perhaps I was reading it wrong. I couldn't accurately assess the situation based on one statement I barely heard through the ceiling.

I had to move forward as if Gil was the second man and let him try to convince me otherwise. If I didn't, I was back to where I started, with no suspects, which was nowhere at all. Still, was that a good enough reason to accuse a potentially innocent man? Because I had nobody else? That would make me no better than Havermayer. I'd have to tread lightly.

"I'm sorry I missed the memorial yesterday."

He gripped his fingers together, forcing the blood out of his knuckles. "It's okay. I understand why you wouldn't want to be there."

No, he didn't. If he knew why I hadn't attended, this conversation would take on a very different tone. "I didn't think I'd be welcome. I've been arraigned for Mara's murder."

Gil winced. "If it matters any, I don't believe you killed her. Did you know my sister was afraid of her husband? Fredo should be arrested, not you. I'm sure he did it, but if I say anything, he'll kill me too." He covered his face with his hands. "I don't know what to do."

Maybe that was why he helped Fredo the other night. Fear. "You need to go to the police. Tell them what you know."

"That's just it. I don't *know* anything. I wasn't here. I didn't see it."

Though I agreed with him 100 percent, I played devil's advocate. "Then how do you know he's guilty? What makes you so sure it's not me? Or somebody else?"

Anger flashed across his face. "I don't know. But I'd like to believe you wouldn't be standing here right now, if you were guilty. As far as somebody else is concerned, who? Who else would want to kill my sister?" He stood with his hands flat on the desktop. "I think you'd better get your stuff and go before I change my mind."

I raised my hands in surrender and backed out of the office.

What just happened?

Gil's volatile reaction knocked me off balance. How did I proceed from here? I couldn't bring up the subject of the kidnapping or my idea for a deal with the prosecutor. Especially since he claimed to have no direct knowledge of Fredo's involvement in Mara's death. If he was telling the truth, I had to keep digging.

Fredo must've left some evidence behind, somewhere. But I'd been searching for a week. Surely, I'd have found *something* by now. Of course, there was always the possibility Gil was only trying to change the subject. It wouldn't be the first time someone pretended to be angry to end a conversation with me. Although, usually, they really were angry.

I loaded cartons, one at a time, into the truck bed. Having not considered how heavy boxes of books could be, I chided myself for not bringing the hand truck with me. Three cases down, and my arms were already tired. I had to keep going, though. Gil could change his mind anytime, and Lacey wanted the bookcases to expand the kids' section. This was the only way we'd be able to get them.

The fourth box was heavier than the others and slipped out of my hands when I lifted it. When it landed on an edge, the cardboard split and the contents spilled out. I had no time to deal with the situation now, so I pushed the carton to the side and grabbed another. When I took this load to the bookstore, we could unpack one and bring the empty back when we came to get the bookcases. Problem solved.

By the time I'd finished loading the rest of the boxes, my arms and legs dragged as if I'd just won an Olympic medal for weightlifting. Charlie was definitely coming back with me for the bookcases. Especially since I'd angered Gil, though I still had no idea how.

I knocked on his office door and waited for him to invite me in. No sense taking chances in his current mood. When he called me in, he sat behind the desk holding the same framed photo he'd had earlier, his face wet with tears. That picture meant a lot to him, it seemed.

"I'm taking this load to the store, and I'll be back for the bookcases. Will you be here a while longer?"

He nodded. "I have to run an errand later, but I'll wait for you to get back." His mood had shifted again, anger replaced by melancholy.

"Thanks." I left before his demeanor could change for a third time. Everyone processed grief differently, but his method seemed to include switching without warning from Jekyll to Hyde and back again. Was he unstable enough to have murdered Mara himself in a fit of pique?

I traversed the three blocks to Ravenous Readers, parked in the alley behind the store, and walked around to the front since I'd given Lacey the only key to the back door. I had to remember to have a copy made one of these days. On the sales floor, an assortment of books dotted the landscape, left by browsing people who'd decided not to buy. Lacey was helping a mother and daughter in the kids' section while Charlie cleared tables and straightened chairs.

"Busy afternoon?" I asked Charlie as he slid the last seat into place.

"It has been, actually."

"You got a minute to help me unload this truck?"

"You bet, boss."

I retrieved the hand truck on our way through the stockroom to the back door. Better late than never. Someday, I'd learn to think things all the way through before acting, but probably not anytime soon. Something to strive for, though.

With the proper equipment and another pair of hands, transferring the cartons to the stock room only took a few minutes. Charlie helped me empty a box to take back with me to replace the damaged one.

We headed back to the main floor. "Would you mind helping me with the bookcases? It'll go a lot quicker with two of us."

"Sure. Let me check with Lacey first to make sure she can spare me."

While he did that, I went back to the office to get a check for Gil. Five hundred dollars was a lot of money in our current financial position, but we couldn't buy eight matching bookcases for three times that much anywhere else. And it would make Lacey happy. Given all she'd done for me, I owed her a little joy.

Lacey cleared Charlie to help me and we took off for Gil's place. We pulled up to the building to find Gil waiting outside.

I climbed out of the pickup. "Sorry to hold you up." I reached into my pocket and retrieved the check. "Here you go. Five hundred, right? I didn't know who to make it out to, so I left it blank. I hope that's okay."

"That's fine." He folded it to put in his back pocket. "The door's open. I should be back before you're done."

"Probably so. It's going to take us a few trips."

He got in his gray Honda Accord and drove away.

I glanced at Charlie, and we both shrugged. Mr. Hyde had returned. I collected the empty box from the truck bed and carried it into the store. Having a perfect opportunity to examine the photo Gil found so fascinating, I handed the empty to Charlie and pointed to the damaged box. "Would you repack that for me, please? I want to take a look at something while he's gone."

He nodded with a smile and set to work.

The office was unlocked, and I slipped inside, closing the door behind me. Charlie would let me know if Gil returned before I came out. The desktop had been cleared, except for the blotter, as had the drawers beneath. When he left, Gil was empty-handed, although he could've already loaded the car while waiting for us to return. Even so, I searched for boxes he'd packed to take with him later just in case. The room was empty, but a closet door caught my eye.

I opened it and found three small boxes on the floor inside. Luckily, rather than seal them with tape, he'd only folded the flaps to close them. The first had office supplies of all shapes and sizes—pens, pads, sticky notes, etc. The second was filled with the kind of paperwork you'd expect for a newly opened business: inventory invoices, repair work orders, business license applications, et cetera. The one on the bottom held the desktop contents, including three silver-framed photographs. *Bingo!*

I pulled them out one at a time, careful not to smudge the glass. There was one of Mara and Tony, smiling on a beach somewhere. The one he'd been upset about? Probably, since they were both gone now. The second one had Mara, sporting her Libra necklace, beside Gil with a matching bracelet, on a boat, hair blowing in the wind.

The odd thought I'd had when I discovered Mara's body finally came to me. Mara wasn't wearing her necklace when I found her. She'd been wearing it that morning, but not after she died. What had happened to it? Could it be the one Gil had on when I spoke with him a few days later?

The third photo had Mara, Gil, and an older couple. I couldn't tell where from, but the older couple seemed familiar. I searched my memory until I found the answer. They were the two people in the pictures I'd found when I was searching for a tool to help me escape the basement.

The items in the boxes belonged to either Gil or Mara. Or both. Fredo and Mara had moved into

Tony's Walnut Street house, so it seemed likely that the basement I'd been imprisoned in belonged to Gil. My assumption now seemed confirmed. Gil was the second kidnapper.

I repacked the boxes and left them in the order I'd found them, then returned to the storeroom to help Charlie. I found him sitting on the floor, holding a small fireproof lockbox.

He held the gray container out to me. "Look what I found mixed in with all these books."

Strange. Why would a lockbox be hidden in a carton of used books? I shook it. It had weight, but nothing rattled. Safe to assume it was filled with important papers rather than the Scavuto family jewels. "Did you happen to find a key with it?"

"No, but it's not exactly gun safe. I should be able to pop that lock with a screwdriver."

"Maybe, but we should probably return it to Gil. It doesn't belong to us."

Charlie stood. "Technically, it does. You purchased all the boxes and their contents. And the contents weren't specified, were they?"

"No. I assumed they were filled with used books, so I never asked."

"There you go. That lockbox is yours to do whatever you want with it. So, what do you want to do?"

My conscience told me to return the box to Gil. But it might have a clue as to who murdered Mara. A clue I could get no other way. "I don't know, Charlie. Let me think on it a while. I'm not sure I feel comfortable keeping it."

"Okay." He took the lockbox, packed it with the books, and carried it to the truck.

We took four trips to carry the eight bookcases back to the bookstore, loading two at a time in the two-foot-deep truck bed. The only way to ensure none of them slid off onto the road. Gil returned as we packed the last load. His melancholy mood had returned, and I thanked him and left before I could upset him again.

Lacey had already begun emptying the small cases in the kids' section by the time we returned with the last two replacements. I shared my lockbox dilemma with her. Charlie brought it to us, along with a screwdriver.

"Well," Lacey said, wiping her dusty hands on her khakis. "You're both right. The box belongs to you, and the right thing to do is return it to the family."

Big help. "Gee, thanks, pal."

She held up her forefinger. "However, you suspect a family member of committing the murder, and that box might contain evidence that a family member would destroy. Perhaps you should give it to the police instead."

I shook my head. "Even though they probably have the key on Mara's keyring, they'd need a warrant to open it. Since they've already arrested me for the crime, it's not likely a judge would give them one."

Charlie waved his screwdriver at me, the question clear on his face.

"Okay, fine. Open it."

As good as his word, he popped the lock in a minute flat. Inside, we found a general assortment of personal papers, including Mara's passport and birth certificate. Near the bottom of the stack was a life insurance policy for half a million dollars, listing Gilberto Scavuto as the sole beneficiary. Fredo didn't get a dime of it.

The last document in the box was marked "Last Will and Testament." It belonged to Mara. I skimmed down to the bequests, and there was only one:

I leave all my worldly goods and possessions to my brother, Gilberto Scavuto.

I was wrong. If Fredo knew about this, he had no motive to kill his wife. But Gil did. A half million dollars and a restaurant's worth.

CHAPTER TWENTY-EIGHT

Since I was too dirty and disheveled after hauling around the bookcases and boxes to venture out in public, I went home to shower and change while Eric picked up pizza for us from the Italian place in Sutton. Savannah greeted me at the door as if I'd just been rescued from a deserted island in the Pacific after being stranded for years with no volleyball to keep me company. Her pure joy warmed my heart every time I walked in the door.

After a quick trip around the block, I fed and watered her, then peeled off my dirty clothes and dropped them in the hamper for washing at a date to be determined later. Much later, probably. That would be one good thing about prison. Unless I got stuck working in the laundry, I wouldn't have to wash clothes. Of course, I'd have no clothing to wash, either. Minor detail.

Savannah stretched out on the couch to sleep off her dinner, and I hopped in the shower. I stood in the steamy water, allowing it to sluice away all my cares. Massaging shampoo into my scalp, I considered all I'd learned today. The photographs, life insurance policy, and will all pointed to Gil as Mara's killer. But it was all circumstantial.

The only hard evidence still directed the investigation toward me. Still, it was worth looking into. If nothing else, it could create reasonable doubt in the jurors' minds at my trial. No matter what Havermayer thought, I still had no believable motive. Gil, on the other hand, had the restaurant and the money.

Eric came in as I dried and dressed in my comfy house sweats. I slipped my arms around his sport coat and kissed the back of his neck. He plated pizza for each of us—pepperoni, mushroom, and extra cheese for me, sausage, onion, and black olive for himself. Guess he wasn't planning on getting lucky tonight.

I filled our wineglasses and followed him into the living room, leaving Savannah to sniff the kitchen floor for droppings. She wore her disappointment on her face when she flopped down at my feet, hoping for better luck.

"How are you feeling?" Eric asked before stuffing a large portion of his first slice into his mouth.

I sipped my wine. "Better. Almost like a civilized human being again. As civilized as I ever get, anyway."

Still chewing, he only nodded.

My first instinct was to broach the subject of the investigation. Then Daniel stuck his two cents in. Better to show some interest in Eric first. Not that I didn't care. These things just didn't occur to me. I'd figure out social interactions sooner or later. Until then, I had to think like Daniel. "How was your day?"

He swallowed. "Frustrating. I haven't made any headway in the break-in case. There's no physical evidence, and nothing of value was stolen, so I don't have anything to work with. This is the first case they've allowed me to handle on my own, and I'm not impressing anyone with my detecting skills. Not even myself."

"With so little evidence, it's a tough case. Give yourself a break. But I have an idea that might help. One I mentioned before that we dismissed."

"Oh?"

"What if it was someone searching for something? It happened right after Mara's death, right? What if someone was looking for her will?"

Eric shook his head. "Her attorney in Chicago has her will. She left everything to Fredo. That's why we discounted it the first time you brought it up, remember?"

"I do, but what if I told you there's another one leaving everything to her brother?"

He set his plate on the coffee table, still holding one slice of pizza. "How would you know that?"

"I found it in a lockbox packed in one of the cartons of books I bought today."

He dropped the crust onto his plate. "So, you think Gil knew about the will but not where to find it?"

"It's possible. That would explain your break-in." I bit into my pizza and tucked it into my cheek. "And it's a motive for murder. There was also a life insurance policy with Gil as the only beneficiary. He probably knew about that too."

"If Fredo didn't know about the new will, that gives us two viable suspects besides you. Fredo could've murdered her thinking he'd get everything, and Gil *knew* he would, leaving Fredo as the perfect patsy." Eric swallowed some wine. "Too bad it's all circumstantial."

"Cases have been made on less. If nothing else, it's a good reason for the ADA to drop the charges against me. I'll never take a deal, and he'll never convince a jury I'm guilty beyond a reasonable doubt."

"I'll need that paperwork to show Havermayer."

"It's at the store. It seemed safer to leave it there than bring it home with me. In case I was being followed or something. We can run over there after dinner and pick it up." I reached for another slice. "But, before we do, I have more information that might help."

He lifted his eyebrows and took another bite.

"I found some pictures in Gil's office today."

"Just happened across them, did you?"

My cheeks and ears caught fire. "Well, sort of. I caught Gil looking at a photo several times when I walked into his office. When he left us alone in the store, I was curious."

"Of course you were."

I took the high road and ignored him. "I'm not sure which one, in particular, he found so fascinating, but there were three framed photos packed in a box. One of them showed an older couple with Gil and his sister. I'd seen a picture of the same couple in the basement while searching for something to help me escape. That means the house I was held in likely belonged to either Mara or Gil, despite the registered owner being a shell company. Except Fredo and Mara had moved into Tony's old house on Walnut, so that leaves Gil."

Eric chewed thoughtfully, then swallowed. "Okay, what else?"

"Mara was wearing a necklace the morning I went to see her that she didn't have on when I found her body. Gil was wearing the same necklace when I went to see him Monday afternoon. When I asked him about it, he said he and Mara each had one because they were both Libras. But one of the pictures I found today showed Mara with the necklace, and Gil had a matching bracelet. Not a necklace. He lied to me. And if the one he wore Monday belonged to Mara, he had to get it from her between when I saw her that morning and when I discovered her dead."

"That doesn't mean he killed her."

"No, but it's curious, don't you think? Why would Mara suddenly decide to give him her necklace? I think it's much more likely he took it after strangling her because it meant something to him. A personal memento or something."

He wiped his mouth with a napkin and sat back on the couch. "I'll mention it to Havermayer when I show her the paperwork, but I wouldn't hold out much hope if I were you. This is all very interesting. However, none of it is evidence."

"No, but it's a whole lot of smoke."

"And where's there's smoke, there's fire."

"Precisely."

When the last crust from the last slice of pizza hit the empty box, I snuggled up next to Eric and relaxed in his arms. I was all-the-way-to-the-marrow-of-my-bones tired. Not only from moving the furniture and boxes. More an accumulation of fatigue caused by the week from hell. Every time I'd recovered from one thing, something else had happened. I'd had enough.

Eric pulled me into his chest and kissed the top of my head. I squeezed him and burrowed in, enjoying a rare moment of feeling safe and protected. Something I hadn't experienced very often in my life until now. Perhaps that contributed to my inability to show Eric how much I loved him. I had to learn, though, or I'd lose him.

I dozed for a while, hovering in that gray area between sleep and wakefulness until he shifted under me.

"Hon, we need to get that paperwork for me to show Havermayer."

I held on, not wanting the moment to end.

"Jen, it's getting late. Let's pick up the stuff; then, we can come home and go to bed. I know you're tired."

He was right, of course. That paperwork could solve all my legal problems. Havermayer had to see it. I sat up and stretched my arms over my head. "Okay. I'm ready."

I drove us the two blocks to the bookstore, too worn out to walk. A deserted Main Street made Riddleton seem like a ghost town minus the saloon and the barber shop. Eric kicked at the clutter beneath his feet on the passenger side floorboard without a word of complaint. Smart man. Now wasn't the time to bother me about how I kept my car. It'd be sure to start an argument, no matter how hard I tried to be reasonable.

Ravenous Readers was dark when I let us in and I flipped on the lights. A glance toward my favorite table by the window, where I'd spent so many hours trying to write *Twin Terror*, opened a hole in my chest. So much had happened since those days when writing that book had been my only concern. Some bad, but some good too.

I took Eric's hand.

He squeezed mine. "Are you okay?"

"Yeah, just remembering the good old days. Aletha must've brought me a million cups of coffee while I sat in that corner over there. She worked so hard to build up this place, and now I might lose it all without ever achieving her goal."

"That's not true. This bookstore has made a huge impact on the town. The kids love coming here, which is what she wanted. And we're going to keep it open, no matter what."

We? That's what Lacey said too. And though he never said it, I suspected Charlie felt the same way. For the first time, I had good people willing to do whatever it took to succeed on my side. Now I had to step up and do my part. But to do that, I had to clear my name.

"We left the lockbox under the coffee bar." I headed that way, fished it from under the counter, and retrieved the insurance papers and the will. "Here they are."

Eric took the paperwork from me and skimmed through them. "Well, you're right. They're pretty damning. Not evidence, but they present a strong motive for Gil to eliminate his sister. With luck, Havermayer will agree and reopen the case." He placed the papers back into the box and closed the lid.

His words energized me as hope peeked out once again. "While we're here, let's look through some of those boxes I picked up. Maybe we'll find something else we can use. Some real evidence."

"I thought you were tired. It can wait until tomorrow."

"I was. I mean, I am, but the more we give Havermayer to think about, the more likely she'll look into it, right?"

"Possibly." He recognized the enthusiasm on my face. "You're not going to let this go, are you?"

I twisted my lips into a smirk. "What do you think?"

"All right, but just for a minute." He waggled his eyebrows. "I can think of a few more interesting things to do with your newfound energy."

So could I, but not while distracted. We picked our way around the chaos in the stockroom. I opened the first carton I came to while Eric started at the other end of the line. The books were high-quality used, and Mara had done an excellent job with the selection. Mysteries by Janet Evanovich and Sue Grafton. Romances by Danielle Steel and Nicholas Sparks. Even a few Louis L'Amour thrown in for the more historically inclined. We'd have no trouble at all selling these at a reasonable price.

The next box I opened had biographies and how-to books. The third contained the classics. Sitting right on top was a copy of *To Kill a Mockingbird*. My favorite book. I ran my fingers over the cover, and all the hours of enjoyment I'd experienced reading and rereading this story came flooding back. I opened it and immediately immersed myself in the fictional world of 1930s Macon, Georgia.

Somewhere in the distance, I heard a cell phone chirp. Who was texting Eric at this hour on a Saturday night? *Who cares?* I turned the page.

"Jen, I have to go."

"What?"

"I have to leave. There's a problem at work."

I tore myself away from the adventures of Jem and Scout. "What kind of problem?"

He frowned and shook his head. "I can't say right now. I'll call you in the morning."

Typical. "Okay. Be careful."

He bent to kiss my cheek. "Come lock this door behind me. And don't stay too late."

"Yes, sir." I gave him a left-handed salute. "I'll be right there."

"I'm serious, Jen. Don't forget to lock the door."

"I will," I said, annoyed at being treated like a child.

He took off and closed the front door behind him. I picked up reading where I'd left off. Just one more page, and I'd go back to work.

Eight pages later, the bells over the door jingled. Eric had returned. Must've been a false alarm. I quickly dropped the book back into the box and opened the next carton so he wouldn't think I'd ignored his instructions. Although, I never did lock the door.

A figure appeared in the doorway. "You have something that belongs to me, and I want it back."

Definitely not Eric.

My heart sank into my belly, and fear rushed down my spine. "I don't know what you're talking about, Gil."

CHAPTER TWENTY-NINE

Gil observed me over the tops of his thin, black-rimmed glasses. "I think you know exactly what I'm talking about. You found something in one of those boxes, and I want it back."

I waved my arm around the cluttered stockroom. "As you can see, I haven't unpacked them all yet. I have no idea what's in them, but whatever it is belongs to me."

"How do you figure?"

"I bought them as is, taking your word for it they were filled with books. Could've been horse manure, for all I knew. If it were, I'd have been stuck with that too."

Fire from his coal-black eyes bored into my blue ones. "I think perhaps you're mistaken," he said, reaching under his untucked pinstriped shirt to pull out a gun.

I stared into the barrel of a large automatic, model unknown. When I tried to look away, it drew me back like a black hole. I braced myself against the paralyzing fear. No way I'd let him see me scared. I raised my hands to shoulder level, showing him my empty palms. "Take it easy, Gil. Tell me what you're looking for," I said, knowing full well it had to be the life insurance policy and the will. What else could it be?

He waved the weapon toward the cartons. "Empty those boxes. My sister's lockbox has to be in there. I've looked everywhere else."

Looked everywhere else? Then it dawned on me, I'd guessed right. "You *were* the one who ransacked Fredo's house."

His eyes narrowed. "I was desperate." He raised the gun to my eye level. "Still am. Get to work."

I had to stall for time. The sooner I started emptying those boxes, the sooner he'd know we'd already found the lockbox. "How did you know I was here?"

He sneered, a tiny lift of one side of his upper lip. "I didn't. My intention was to break in and search myself. A stroke of luck had you here already to do it for me." His eyebrows dropped behind the rims of his glasses, and hate poured out of his coal-black eyes. "But it's up to you. I don't really need you, after all. I can still do it myself."

"Okay. Okay, relax. I'll go through the boxes." Bile gurgled as I considered what might happen when the lockbox wasn't in them. Should I tell him we found it already? Perhaps, but then I risked his wrath when he discovered the paperwork was gone. I never should've listened to Charlie. However, if I hadn't, we wouldn't have found the evidence Havermayer needed to reopen the case. Assuming she did. "Why is this box so important to you, anyway? What's in it? Gold? Jewels? Your dog's favorite toy?"

Gil stared at me, his face impassive, then sighed. "I don't have a dog, and the only thing in that box is papers that have no value to anyone else. Please find it, or tell me what you've done with it. I really don't want to have to hurt you, so cooperate." He waved the pistol. "Empty the boxes. Now!"

I stepped toward a carton. Emptying the boxes would at least buy me some time. Eric might come back and rescue me. I instinctively glanced toward the door to the sales floor.

Gil followed my gaze. "Forget about it. Your boyfriend's too busy to save you this time."

"What makes you think that?"

"I overheard him talking to his partner in front of the police station. A little girl is missing. Everyone's out looking for her." He lifted his upper lip into an evil abomination of a smile. "No help for you, I'm afraid."

I shuddered. Gil had hidden this side of himself well. "Did you have something to do with that child going missing? To keep the police busy?"

He scowled and narrowed his eyes again. "Of course not! I'd never do something like that to a little girl."

Nice to know he only kidnapped *big* girls. I began to pull books out of the carton I'd opened when he came in. "I guess you're not the teary-eyed grieving brother you wanted us all to believe you were."

He faltered. "I loved my sister."

"You have an interesting way of showing it."

"She's gone. There's nothing I can do about it now."

When the box was empty, I turned it over to show him that nothing was left. "What's so important about this lockbox anyway? Seriously, what's in it?"

"My sister's personal papers."

"As in what? Her Sam's Club card? What do you need that for, anyway?"

"It's none of your concern." He switched the gun from his right hand to left, then wiped his right hand on his khakis.

He was nervous. I might be able to work with that. "Why don't you put that thing away?" I said, pointing at the pistol. "I'm no threat to you."

"Call it an incentive to keep looking."

I stood up straight and faced him. "I don't work well under pressure. Ask my publisher."

Gil leveled the gun at me again. His hand shook slightly. "Shut up and get those boxes emptied."

"You won't shoot me." I swallowed hard and willed myself forward a step. "You don't have it in you."

"And you don't know anything about me." He shifted the weapon to the right and fired, striking the back door. The bullet ricocheted off the steel and buried itself in the wall. "Don't mess with me. The next one won't miss."

I glanced down to ensure I'd maintained control of my bladder. I had, but it was close. "All right. Don't do anything you might regret, okay?"

With only a couple of cartons left to unload, my mind whirled. I had to find a way out of this mess before he realized I'd turned the insurance policy and will over to the police. But first, getting him to confess was a priority.

310

As long as I kept him talking, he wouldn't be shooting at anything. Especially me.

A recorded confession would put him away, and since South Carolina was a one-party state, as long as one of us knew the conversation was being recorded, the police could use it. But my phone was in my back pocket. I had to get it out without Gil noticing.

Standing in front of an open carton, I stretched my arms over my head, then touched my toes a few times.

Gil glowered. "What are you doing?"

"Stretching. I was getting stiff, and my back hurts."

"Knock it off and get back to work."

"Okay, just give me a minute." I rested my hands on my lower back, leaned backward, and stared at the ceiling. In my peripheral vision, I saw Gil follow my gaze. I quickly pulled my phone out of my pocket and dropped it into the box behind me. I straightened up and shook out my arms. "That's better. Now I'm ready."

He nodded toward the open box.

I dug through reference books with one hand while opening my voice recorder with the other. Now for the hard part. Squeezing a confession out of him. I wasn't convinced he intended to kill me, but on the other hand, what choice did he have? If he let me go, I'd run straight to the police, and he'd be arrested for holding me hostage at gunpoint at the very least.

He could be planning to skip town, though. Except, the only way he benefited from owning Antonio's was if he stayed here. I had to assume his plan included getting rid of me in a way he wouldn't be caught. He had no other options.

I removed the paperback dictionaries and threw them on the floor. The heavy hardcover books I set to one side of the box. They might come in handy. I took a deep breath and ventured into my first question, hoping to surprise him into saying something revealing. "So, Gil, why did you kidnap me the other night?"

His eyebrows shot up over widened eyes, then quickly recovered.

I smiled. "You didn't think I knew, did you?" I dropped another book on the floor. "I heard you and Fredo arguing and recognized your voices."

"That's ridiculous."

"Fredo wanted to kill me, but you stood up for me. Why?"

"Because killing you would cause more problems for us. I only wanted you to stay gone long enough for them to think you jumped bail and lock you up," he blurted, then pressed his lips together, shaking his head.

Got him! For the kidnapping, anyway. Now for the murder. I checked my phone. Still recording. "Why did you want me locked up? They already had me for Mara's murder. Once I was convicted, you'd get away with it."

His upper lip curled. "You wouldn't leave it alone. I had to get you off the street until your trial. Then I'd be safe. You'd never convince anyone you weren't guilty."

"Yeah, you took care of that pretty well. I have to wonder, though, why did you want to kill your sister? You two seemed so close."

"We were." His eyes misted over, and he turned away. "It was an accident. We argued, and I grabbed her but never meant to hurt her."

I took a page out of Havermayer's playbook. "I get that. These things just happen sometimes. What were you arguing about?"

Gil shook his head again. He wouldn't fall for it, either. Time for the cops to come up with some new plays. "You wouldn't understand."

"Try me." It didn't matter what he said, though. I had what I needed to clear my name. Let the police figure out why he did it. My priority now was getting out of here alive.

"Believe it or not, I was trying to save your beloved Riddleton."

Save Riddleton? "How? Save it from what?"

"Drugs. Mara wanted to bring the drug trade to Riddleton. I stopped her."

That explained where they got the money for all those vacations. And the trip to South America right before they moved here. She was setting up her pipeline. "Why? You knew that's what she planned when you came here. What changed your mind?"

"I fell in love with this idyllic town. The first place I felt like I belonged in a very long time. I didn't want to see it destroyed."

Huh. Maybe he did have a heart in there someplace. "I guess I should thank you. It would be a lot easier, though, if you weren't pointing a pistol at me. Put the gun away. Let's talk about this like reasonable people."

He glanced down at the weapon, seeming to consider my request. Then he lifted it again. "Shut up, and find the lockbox."

I'd tried to talk my way out of this situation, but he wouldn't cooperate. He'd left me no choice but to take action. I eased my phone out of the box and slid it into my front pocket, then lifted the hardback dictionary and thesaurus out of the carton and turned back toward him. Pretending to stretch again, I cocked my arm and flung the dictionary at his gun hand. As it connected, I threw the thesaurus at his face and ran for the door.

When I glanced back, the gun had skittered away, and blood flowed from his nose. He yelled and came after me. I sprinted along the wall, pulling books off the shelves to throw at him. He dodged them, protecting his face.

Gil caught up to me when I turned the corner at the window. He grabbed me from behind, and dragged me down to the floor. Hand on the back of my head, he pushed my face into the carpet. With my nose and mouth pressed against the floor, I couldn't breathe. I flailed my arms, smacking my left wrist against a table leg. Pain shot up my arm. I tried to turn over, but his knee wedged into my back. He had me trapped.

My only hope was to fool him into thinking I'd given up. I went limp, playing possum.

Gil cackled like the witch firing up her oven to roast Hansel and Gretel. "Smart girl! You know when you're beaten."

He crunched my wrists together in one hand, sending another bolt of pain up to my shoulder. Then he grabbed my hair and yanked me to my feet.

My arms felt like they were separating from my shoulders. I bit back a scream.

Dragging me backward toward the stockroom, Gil said, "You're about to have a terrible accident trying to move those bookcases. You really shouldn't try to do things like that by yourself. You never know what might happen."

"Thanks for the advice," I said through gritted teeth, digging my heels into the carpet, trying to slow him down but only succeeding in making him angrier.

When we squeezed through the doorway, he stumbled over one of the books I'd thrown at him. I jerked my wrists out of his grasp and punched him in the stomach. His breath rushed out in a grunt, and he lost his grip on my head.

I pushed him away and scrambled toward the door.

He tackled me, slamming my skull into the floor tile.

Lights ricocheted behind my eyes as the pain overwhelmed my consciousness. I groaned, unable to move.

Gil stood and levered the top bookcase off the stack by the wall, humming to himself.

My head cleared. It still hurt, but I could think again. I turned to the side so I could sit up and spotted the pistol where it had slid into the wall, four or five feet away. I glanced back at Gil, who was still busy arranging my "accident" with his back to me.

I didn't trust myself to stand. A quick turn of my head sent a wave of dizziness and a bolt of pain through it. Besides, I couldn't move fast enough that he wouldn't catch me again. I had to get to the gun without him realizing it.

Resting my elbows on the floor behind me, I eased myself toward the wall, cringing at the tiny sliding sound my jeans made. No sign Gil had noticed, though. I kept going. Only two feet to go until I could reach the weapon.

Pain pulsed through my head, and my injured wrist throbbed. I reached for the gun, but my fingers fell a few inches short. One more slide should do it. I heaved myself forward. A grunt escaped my lips.

Gil turned. "Hey! What are you doing?"

He crossed the distance between us in two strides and dove for the gun.

My fingers made contact. I grabbed the pistol and swung it up.

He was still in midair when I fired. A crimson rose blossomed on his shirt. The last thing I saw before he landed on top of me, forcing the air out of my lungs. I struggled to breathe, but his weight constricted my rib cage. When I tried to push him off, he didn't budge. The man was too heavy. How could such a skinny guy weigh so much?

The bells over the front door jingled, and Eric shouted, "Jen! Jen, where are you?"

"Back here," I whispered, unable to generate enough airflow to yell. It was okay. Eric would find me. He always did.

When he burst through the door, I lifted my hand.

He rolled Gil off me and checked his pulse.

I filled my lungs with air. "Is he dead?"

"No. He's in bad shape, though." He called for an ambulance, then helped me up. "Are you okay?"

"Yes." I stared at Gil's inert body, my injured arm cradled across my belly, the gun on the floor at my feet. "Are you sure he's not dead?" The idea I might've killed someone else, even in self-defense, sent a spike of pain through my skull.

Eric placed his hands on my shoulders and gazed directly into my eyes. "He's not dead. The paramedics will be here in a minute. He'll be fine."

A wave of gratitude filled my chest. All I could do was nod in response.

He wrapped his arms around me.

I laid my head on his shoulder. "Did you find the little girl?"

He eased away. "How did you know about that?"

"Gil heard you talking to Havermayer. What happened?"

Eric smiled. "She didn't want to go to bed, so she hid in her toybox. Her parents couldn't find her and panicked. She's fine."

The paramedics rushed in, followed by Havermayer.

Eric picked up the pistol and handed it to her. "This belongs to him." He pointed to Gil, who was being loaded onto the stretcher.

She took it and looked at me. "I guess this is your doing?"

"He attacked me." I pulled my phone out of my pocket and handed it to her. "I recorded his confession. It should be all you need to convict him for Mara's murder."

Havermayer accepted the cell and turned off the recorder.

Eric put his arm around my shoulders. "I guess this means you're going to have the ADA drop the charges against Jen?"

She turned to him and smiled. "I guess it does."

Maybe she has a heart in there someplace too.

CHAPTER THIRTY

I sat by the bookstore window at my table, sipping coffee and watching the traffic go by. Not too much of it on a Monday, but I'd already had my share of excitement for the day. I'd spent the first part of the morning at the courthouse in Sutton, watching the ADA drop the charges against me. One problem solved. Two to go.

Now that I was no longer huddled under the cloud of a murder indictment, I could approach the bank about a loan for the bookstore. The loan officer might still turn me down, though, since they usually required a steady source of income and collateral. Neither of which did I have very much of. Not quite ready to follow a victory with a defeat, I fueled my courage with a large dose of caffeine.

I glanced around my newly refurbished bookstore. Lacey had done a terrific job redoing the kids' section, and Eric had spent all afternoon yesterday bracketing the small bookcases together for display. The new

Used section was divided by genre shelves with books alphabetically ordered by author. Would they sell? More important, would they sell in place of the new books? If so, how much longer would I be able to keep the store open? Of course, I suspected Gil would never cash that five-hundred-dollar check, so that would keep us going for a day or two.

Lacey plunked down in the seat across from me, wearing a wide grin, and Charlie grabbed my mug for a refill. Something must be up. I never rated that kind of service. I turned to Lacey. "What's going on?"

Although I didn't believe it possible, her grin grew even broader.

She waited until Charlie returned, set my mug in front of me, and sat beside me before replying. "I want to talk to you about something, and I want you to know it's perfectly okay if you say no. Nothing will change around here. Okay?"

Intriguing. She'd already told me she was pregnant and asked for maternity leave, so that couldn't be it. What else could it be? "Okay."

She took a deep breath and rolled her cup between her hands. "Ben and I talked last night, and we want to invest in Ravenous Readers."

Disco Charlie jumped up and danced a circle in his purple platform shoes. "Yippee!"

"Hold on, Charlie. We have some details to iron out before we get too excited." I laughed, happy he was himself once again. As Charlie returned to his chair, I said to Lacey, "What did you have in mind?"

Another deep breath and a palm-wipe down her khakis. "We want to give you a hundred thousand dollars for a third stake in the business."

A hundred thousand dollars? The whole store wasn't worth that much, at least according to Simeon Kirby. My jaw relaxed, and my brain froze. I had no words to reply with.

Lacey caught my expression and stammered, "If . . . if that's too much, we'll take 20 or 25 percent. Whatever you think it's worth. We just want to help."

Charlie fidgeted, his eyes flying back and forth between us like he was watching a pickleball match.

Could I accept this deal? No, not under those conditions. "I'm sorry, Lacey. None of those numbers work for me. I can't accept."

"Oh." A tear formed in the corner of her eye as she studied her cup. "I'll talk to Ben, but I don't think he'll go any lower than 20 percent."

"I understand." I watched her, hoping she wouldn't glance up to see a twinkle in my eyes. "Tell him I won't accept anything less than a fifty-fifty split. You take half or nothing. Okay?"

Lacey and Charlie both flew out of their chairs at the same time. Charlie wrapped his arms around her, lifted her off the ground, and spun her around. Tears poured down her cheeks. I smiled so hard my jaws ached.

When Charlie finally brought her in for a landing, she hustled over for a hug. "Thank you, Jen. I'm so happy!"

"Me too. Thank you for saving us."

Charlie clapped his hands. "Me three!" He joined our hug. "Although, now I have two bosses."

"You always had two bosses," Lacey and I said simultaneously.

The front door opened, and Eric came in. "What's going on here?"

Charlie and Lacey pulled out of our group hug.

"Lacey and Ben are investing in the bookstore. We're partners now," I said through my ear-to-ear grin. "I don't have to try to get a loan from the bank."

"That's wonderful!" He took Lacey's shoulders and kissed her cheek. "Congratulations. You two will make a terrific team."

"Thank you," Lacey said, wiping away a fresh torrent of tears.

Yes, we would, and I was determined to do my share and make us a true team. Lacey had shouldered more than her share of the responsibility for long enough. It was my turn.

A mid-forties woman sporting a dark-brown bob came in, smiled at our group, and headed straight for the Mystery section. The best place in the store, in my opinion. Eric strolled to the coffee bar and filled a cup from the urn.

Lacey wiped her eyes and smoothed her hair. "Do I look okay? I don't want to scare the poor woman off."

Her eyes were a bit red but not puffy, and she wore little makeup, so no mascara streaks decorated her cheeks. "You look fine. And you're smiling. She'll know whatever happened was a good thing. If she even notices."

Eric returned with his coffee, and we settled in at the table.

Charlie turned to head back to his post at the coffee bar.

"Hey, Charlie, wait a minute."

He stopped and did an about-face. "What's up?"

"Did your girlfriend ever show up?"

His expression twisted into confusion.

"You know, the one you met online."

"Oh! No, she never did, but I'm glad I took your advice and decided to be myself anyway."

"Me too."

Eric grinned at him. "That's always the best way to go. Then there are no surprises."

Charlie nodded, then clumped back to work.

I looked at Eric. "I don't know how he gets around on those shoes. My ankles would give out after fifteen minutes."

He shook his head. "Beats me. Although, I don't think the cowboy boots are much better. He must have some really strong legs."

"No doubt. What have you been up to since we got back from Sutton?" I asked.

He sipped from his cup. "Helping Havermayer tie up loose ends. Gil should be out of the hospital in a few days. His arraignment's set for Friday. Fredo's going to testify against him when it goes to trial."

"Where did you find him?"

"We didn't. He heard what happened and turned himself in. Turns out he was hiding from Gil, not us."

"Why didn't Fredo report him to the police to begin with? And why did he work so hard to make people believe I did it?"

"Well, at first, he thought you did. He didn't learn the truth until Gil couldn't find the will naming him the sole beneficiary. By then, he was afraid to tell anyone. Gil threatened to kill him too. That's also why he participated in your kidnapping."

"Yeah, but wasn't it Fredo's idea to get rid of me? I heard him say it."

"Havermayer asked him about that, and he said he was only trying to push Gil into panicking and making a mistake."

I took a swallow of coffee to consider his words. "I'm not sure I believe that. He seemed pretty serious to me."

"Could be, but even with your recording, we need his testimony to guarantee a conviction. And since you weren't harmed, I think Havermayer and the ADA will look the other way if that's what it takes. Sometimes you have to compromise to get what's really important."

It made sense, but I still didn't like it. "I guess."

"Besides, I think the prosecutor's going to take the death penalty off the table to give Gil an incentive to plead guilty. If he does, there won't even be a trial."

"What happens to Fredo then?"

"I don't know. That's up to the ADA."

Over Eric's shoulder, I saw the brown-haired woman perusing the Used book section empty-handed. Looked like we were about to lose our first new-book sale to a cheaper used one. Maybe this wasn't one of my better ideas. Still, whatever we made on the deal was pure profit since we hadn't paid anything for the books. It was better than nothing.

"I guess we'll have to wait and see what happens. And what about his loan issue in Chicago?"

Eric laughed. "That loan was from the Chicago Bank and Trust. And he's made every payment in full and on time."

"So much for my enforcer theory. I'm glad I was wrong about Simeon Kirby, but still not thrilled about his plans for Riddleton."

"We don't know that he has any plans. He hasn't done anything yet. And you must admit, new development would be good for business."

And terrible for our way of life. "At what cost, though?"

He reached over and took my hand. "Let's wait and have this argument when something actually happens, okay?"

"Okay, but I still don't like the idea."

"Got it." He squeezed my hand, then pulled his away. "I have something else you're not going to like too."

"What's that?"

"The cold-case squad in Sutton has given up on your skeleton. They can't find anything, so they're shelving the case for now."

"That means it's no longer an active investigation, right?"

Eric narrowed his eyes at me. "What're you thinking, Jen?"

I could check into it myself without being accused of interfering in a police investigation. "Nothing." My lips twitched. "I'm not thinking anything at all."

He shook his head and took our cups to the coffee bar for refills.

The brown-haired woman finished checking out at the register and headed to the door holding two brand-new hardcovers and one used paperback.

Maybe it isn't such a bad idea after all.

ACKNOWLEDGEMENTS

Many thanks to:

My agent Dawn Dowdle, my editor Rachel Hart, and the Avon team for all their hard work and support.

Ann Dudzinski and Julie Golden for brainstorming and suffering through first drafts and always offering me cheese to go with my whine.

Sadie for all of the above and much, much more.

She can write the perfect murder mystery... But can she solve one in real life?

Crime writer **Jen** returns to her small hometown with a bestselling book behind her and a bad case of writer's block. Finding sanctuary in the local bookstore, with an endless supply of coffee, Jen waits impatiently for inspiration to strike.

But when the owner of the bookstore dies suddenly in mysterious circumstances, Jen has a real-life murder to solve.

The stakes are suddenly higher when evidence places Jen at the scene of the crime and the reading of the will names her as the new owner of the bookstore...

Can she crack the case and clear her name, before the killer strikes again?

Don't miss Sue Minix's debut cosy mystery – available now!

I wrote murder mysteries. I didn't investigate them. Until now...

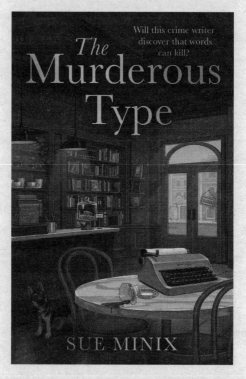

Crime writer turned amateur sleuth, Jen, has taken over the running of the local bookstore in her hometown of Riddleton.

But balancing the books at Ravenous Readers is nothing compared to meeting the deadline for her new novel.

Dodging phone calls from her editor takes a back seat, however, when the local police chief is poisoned. To solve the murder, Jen must dust off her detective hat once more.

With everyone in town seemingly a suspect, and evidence planted to incriminate local police officer and close friend Eric, Jen is working against the clock. Can she find the killer and beat her own writer's block before it's too late?

Don't miss the second instalment in this cosy mystery series – available now!